Wedding Night
WITH THE Earl

Amelia Grey

St. Martin's Paperbacks

WEDDING NIGHT WITH THE EARL

Copyright © 2016 by Amelia Grey.

All rights reserved.

For information address St. Martin's Press, 175 Fifth Avenue, New York, NY 10010.

ISBN: 978-1-250-04222-4

Our books may be purchased in bulk for promotional, educational, or business use. Please contact your local bookseller or the Macmillan Corporate and Premium Sales Department at 1-800-221-7945, ext. 5442, or by e-mail at MacmillanSpecialMarkets@macmillan.com.

Printed in the United States of America

St. Martin's Paperbacks edition / March 2016

St. Martin's Paperbacks are published by St. Martin's Press, 175 Fifth Avenue, New York, NY 10010.

10 9 8 7 6 5 4 3 2 1

Chapter 1

There's a divinity that shapes our ends,
Rough-hew them how we will,—
                    —Hamlet, act 5, scene 2

Early Winter
Northern Coast of England

Adam Greyhawke supposed there were worse deaths than being shot by an irate husband. He'd looked down the wrong end of a clumsily held pistol barrel more than once in his thirty years. Fear wasn't something that ever crossed his mind.

For the past two years he'd welcomed death. Maybe he'd even longed for it, because guilt was a hell of a friend. Now that the moment was actually close at hand, perhaps it would have been more acceptable if he had met his end saving the life of an innocent child from the path of a runaway carriage or something equally heroic, but Adam had seldom had the opportunity to be so noble.

"Give me one good reason why I shouldn't blow your

head off your shoulders right now," the short, slim man barked.

"I can't think of one," Adam said calmly.

Though his eyes were blurry from all the brandy he'd consumed and his head was pounding, Adam noticed the man's gaze dart to the young woman standing beside him in the dimly lit upstairs room of the tavern and inn. They exchanged furtive glances. Clearly they hadn't expected him to be so accommodating. Adam really didn't give a damn whether the man pulled the trigger.

Somehow, it seemed fitting that today would be his demise. It had been hellish. Not only had his wife and child died on this day two years ago, this morning he'd received word that a young cousin had succumbed to consumption a few weeks ago and Adam was now the eighth Earl of Greyhawke. Once, that would have meant something to him. When Annie was alive, when life meant something to him. Now, it meant nothing. The thought of being an earl without all that he used to hold dear was excruciating.

"If I agree to let you to live," the husband challenged, "how do you plan to repay me for the harm you've done to me and my wife?"

Adam's feet were well planted, yet he swayed and grunted a hollow laugh into the stale air of the chilled room. So now they were to the heart of this unsavory matter. Money. The infuriated man before him wasn't a cuckolded husband after all. He and his partner were tricksters and Adam was their prey for the evening.

Obviously the nodcocks didn't know Adam's state of mind.

It bothered him a little, and a very little, that he'd

been caught in a snare laid by a duo of schemers out to pad their pockets by pilfering his for what they could get. Adam's intuitive senses were sharp, and he was usually quick to know when he was being set up. Maybe it had been the overindulgence in drink or the fact that he hadn't been with a woman in a very long time. Perhaps he'd deliberately shaken off the pervading sensation that something wasn't quite right about the woman's story of being a widow and in need of warmth and comfort to see her through the long night. And then, just maybe this unpleasant end was the best he deserved.

Whatever the reason, he wouldn't complain. Fate had been good to him in his youth, saving him from more dangerous escapades than his ill-spent life warranted. It was only recently that fate had taken a disliking to him. And he no longer cared. Everyone knew that life stopped, bowed, and paid homage to some and rolled right over others, leaving them to gather up the broken pieces.

"I'm afraid there is nothing I can do," Adam remarked, indifference dripping from his words while he tucked the tail of his shirt into the waistband of his trousers. "I'm in her chamber with both of us in a rather accusing state of dishabille. Her reputation is already ruined beyond any suitable repair I could suggest."

The man's eyes widened, and his face flushed with a sudden flash of anger. He took a menacing step closer to Adam and glowered fiercely. "I demand you do something for this injury."

Adam swayed again. He glanced at the barrel of the pistol, then looked back at the man. "Perhaps I could apologize for not knowing the young woman was happily married and not a lonely widow after all."

The two flimflam artists exchanged panicky glances once again. Apparently, Adam wasn't the first quarry in their game of chicanery. No doubt they had expected him to quiver, deny any wrongdoing, and jump at the chance to buy his way out of a bloody and most assuredly painful death.

Most gentlemen probably would.

Not Adam.

He should have known this would not be a good evening to find a tavern, drown in a bottle of brandy, and console himself with a willing woman. At the time, the thought of one more lonesome evening in that cold, godforsaken cottage was more than he could bear. Death could not be worse than the utter feeling of despair that had gripped him for two years.

Though Adam and the woman had barely made it past a few uninspiring kisses and several hastily felt caresses, he liked to think he was on the verge of forgetting his torment for a few moments and simply enjoying the lust of being a man.

"You can bloody well give us your money, and be quick about it, too," the trickster demanded, rolling his right shoulder, making the pistol bobble carelessly in his hands. "You're a wealthy gentleman. She heard you talking in the tavern. You've a big estate north of here. Now hand over your purse."

Adam had willingly given up his wild and undisciplined behavior of bachelor life when he'd met and married Annie. He'd left the proper, respected life of a gentleman after she died. For two years he'd been just a man. An ordinary man who looked after his estate and occasionally astounded his tenants by herding his own sheep. But what he'd never left behind was his honor.

He would die with that intact.

He turned his weary attention back to the threatening man and his conspirator. "I'd rather be shot."

"You don't believe I'll do it, do you?" the crook said gruffly, almost poking Adam in the chest with the barrel.

"On the contrary," Adam said. "I'm asking you to." He held out his hands palms up. "My pockets are empty," he said unapologetically, even though it was a bold-faced lie. "I came up here believing I was going to pay the lonely widow with a shot of brandy and an evening in a soft bed enjoying my favors."

"Oh, you despicable brute!" the woman screamed at Adam, and then whirled to confront her husband. "Give me the pistol, you coward! I'll shoot him myself!"

She pulled him toward her and grabbed for the gun. The man jerked away and shoved her to the floor.

Despite his unsteady legs, Adam lunged for the husband and quickly deflected the weapon from his chest with his hand. The ball exploded from the barrel with a crack loud enough to wake the dead and landed harmlessly in the wall.

Adam was head and shoulders taller than the thug and outweighed him by at least two stone. It really wasn't a contest to take the spent firearm away from him, toss it to the floor, and flatten him against the wall. Adam pressed a forearm against the man's throat and gazed into his shifty, frightened eyes.

A frown tugged at the corners of Adam's mouth and he released the culprit and stepped back. It didn't look as if this were going to be his lucky day to die after all.

Chapter 2

Who alone suffers suffers most i' the mind.
—King Lear, *act 3, scene 6*

Late Winter

It was seldom warm on the northern coast of Yorkshire and the breeze never completely died away. Sunshine wasn't a regular visitor to the area, either. It didn't matter. Gray skies and cold, damp wind suited Adam.

His cottage was less than a half hour's trudge from the craggy cliffs that lined the shore below. He knew the way as well as he knew the back of his hand. Over the past two years, he'd made the trek to the water so many times that his footsteps had beaten a path across the stony, uneven ground. Looking out across the vast North Sea brought him a measure of peace he'd found nowhere else.

The first time Adam had made the short journey, it had crossed his mind to jump into the turbulent waves below. But he had never been a coward. And leaving this world would have been the easy way out of his pain. Living meant bearing the agony and misery of his wife's death and his part in it.

He reached down and patted Pharaoh's warm back. The large blond Pyrenees had been his faithful companion since Adam and his friends had saved him from a cruel shopkeeper's whip a year ago. Adam could still feel the scars across Pharaoh's shoulders from the deep lashes he'd received before they'd rescued him.

Several times a week, he and the dog would make their visit to the sea. Most often he would let Pharaoh set the pace. The tall, lanky dog liked to run. Pharaoh was still a pup at heart and always eager to stretch his legs with his master. But while on the peak of the cliff, Pharaoh never left Adam's side to sniff, scratch, or hunt. It was as if he knew they were there to stand, to think, and to remember.

"Come on, boy," Adam said, patting Pharaoh again. "Time to head back and see what Mrs. Leech left for us to eat tonight. I'd wager it's mutton stew again, wouldn't you?"

The dog barked once and then dutifully turned around and they began their journey to the cottage at a slow walk so Pharaoh could wander the landscape.

When Adam topped the ridge, he saw a black-lacquered coach trimmed in red and gold paint sitting in front of his house. A handsomely liveried driver and guard sat high on their perches. It was close to the time his friends Bray and Harrison had visited him for the past two years, but they wouldn't come all the way to

Yorkshire in a carriage. It would take that conveyance more than twice the time to make the journey as it would on horseback.

Pharaoh saw the coach about the same time as Adam. He stopped, bristled, and barked a loud, low-toned warning.

"Easy, Pharaoh," Adam cautioned, rubbing the dog's head. "I don't like strangers either, but I can't see trouble coming out of anything that fancy. But since you're dying to find out who it is, go on ahead and check it out. Just don't frighten anyone until I get there."

The dog loped down the hill, barking as if he were a terrifying hound from hell. Adam picked up his pace, too. More than likely it was someone who had lost his way while looking for an estate. Adam would help them if he could and then quickly send them on their journey. By the time he made it to the vehicle, Pharaoh was standing in front of the carriage door, alternating between barking and growling.

"Pharaoh, that's enough of that," he told the dog, and gave his head a slight push to send him on his way. "Go find something to do. I'll take over from here."

A window in the door pushed open and a round-faced gentleman with big, slightly bulging eyes stuck his head out and said, "A pleasant afternoon to you, my good man. Could you please tell me if this is the house where the Earl of Greyhawke is residing?"

Adam thought about lying and sending the gentleman on a fool's search for a nonexistent cottage somewhere on the other side of the valley, but what good would that do? The man would eventually discover he'd been duped and return. Better to get rid of him now and not have to deal with him again later.

"Who's asking?"

"I'm Mr. Alfred Hopscotch, the Prince's emissary. He's sent me to see the earl on an urgent matter."

Adam tensed. The Prince? Sent someone to see him? He certainly hadn't expected that. He eyed he man curiously. "What does the Prince want with me?"

The man's wide, bushy brows shot up. He looked Adam up and down. Adam knew Hopscotch was thinking that he'd never seen a gentleman dressed in commoners' clothing with shoulder-length hair unbound. But Adam didn't give a damn. His appearance suited him.

Mr. Hopscotch eyed Pharaoh again, too, as the dog sniffed around the carriage wheels, trying to decide which one was best for marking his territory.

"I will be happy to explain. I'm afraid the dog wouldn't let me out."

Adam shrugged. "He doesn't take kindly to strangers poking around."

"Will he bite?"

"Only on my command."

"In that case, I suppose I will have to assume you won't issue that order and it's safe for me to come out."

The rotund man pushed the door open and stepped down from the carriage, then shut the door behind him. He swept his hat off his head, bowed, and looked up pleasantly at Adam. "Lord Greyhawke, pardon me for not recognizing you. I expected someone a . . . Well, never mind. The Prince received your letter asking that the title Earl of Greyhawke be bestowed on your heir.

He sent me to tell you that you cannot disclaim a peerage."

"I have no use of it," Adam said flatly.

Mr. Hopscotch watched Pharaoh wander over to him and sniff around the tail of his coat. The Prince's man cleared his throat uncomfortably and said, "Still, it is yours and you simply cannot just give it up. You don't have to take a seat in Parliament right away, of course, but someone has to take care of the entailed property of the title, as well as the other estates, properties, and businesses associated with it. Legally you are the only one who can do that."

Adam frowned. His quiet life away from Society suited him. He had no son to leave the title to, and he didn't plan to ever marry again and have a son. He didn't want the title. Why couldn't it pass to someone who actually wanted it?

"Are you trying to tell me there are no other male Greyhawkes in England who can accept this responsibility?"

"There's always someone next in line for the title," said Hopscotch, drumming his fingers nervously on the rim of his hat while Pharaoh continued to sniff around his legs. "You have an heir, my lord. In fact, he is the reason for my visit today."

Making sure he didn't come in contact with Pharaoh, Mr. Hopscotch slowly reached behind him, opened the carriage door, and motioned with his hand for someone to come forward. "Come, come. Don't be frightened. The dog is large but harmless—at least while by his master's side," he added under his breath.

Adam watched a small, skinny, terrified-looking lad

about the age of three or four step down onto the footstool. His large brown eyes appeared too big for his thin, pale face. Dark brown hair fell across his forehead. It was neatly trimmed above his brows and just below his ears. His clothing, while not expensive, was clean and pressed. Pharaoh immediately approached him for a sniffing inspection, and the child leaned closer to Mr. Hopscotch, almost hiding his face in the man's coat.

"Come now, none of that. Behave as a young man." Mr. Hopscotch took hold of the lad's shoulders and made him face Adam. "Lord Greyhawke, may I present your cousin Master Dixon Greyhawke."

Adam stared at the little fellow. He didn't like seeing the frightened look on the boy's face. Pharaoh didn't like strangers coming around the cottage, but as long as Adam was calm, Pharaoh would be, too.

Adam pointed to the house and said, "Pharaoh, to the door." The Pyrenees looked around at Adam as if to say, *Do I have to?* "Go on. By the door."

The dog hesitated, grumbled, and then trotted over to the door of the cottage and curled up in front of it.

Mr. Hopscotch looked up at the driver and snapped his fingers, then turned to the boy and said, "Master Dixon, you must greet your guardian properly."

Adam's head jerked around to the man.

Guardian?

Hell, no.

Not Adam.

The lad timidly stepped forward, bowed low, and said, "It's a pleasure to meet you, my lord."

"Well done, young man," said Mr. Hopscotch, patting

him on the shoulder. "I'm sure the two of you and the dog will be getting along fine in no time at all."

Adam stood six feet four in his bare feet and taller in his walking boots. He rose over Hopscotch and peered down at him. "You aren't leaving him here."

Mr. Hopscotch blinked but didn't cower. "I have no choice in the matter, and neither do you. He is next in line for the title. Until you bear a son, he is officially your heir. Even if you somehow managed to do the impossible and pass the title on to him while you are still living, as his oldest living male relative you would be responsible for him, his education, and all that comes with the property until he comes of age."

"I'm responsible for no one," Adam argued with a snort of derision.

"You are now," Mr. Hopscotch answered quickly. "It is your duty to manage, protect, and prosper the estate and all it entails until the next earl takes over."

Damnation, it never dawned on Adam to think about who might be next in line for the title. He hadn't really thought about anything in a long time except what had happened to Annie and his child. Hell, he hadn't even known he was in line for the title until he'd received a letter several weeks ago stating he was the new earl. The Greyhawkes had never been a large or close-knit family. Adam had assumed the next heir would be someone older, bigger, and stronger-looking than the tyke standing beside Hopscotch, trying his best to be brave.

"He's too young for Eton, of course," Mr. Hopscotch continued, "but you can start teaching him the usual things a boy needs to know, such as how to ride, shoot, hunt, and play chess. A tutor can take care of everything else he should learn."

"I don't know anything about teaching a child how to ride a horse or hold a bow, even if I wanted to," Adam muttered impatiently. "Which I don't." The driver placed a trunk at Adam's feet. He frowned, looked up at Hopscotch, and asked, "What's this?"

"I'm really not sure," the Prince's man said, staring at the trunk. "But I would suspect it's some of whatever is left of Master Dixon's possessions. I think there are more things at the orphanage, but I'll leave it to you to look into that for him."

Mr. Hopscotch reached for the handle to the carriage door. Quick as lightning, Adam slammed his open hand against it, holding it shut. Hopscotch and the boy flinched from the loud crack.

Adam's gaze zeroed in on Hopscotch, and he leaned his face dangerously close to the older man's.

"I said, you aren't leaving him with me." Adam's voice was low and calm, but there could be no doubt that he meant what he said.

"In this you have no choice, my lord." Mr. Hopscotch calmly pointed to the top of the carriage.

Adam glanced up and saw the guard had his musket trained on Adam's chest. He didn't think for a minute the sentinel would shoot him, but he would keep Adam from harming Hopscotch.

"Unfortunately, he's on the Prince's orders, not mine. I can't tell him what to do. As far as the Prince is concerned, *you* are the Earl of Greyhawke and this child is *your* heir and *your* responsibility."

Responsible? For this bony snip of a lad?

Adam had barely been able to take care of himself the past two years. He no longer drank all night and all day, as he had when he'd first arrived in Yorkshire, but he certainly wasn't capable of taking on the care of a young child.

"What you do with him from here on out will be your choice. If you don't want to care for him," Mr. Hopscotch continued in an irritated voice, "hire him out as a servant or take him to London and put him back in the orphanage. Quite frankly, Lord Greyhawke, I wouldn't have the stomach to do something like that to him."

A servant or orphanage? What kind of man did Hopscotch think he was?

Adam turned to Dixon. His big eyes were wide and staring straight ahead. He looked so stiff and brittle at the moment, Adam feared he'd break if anyone touched him.

"An orphanage?" Adam asked from between clenched teeth. "Where the hell . . ." Mr. Hopscotch's brows lifted. Adam stopped and swore silently as he cleared his throat. "Where's his mother? He needs to be with her until he's old enough to be sent to school."

"She's no longer with us," the Prince's man answered almost under his breath.

"You mean she's—"

"Yes," said Mr. Hopscotch, cutting off Adam's words quickly. "From what we've been able to discover, she was the only family he had, except for you, of course."

Adam looked at the young lad standing so stoically. There was no doubt the boy knew what they were talking about. His eyes held a glistening gleam, though he never moved or said a word. For the first time in over two years, Adam felt his heart soften. He didn't want it to, but he felt the boy's pain of loss and knew that someone so young shouldn't have to feel that overpowering sense of helplessness.

Adam wanted to reject the pull of compassion that gripped him, worming its way into his soul. "I don't know what to do with him," he grumbled. "Doesn't he have a nurse or governess? Look at him. He can't be more than three or four years old."

"I'm five," Dixon said defiantly in his first show of any kind of emotion as he looked up at Adam with glaring brown eyes. "I don't need a nurse. I can take care of myself." He then jerkily folded his arms across his chest and set his lips in a thin, firm line.

"Good," Adam responded. "If you stay here with me, you'll probably have to."

"We hope it won't come to that, my lord," Mr. Hopscotch said, and then stopped and sighed heavily. "The Prince is happy to assist you in any way you might need."

"Me mum said I was small for my age," the little boy said, obviously not ready to forgive Adam for thinking him younger.

"That you are."

"I'll grow," Dixon insisted. "I'll be taller than you one day."

"Let's hope so," Adam said more to himself than the lad.

"We found out that Master Dixon was living in an orphanage. Apparently, a neighbor, who unfortunately didn't know what to do, placed him there. He certainly didn't have the means to bring Master Dixon up in the proper way an heir to a title should be educated, protected, and nourished," Mr. Hopscotch said. "For more than two months now, my lord, the extensive Greyhawke estates have been left in the hands of solicitors, managers, and all manner of overseers. You need to come to London, talk to your solicitors, and start seeing to all your properties. If you don't want the lands and businesses kept up properly and in good stead for the benefit of yourself, at least do your duty, as a man of honor, for your staff who takes care of your homes, the tenants who work your lands, and for Master Dixon until the time he comes of age."

Adam had never really thought about the responsibility that came with the title he'd never expected to hold. Tenants, lands, and businesses? A five-year-old homeless heir?

He vacillated again. He didn't want to take care of the lad, but Hopscotch knew he'd never send Dixon to an orphanage. Adam was a man of honor. That was about the only thing he hadn't denounced when he'd moved to the coast.

Adam had done a lot of things in his thirty years of life. Some good. Some bad. But he'd never run from a fight or from an obligation, and he couldn't now.

His gaze swept over to the defiant little lad again, and his mind started swirling with thoughts. As the earl, it was his duty to beget an heir. Yet he'd vowed never to marry again and put another woman through the hell Annie went through trying to have his babe. And now he didn't have to. He had an heir. Through no fault of either of them, Dixon was suddenly Adam's responsibility. So was this fate's way of trying to make up that loss to him and grant him an heir?

Adam grunted a short, humorless laugh. Obviously fate was not through with him yet.

He might not want to be Dixon's guardian, but how could he leave the lad to suffer in an orphanage or worse? He couldn't. Dixon needed to be nurtured as if he were Adam's own child.

And just that quickly, Adam knew he would give up his solitary life and satisfy tradition. He would move back to London as the Earl of Greyhawke and be responsible for all it encompassed. Maybe at last, through this deed of caring for Dixon, he could find some measure of happiness, if not redemption, for what he'd done to his wife.

Adam took in a large breath, knowing what he was facing. He looked down at the boy and said grudgingly, "Come with me. It's best you make friends with Pharaoh."

Chapter 3

I have set my life upon a cast,
And I will stand the hazard of the die.
—Richard III, *act 5, scene 4*

Adam's first full day in London had been a challenge, and thankfully it was coming to an end.

Between solicitors clamoring for his undivided attention, tailors measuring him for new clothing, and a surprised bevy of servants—who, he felt certain, weren't sure they believed him to be the new earl—scurrying about, Adam's head was pounding. Dixon had managed to stay out of the fray by playing in his new room with the wooden soldiers Adam had bought him before leaving Yorkshire.

Pharaoh hadn't been as accommodating. Adam had to keep the dog close to his side. The new surroundings and activity of so many strangers in the house had him either barking or pacing for most of the day. Adam kept thinking he'd have time to take the restless Pyrenees for a walk, but that hadn't happened.

One good thing about coming back to London as the new Earl of Greyhawke was that Adam didn't have to go back to the house he'd shared with Annie. He knew he had to do something with the property one day, but not right now. Learning that as Lord Greyhawke he had a well-staffed house in Mayfair waiting for his arrival made his decision to return to London a bit easier to shoulder.

When he'd arrived yesterday, Clark, the butler, and Mrs. Goodstone, the housekeeper, had stared at him as if he'd come from a strange part of the world. He guessed that to some extent, they were right in their assessment of him. His best commoners' clothing didn't come close to the quality of a poor nobleman's frock, let alone the finery of a prosperous earl. Adam had pulled his hair back in a queue like a proper gentleman, but by the expressions on the servants' faces, it did little to alleviate their fears that the earldom had been commandeered by a common mischief maker. Which was the main reason he'd sent for a tailor right away.

He could have told them that he was more shocked than they were about the turn of events. Bearing the title of earl wasn't the way he'd envisioned living out his life. But now that he had accepted the role, he would be a good and proper custodian of the earldom and guardian for Dixon.

Now the solicitors and tailors were gone and the day was late. Lamps and fires had been lit, and the house was quiet once again. But there was one more thing Adam wanted to do before he poured himself a much needed glass of port. He had to take Pharaoh for a long walk, and it would probably be good for Dixon to get out of the house for a while, too.

Adam closed the ledger he'd been studying and placed the quill in its holder. He was about to push his chair away from his desk when Pharaoh started barking from the front of the house.

At the cottage, Adam would have ignored such an outburst from his dog because he often barked at squirrels, rabbits, and other small animals that roamed the land. But because Mrs. Goodstone and the other maids were still wary of such a large dog in the house, Adam rose from his desk to investigate.

Before he made it across the room, he heard familiar male voices and laughter join the barking. His steps lightened. Rounding the doorway, he saw Bray and Harrison standing in the vestibule. Pharaoh jumped on first one and then the other as they patted his head and shoulders and rubbed his back. The quiet butler stood to the side, looking mystified by the merriment taking place.

Adam smiled at the sight of them. Shortly after Mr. Hopscotch's visit, Adam had penned short messages to both his friends, saying he would be returning to London but his arrival date was uncertain. He should have known they would be keeping watch for him.

"How did you two blackguards know I was in Town?" Adam asked, walking down the corridor toward them. "I only arrived late yesterday afternoon."

"Don't you remember, my friend?" Bray said as Pharaoh continued to jump up on his chest, demanding attention. "There are no secrets in London."

"And keep in mind there are no hiding places, either,"

Harrison added as Adam shook hands with him and clapped Bray on the back, greeting them both warmly.

It was always good to see his childhood friends. Adam had never told them, but he'd appreciated their visits to Yorkshire to see him the past two years. He knew they feared they'd be intrusive, but they hadn't been. They'd been welcomed. He didn't think he'd ever let them know that, and he should have.

"Pharaoh, down," Adam said as the tall, strapping men tried to shrug out of their coats and gloves and give attention to Pharaoh, too. The dog woofed and jumped on Adam, wagging his long, sweeping tail excitedly. "Sit, Pharaoh, sit," he said, and rubbed the Pyrenees's head when he quickly obeyed.

"It's been too long, Adam," Harrison said. "It's about time you decided to come back."

"And I'm damn glad you did," Bray added, clapping him on the back again. "I wasn't looking forward to that long, cold ride up to the north country this spring."

"Now you don't have to," Adam answered. "Come into the drawing room where there's a fire. We'll have a drink."

The coats were handed off to Clark, and the three men and Pharaoh walked into the drawing room. Harrison and Bray settled into the comfortable wingback chairs that faced a settee. Adam strolled over to the side table to pour three glasses of port. He heard his friends talking in low tones and looked up. Bray was leaning toward Harrison and seemed intent on whatever he was saying.

"What are you two whispering about?" Adam asked, replacing the stopper on the decanter.

"Nothing," Bray said quickly, and sat back in his chair.

"It didn't sound like nothing." Adam picked up the three glasses between his two hands and started toward them. "I'd say that one of you is looking to pick a fight with me and that the other is wisely trying to talk him out of it."

Harrison chuckled and took the drink Adam offered. "We've certainly done a lot of that in our lives, but not today. Bray was just saying that now you're in London we must get you down to the Heirs' Club so you can officially apply for membership."

"Yes," Bray agreed, and took his glass. "But Harrison thought it might be a little too soon for you to do that." Bray looked at Harrison. "He knows I think the sooner the better."

"Then once again, I bow to you being the duke and knowing more about this than I do," Harrison said, and lifted his glass in a mock salute to Bray. "Let's just go ahead and do it right now."

Adam had no reason to doubt what they were saying, but the two men seemed oddly uncomfortable with each other. "No. Wait a minute," he said, lowering his frame into the blue velvet settee. "While it might be good for you right now, it's not good for me. It's been a hell of a day. Not only that, as you can see I don't have proper clothing yet. I would like to take my time and settle into London quietly, if you don't mind."

Harrison threw another glance in Bray's direction. "He needs more time. We'll take it slowly."

"Good," Adam said. "I want to be able to walk through the door of that club and order a drink without having Bray by my side, but it won't be today or tomorrow."

"Why don't we make the Heirs' Club your first outing in London?" Harrison asked. "We'll meet there whenever you—"

Harrison stopped, and Adam looked behind him to see what had caught his friend's attention. Dixon stood quietly in the doorway, twisting his hands together and looking at them curiously. Like Adam, he had been fitted for new clothing, but today he was still dressed as a commoner.

"Perhaps there's something you need to tell us first," Harrison said, raising his brows in surprise.

"I might as well." Adam motioned for Dixon to come into the room. When the boy stood beside Adam, Adam turned to his friends and said, "Your Grace, my lord, may I present Master Dixon Greyhawke. Dixon, the Duke of Drakestone and the Earl of Thornwick. My oldest friends."

The lad bowed low, rose, looked up at them, and said, "Pleased to meet you, Your Grace, my lord."

Harrison and Bray put down their glasses, stood up, and greeted Dixon, who promptly said to them, "I'm going to be as tall as you are one day. My mum said I would be."

"I suppose she was right," Bray agreed.

"How old are you?" Harrison asked.

"Five," Dixon said, displaying the fingers on one small hand for them. "I'll be six before year's end."

Adam knew his friends were curious about Dixon, but Adam couldn't talk freely in front of the lad. He excused himself and went to find Clark. He asked the butler to have a footman go with Dixon and Pharaoh for a walk in the park. Adam then returned to the drawing room, made himself comfortable on the settee again, and picked up his glass of port.

"So tell us about the boy," Bray said.

"He arrived at my door little more than a month ago with a man by the name of Mr. Alfred Hopscotch."

Bray and Harrison looked at each other, and Adam asked, "You know him?"

"The Prince's emissary who takes his job very seriously," Harrison said, then took a sip of his drink.

"We've both had encounters with the man for different reasons," Bray added. "We should have known he would eventually get around to seeing you about something, too."

"He's a difficult man to say no to."

"We know," Bray and Harrison said at the same time.

"So tell us who Dixon is and why he is here with you in London," Bray said.

"I'll make this short. He's my cousin and next in line for the title, and thereby my heir."

Bray and Harrison exchanged uncomfortable glances again.

"Maybe you should settle back with your drink and tell us the long version of the story," Harrison suggested.

"There's not that much to tell. I had never met Dixon. I can't say I even knew about him until Hopscotch brought him to my house."

Adam briefly told them about his long conversation with Mr. Hopscotch and that because of Dixon, Adam had accepted his duties as the Earl of Greyhawke so that he could one day hand over a wealthy, thriving legacy to Dixon. Adam ended by saying, "The easiest explanation is that, once again, fate gave me no choice about my life."

"It seldom does," Harrison said solemnly.

Harrison would know something of what Adam was feeling. Harrison's brother and family had died from the ravages of a fever just over a year ago, unexpectedly making Harrison the new Earl of Thornwick.

"So when you say Dixon is your heir, you mean that he is until you marry and have a son."

Adam held up his hand and shook his head for good measure. "No, I mean my heir to take over the title. There will be no more marriages, no more babes, for me. I will not go through that hell again."

"Surely you don't mean—"

"I do," Adam cut in. "Dixon is my heir."

Bray and Harrison shifted in their chairs. He supposed he could understand their unease. They were both happily wed. "Now when will I get to meet the duchess and the countess?" Adam asked.

"Soon," Bray said, looking at Harrison before taking a sip of his drink.

"Do you plan to enjoy the parties, balls, and other festivities of the Season?" Harrison asked.

"I will," Adam said, and looked down at his worn clothing and laughed. "But only after I've made a transformation and become a proper earl. I doubt I'd be welcomed in anyone's house dressed as I am." He stopped and smiled. "Just because I don't plan to ever marry again doesn't mean I don't want to enjoy the company of sweet-smelling, beautiful young ladies at a ball or the warm bed of a mistress. I am still a man, after all."

Chapter 4

Society is no comfort
To one not sociable.
—Cymbeline, *act 4, scene 2*

News of the Earl of Greyhawke's arrival in London spread across the Town like a whirlwind. Within a few days, Adam had more invitations to dinners, card parties, and balls than he could possibly attend. He'd discounted them all until the one that had arrived earlier in the day. Luckily, some of his new clothing had arrived, too.

Tonight was his first foray back into the social world of the ton in over two years. A part of him was looking forward to the activity surrounding London's Society Season after living in solitude for so long. While he'd been satisfied with his quiet life in Yorkshire, the isolated existence had often been lonely; but at the time, he supposed, he'd needed it to be that. However, it was no existence for a child to learn how to grow up to be a gentleman.

Adam left his hat, cloak, and gloves with the attendant at the front door of the Duke of Quillsbury's home and sauntered down the corridor to the room where the music, laughter, and chatter were coming from. He stood at the entranceway and stared out over the sea of swirling, colorful skirts, black coats, and white shirts. He scoured the faces in the room. All the furniture had been removed except for a few chairs lined up against the wall. He didn't see Bray or Harrison, but he noticed several other faces he knew in the swarm of people.

Adam had missed two Seasons, but it didn't look as though anything had changed. The widows, dowagers, and spinsters sat in chairs near the dance floor. The older gentlemen stood in groups of three and four, talking, laughing, and eyeing every female who passed. Young ladies chatted behind their hands and fans, while all the eligible bachelors looked them up and down with long, approving glances.

He smiled to himself. Yes, now that he was here, he knew there were things about London he'd missed. And there were things about London he was looking forward to enjoying again.

"Adam, this is a surprise."

He turned to see Bray coming up behind him.

"I didn't expect to see you here. I thought your first outing in London would be when we meet at the Heirs' Club."

Adam greeted Bray and said, "I thought so, too, but when the invitation to the duke's dinner and my first new clothing arrived this morning, I couldn't resist the temptation."

Bray looked around the room. "Good, but I thought we'd have a chance to talk again before you attended any of the parties."

That was a strange thing for him to say, Adam thought, but he smiled and answered, "Are you saying I should have come to see you before anyone else?"

"No. Yes. Maybe. Have you spoken to anyone yet?"

Adam didn't know if he was being overly suspicious or if Bray was really acting a little strange. "I just arrived. Why?"

"No reason." Bray stopped and laughed. "I just arrived, too."

"I was looking to see how many faces I recognize."

"Most of them, I'd venture to say. I should have known the Duke of Quillsbury's dinner party would be your first evening out. No doubt you remember he has the best cook in all of London."

"I remember well. That's why I'm here. After too many meals of mutton stew the past couple of years, I couldn't resist the opportunity to dine at the duke's table once again when the invitation came this afternoon."

"And drink his wine," Bray added.

Adam grinned. "Without a doubt."

"Why don't we go get a drink? The table is on the other side of the dance floor."

Adam was about to turn when from over Bray's shoulder he saw Harrison taking off his cloak at the front door. Adam's eyes narrowed and he was suddenly washed with a feeling that something wasn't quite right. "I see Harrison has just arrived. And he's alone. I wonder why his wife isn't with him."

Bray looked down the corridor but didn't respond to Adam as Harrison walked up and greeted them.

Harrison glanced at Bray before saying, "This is a surprise, my friend. We didn't expect to see you tonight."

"So Bray just said," Adam commented cautiously. "And I'm wondering why." Just as during their brief visit to his house a few days ago, something didn't feel right between his friends. Adam looked at Bray. "Where is Louisa?" And to Harrison he said, "Where is Angelina?"

"Home," they answered one after the other.

Dinner at the Duke of Quillsbury's house was a sought-after invitation each year. Bray's and Harrison's wives wouldn't miss it unless there was a very good reason.

Adam frowned. "What's this? Both of you here and your wives not by your sides?"

Bray and Harrison looked at each other again, and Adam didn't like the signals they were sending each other.

"Why aren't they here?"

Harrison shifted his stance. Bray avoided Adam's eyes and sipped his drink.

Neither man spoke.

"Someone had better start talking right now," Adam said.

"Oh, hellfire," Harrison muttered. "We tried to tell you the other afternoon and we just didn't know how."

Adam stiffened. "Tell me what?"

Bray sighed. "Both Louisa and Angelina are with child and not attending the Season."

The words hit Adam like a horse kick to the stomach, but he was sure he masked it well. "Both of them?" he asked with a steady voice. "At the same time?"

Harrison nodded. "It's not like we planned it to happen this way. It just did."

"Louisa and I were shocked," Bray added. "We've

been married almost two years, we were beginning to wonder if . . . well . . ." He let his words die away.

"Why didn't you tell me this the other day when you were at my house?"

"I wanted to," Bray said. "Harrison thought we should give you another day to get settled, so we decided to go see you and decide after we got there if it would be a good time to tell you."

"Then we met Dixon and you said he was your heir and that you'd never marry again and have a son. We just couldn't bring ourselves to do it."

Adam had suspected something was wrong that afternoon, but he'd let the uneasy feeling pass, thinking it was because he'd been gone from London so long. They were his friends, they were—"Cowards," he accused. "You were both cowards."

"Hell, no," Bray said.

"Those are fighting words, Adam," Harrison said calmly.

He knew it, but he added, "If you think you can take me, we'll step outside right now."

"That's enough of that from both of you," Bray said. "What Harrison told you is true, Adam. We didn't know how to tell you about our wives after what you went through. We didn't know you'd be here tonight. "

Adam wasn't sure what he was feeling except that they should have told him. "When the hell were you going to let me know? Or were you hoping someone else might tell me and save you the trouble?"

"That's not true. You know us. We thought we'd have a few drinks at the Heirs' Club and then tell you. We were trying to be kind."

"Just the way we have been since Annie died."

Startled, Adam blinked. That was the first time he'd heard her name spoken out loud in over two years.

His throat thickened and suddenly his mind swirled with images and sounds he thought he'd buried for good. He saw Annie lying in bed, drenched in sweat, gasping for every breath. He'd watched her shriek in pain, swearing she hated him for planting the babe inside her. He'd listened to her beg him to save her life, to save her baby's life. He'd heard her screams until he'd thought he'd go insane from the helplessness he'd felt.

Damn, he'd tried. He'd called in every doctor and apothecary in London to help her. And later, near the end, she'd pleaded with him to cut the baby from her and end her life.

Adam . . . Adam . . .

He swallowed hard. The damning, unwanted images from the past faded from his thoughts.

"You have to know telling you about our wives was hard for us," Bray said in a low voice as a couple of young ladies walked very slowly past them.

"Damn hard," Harrison admitted under his breath. "But, all right, we've admitted we should have told you that afternoon at your house."

"Hell, no, you should have written the minute you knew." Adam looked from Bray to Harrison. "Did you think I wouldn't be happy for you?"

"Of course not," Harrison said.

"That's not it at all," Bray added. "We didn't want to—I don't know. Just take our word for it that it wasn't easy to tell you our wives are expecting a babe when you lost yours."

"If I hadn't come to London, when were you going to tell me?" he asked crossly.

"After the babes were born," Harrison admitted.

"And we knew everything was all right," Bray finished. "Adam, I know what hell you went through with Annie those three days. Remember, I was there with you."

Adam remembered.

Bray's mouth thinned in a grimace. He touched Adam's shoulder, but Adam shrugged it off and turned away.

"I'm fine," he said, but he wasn't. They were his friends and he was happy for them. They deserved sons, but he was worried for them, too. Bray and Harrison were built like him. Tall, with wide, muscular shoulders. What if their wives had the same problem Annie had and couldn't deliver the babe?

Adam wanted a drink. He turned to head for the beverage table and his gaze lighted on a tall, slender young lady staring at the dance floor. She wasn't smiling as though enjoying the lively dancers. Her expression was more one of wistfulness. It almost spoke of envy. But why would a stunning beauty have reason to envy anyone?

The neckline of her pale pink gown swept low, showing a gentle swell of enticing breasts. A flowing, frothy skirt seemed to flutter down her legs. Her carriage was straight, but not rigid. Expressive eyes, small nose, and shapely lips all came together beautifully, making a lovely face. But standing there with no one else near her, watching the dancers, she looked very much the way he felt at the moment—totally alone. And suddenly he sensed there were emotions deep inside her that were also in him.

Adam glanced at Bray, nodded in the young lady's direction, and said, "What's her name?"

"Miss Katherine Wright. Niece to our host. She made her debut a couple of years ago."

"I'm going to ask her to dance," Adam said, and turned away.

"No, wait," Bray said. "Don't do that."

Harrison grabbed his arm as he passed and tried to hold him. "Adam, stop. Not her."

Adam shrugged off his friend's grasp and kept walking.

Chapter 5

. . . she, poor soul,
Knows not which way to stand, to look, to speak,
And sits as one new-risen from a dream.
    —The Taming of the Shrew, *act 4, scene 1*

He didn't stop until he stood between the young lady and the dance floor. "Miss Wright?" he asked.

Long, full lashes rose, and she looked up at him with the most vibrant green eyes he'd ever seen. In that instant, Adam's lower stomach tightened perceptibly and his lower body thickened. He hadn't felt that instant rush of deep, aching desire in way too long, and he didn't know if he wanted to embrace it or run from it. He didn't ever remember feeling such a strong pull of awareness, not even when he first saw Annie.

Now that he was standing before her, gazing into those deep green pools, he felt sure he saw not only wistfulness, but a hint of sadness in their depths. That intrigued him even more.

"Miss Wright?" he said again. "I know we haven't been properly introduced, but I'm the Earl of Greyhawke. Would you give me the pleasure of finishing this dance with me?"

She looked stricken by his question, but not fragile. Her eyes opened wider. The softer, more personal emotions quickly faded to surprise. She opened her mouth as if to speak, but it was as if she couldn't find the breath to say the words. She promptly closed her lips again without uttering a sound.

Adam could understand that she was astonished he'd approached her without benefit of a proper introduction. Some people had been banished from Society for less serious infractions. But good Lord, they were eighteen years into the nineteenth century. Surely she wouldn't insist they stand on such an old ceremony. If he was willing to overlook the presentation, why couldn't she?

He said again, "Would you like to dance?"

Still, she remained quiet, searching his face as if trying to ascertain if he were real or a figment of her imagination. Her continued hesitation to speak baffled him.

Adam felt an unfamiliar prickle of rejection. He should have stayed with the easier idea of getting a drink. What had made him think this beautiful young lady looked as lonely as he felt and that she would be agreeable to lightening his load for a few moments on the dance floor?

Damnation, it wasn't that he wanted to dance. He could take or leave a set around the floor. At the moment, he just wanted to do anything other than think about Bray, Harrison, their wives, and their babes.

Suddenly, and maybe more than a little irrationally, but still peeved that his friends sought to leave him out of a very important part of their lives, he bristled and said, "It's a simple question, Miss Wright. I'm not asking you to marry me, just to dance."

Her head tilted back farther and her chin lifted boldly. But rather than being affronted by his terse manner, she seemed amused. The hint of a lovely smile lifted one corner of her mouth and she said, "Then it's my misfortune that it's not a marriage proposal, because if it had been, I'd be delighted to say yes. But since it's merely an invitation to dance, I'll say no. Is that simple enough for you, my lord?"

Her voice was sweet and unhurried, gentler than he'd expected, especially since his last sentence to her had been a bit abrupt. It washed over him as silkily as warm, sudsy water. Adam's irritation melted away. And much to his surprise, he felt another tightened tug of sexual awareness. She had mettle, and that appealed to him.

"In that case, Miss Wright, I suppose it's a good thing I wasn't asking for your hand."

"A very good thing," she answered in the same light tone and manner as before. "You just saved yourself from being taken off the marriage mart tonight."

Her response surprised him again. She obviously wasn't the least bit shy to be talking to an earl. In fact, she was actually impertinent. And blast it, he liked that, too.

He relaxed and took the time to give her a more thorough consideration. Thick, rich-looking auburn hair was attractively swept up with pink ribbons woven through it. Parchment-pale skin, beautiful face, slender throat, ample breasts. From what he could discern from the high-waisted gown she wore, he had every reason to believe she had a shapely body beneath her gown. Yes, she was very pleasing to him.

Adam casually crossed his arms over his chest. "Must I wait for a proper introduction before you will dance with me?"

"I'm not that supercilious, my lord."

That was abundantly clear, yet she'd refused him. "Then perhaps you will indeed need a marriage proposal before you will share a set with me."

She inhaled deeply, and he couldn't keep his gaze from dropping to her chest to watch the rise and fall. He had lived lonely for far too long and she was far too tempting for his precarious state.

"Not even then," she answered.

Then when?

She was frustrating him more than his friends had. He lowered his arms and said, "My apologies if my information was wrong and I'm mistaken and you're married?"

A slight flush heightened her cheeks. "No, my lord. I'm not wed, nor am I betrothed."

That piqued his interest in her even more. "Then I can only assume that because you are the niece of a powerful duke, you have no interest in dancing with a lowly earl."

"A lowly earl?" she questioned, and her eyes sparkled with amusement that was infectious. "I think perhaps you would like for that to be the case. Maybe that way you could say I met your expectations."

Hellfire, he hadn't expected anything. No, that wasn't true. He'd expected a dance. Was that too much to ask? What he hadn't expected was for her to be so charming, so arousing, and he certainly hadn't expected her to refuse him.

But he said, "I had no expectations other than a few steps, skips, and twirls across the dance floor."

"But alas, it's just that I don't dance."

His brows rose in disbelief. His fascination with her was growing with each sentence she spoke. He held her pinioned with his gaze and said, "The niece of a duke and you don't dance?"

"That's right," she said confidently, with no other excuses to follow.

"I find that difficult to believe. Perhaps it's that you just don't care to dance with me?"

A wrinkle formed in her brow. "Wouldn't it be foolish of me to decline a lively quadrille with a handsome gentleman such as yourself and especially an earl?"

Yet you do.

"Well . . ." He crossed his arms again and smiled ruefully. He was actually enjoying their banter and was in no hurry for it to end. "I admit I was thinking that very thing, but still you declined my offer."

"Then don't you think that I must have a very good reason for not dancing with you?"

"Indeed I do, but I don't know what it is. Perhaps you are a young lady who enjoys the thrill of being chased by all the handsome bachelors in England?"

She granted him a soft, teasing smile that showed beautiful even teeth. She even laughed a little, a lilting sound that swept over him like a cooling breeze on a rare, sultry summer day. Chances were she had no idea how instinctively sensual she was. He would love to be the one to awaken her womanly desires.

"I don't run either, my lord."

Though her voice was breathy, her eyes, her expression, challenged him to continue their lighthearted conversation. The devil take it, Adam had never been able to ignore a challenge. She was flirting with him, and he was devouring every moment of it as if he were a hungry animal. And after more than two years on the northern coast, perhaps he was.

All right, she had him right where she wanted him. The lure to play this out her way was too great to ignore. He had to take the enticement she had been laying out before him, whether intended or not, since he'd first caught sight of her. He meant to see she didn't win this battle between their wills.

"I don't like to lose, Miss Wright. What will it take for you to dance with me?"

She looked as if she were pretending to think about that and then said, "It will take a miracle."

Adam blew out a laugh. Softly, but a real laugh. He couldn't remember the last time it had actually felt good to laugh.

"I'm afraid that if I ever had favor with the one who bestows miracles, I lost it long ago."

"So did I, my lord."

Her eyes turned sad again, her words almost wistful again. The way she looked at him changed the rhythm of his heartbeat. Something moved deep inside him, and he knew what it was. Attraction. Deep, primal attraction that sank into his loins and buried there. He didn't want to be drawn to her, but he was. He couldn't stop the pull she had on him, and he didn't want to try.

Right now, more than anything, he wanted to dance

with her, to touch her hand, to caress her fingertips, to circle her waist and twirl her under his arm. He wanted to lose himself in the joy of feeling a woman in his arms, a woman he wanted to be close to.

"Dance with me," he said, and knew the words came from the depths of his heart and sounded far more earnest, and way more desperate, than he'd intended.

She blinked slowly. He could see deep emotions gathering in her eyes and settling on her face. Somehow he knew she was feeling what he felt. She wanted to dance with him, too. For a fleeting moment, his heart soared. Though the quadrille was almost over, she was going to say yes.

Instead, she moistened her lips, swallowed, and said, "I don't dance, my lord. I have never danced and I never will."

Her voice was clotted with emotion and hampered by sudden erratic breathing. He saw a flash of anguish in her eyes. Why did a request to dance evoke such a response from her? A desire to draw her to his chest and soothe her grew inside him.

Before he could respond to her, she said, "Now, please excuse me, my lord."

She turned away, and that was when he saw she used a cane.

Oh, hell!

She relied heavily on it to walk, but her shoulders never dropped and her back never bowed. Disbelief assailed him. All the time he stood in front of her, he never saw the cane in her hand. How had that happened? It must have been hidden in the folds of her gown. He must have been too intrigued by her countenance, her eyes, and her words to notice that she supported herself with a cane.

Adam felt as if all six feet four inches of him flattened to the floor. He let out a frustrated sigh. That had to be the worst blunder he'd ever made. Fate was definitely making it up to him for all the times it saved his life when he was younger. Why hadn't she just told him?

The music came to an end, the sound of hands clapping and feet tamping on the dance floor quieted. He started to go after Miss Wright to apologize, but she'd been too quickly swallowed up in the group leaving the dance floor.

And what would he say to her, anyway?

Damned if he knew, but he had to try to find a way to let her know he wasn't being heartless. That was, if she ever agreed to speak to him again. He turned and looked over at Bray and Harrison. They both quickly glanced away from him. They had watched him stand there and talk to her, and neither of them had made a move to come to his aid. He should kill both of them. Yes, strangling them with his bare hands might feel damn good right about now.

He strode over to them with purpose and said, "You two bloody blackguards let me walk over there and ask Miss Wright to dance knowing she couldn't. You are supposed to be my friends. Which one of you wants to die first?"

Bray and Harrison each quickly pointed to the other and said, "Him."

"I should tie up both of you with a boulder and rope and send you straight to the bottom of the Thames."

"Please, not me," Bray said, clearly holding his laughter in check. "You know I hate a cold swim."

"I'm not interested in such a black, watery demise either," Harrison said, hiding a smile by wiping the corner of his mouth with his thumb. "But you can't say we didn't try to warn you not to ask her to dance."

"Not very hard," Adam muttered.

"I thought we tried very hard, didn't you, Harrison?" Bray said, the edges of his lips quivering.

"I know I did," Harrison agreed. "You'll remember, Adam, I even tried to hold you."

"And that's the only reason I've decided to spare your lives." Adam stopped and hesitated. "What do you know about her?"

Bray cleared his throat and said, "Not much. This is her second or maybe third Season. She seems to spend time at the parties with a group of ladies who call themselves the Wilted Tea Society."

Adam frowned. "What kind of name is that?"

"A dreadful one," Harrison said. "I've heard it's in reference to the fact that the ladies are not old enough to be dried-up weeds on a shelf as true spinsters, but most of them are getting older and still unwed, so they are only slightly wilted."

Adam harrumphed at that idea. Miss Wright was not in any way slightly wilted. "Do you know what happened to her?"

"I'm remembering her leg was injured in a carriage accident, but I can't be sure," Harrison said.

"It was," Bray added. "Everyone in her family was killed but her. And from what I heard, she almost died."

That would be devastating to anyone. "Recent?" Adam asked.

Bray shook his head. "I don't think so, but just how long ago it was I don't know. I'm afraid I don't know any details."

"Sorry, ol' chap. Neither do I," Harrison said when Adam looked to him for more answers.

Adam remembered seeing sadness in her eyes before their conversation had begun. Perhaps she'd been thinking about the accident. And what about the wistfulness he'd sensed in her as well? Why was that on her lovely face? Was it because she couldn't dance?

Suddenly, Adam had the outrageous thought that he could teach her to dance, if she'd let him. He didn't know where that thought had come from, but he let go of it quickly. He didn't even know what was wrong with her leg, or foot, or whatever the hell it was that caused her to limp and need a cane.

Adam would acknowledge that he felt empathy and a tenderness for her. She had obviously been hurt, but pursuing a young lady for any reason was not in his plans.

Would never be in his plans again.

"She lives with the duke, his brother, and their sister," Bray offered. "But for how long I don't know."

"I do know she's not without beaux," Harrison offered. "As you would imagine, being that she's the duke's only unmarried niece. I think several eligible bachelors have called on her the past two Seasons. I heard that more than a handful have put pressure on the duke for her to accept their proposal. She's refused them all."

"Perhaps they've all made as big a blunder as I just

did," Adam said, grumbling more to himself than his friends.

"I doubt that."

"Harrison," Bray admonished with a roll of his eyes and a slight shake of his head.

Harrison cleared his throat. "Sorry, Adam. I mean, I can find out more about her if you want."

"I don't," Adam said quickly. "I'm capable of asking her anything I might want to know."

"Fair enough. We'll leave it up to you."

"Look," Bray said, "why don't we skip dinner here and go over to White's for a few drinks and a game of cards and billiards?"

"I'm staying here," Adam said. "You two go ahead."

He couldn't leave until he spoke to Miss Wright again. She aroused protective feelings in him that were unwelcome and unsettling, but he had to talk to her again. He wouldn't allow himself to be interested in her no matter how lovely and clever she was. All he wanted to do was let her know he hadn't meant to be so lame-headed. And he intended to find out what was wrong with her leg. Was it her hip, her knee, or her ankle that caused her problem?

"I don't plan to stay for brandy after the dinner, but I do plan to stay for the meal. How about you, Bray?"

"Same here," he said. "Unless, of course, Adam needs me to stay."

"Better yet," Adam said with a rumble in his voice, "why don't you two go home to your wives? I'm sure they need you. I just discovered that I can still get in trouble without your help."

"Indeed you can," Harrison said. He tried to hide his

smile again, but the quiver at the corners of his mouth betrayed him, and suddenly he and Bray were laughing out loud.

Adam twitched a smile, too. He couldn't stay angry with his friends. Besides, it was his fault that he hadn't noticed Miss Wright held a cane. She must have thought him a nodcock with the way he was demanding she dance with him.

He'd enjoyed Miss Wright's flirting and banter, and though his body was telling him he desperately wanted to, he couldn't pursue her.

Chapter 6

*That deep torture may be called a hell
When more is felt than one hath power to tell.*
—The Rape of Lucrece, *1287–88*

Katherine was mortified.

No, she was horrified.

No, it was worse than either of those, but she didn't think there was an adequate word to describe just how she felt. The earl had actually asked her to dance!

A weaker woman would have fainted, thrown herself out the window, or jumped off the balcony. All Katherine could do was sigh. Quite heavily, as she gathered her tattered wits about her and, with the aid of her simple wooden cane, walked away from Lord Greyhawke.

She quickly melted into the crowd leaving the dance floor. Not much bothered Katherine anymore, and she couldn't remember a time that anyone had gotten the best of her, but the earl had done just that with his simple, perfectly legitimate question.

Long ago, she'd learned to live with her troublesome leg. After all, it had been more than twelve years since

the accident and ten since she'd reinjured her leg and
made it worse by falling down the stairs when she was
nine. For a while she'd pitied herself, and then for a longer time she'd used it as a shield against other hurts,
and on a few occasions she had been known to wear it
like a badge of honor. Now it had become a part of her
and she seldom thought about it. If she rose to walk, she
picked up her cane first.

Katherine was used to people staring at her, knowing it was odd for someone so young to use a cane. She'd
used it every day since she was nine years old, and she'd
never had anyone fail to recognize that she held it. When
she'd looked up at the handsome, powerfully built gentleman standing before her, her heart had started beating so wildly that she'd thought it might burst right
through her chest.

Of course she couldn't answer him when he first
spoke to her. One, because she was mesmerized by his
gorgeous brandy-colored eyes; two, because no one had
ever asked her to dance before; and three, because at that
moment she would have given everything she owned to
have been without blemish and able to say yes to the
handsome stranger.

As they'd talked, she'd realized the persistent earl
hadn't seen her cane. He hadn't even noticed when she'd
glanced down and seen that it was hidden in the folds
of her gown. When he'd first talked to her, he'd seemed
distracted and perhaps a bit on edge, but after they'd
conversed for a short while, he'd relaxed and seemed to
enjoy their banter.

Why couldn't he have just come up to her and started
a pleasant conversation about the music, or her uncle,

or the weather? That's what a normal gentleman would have done. But no, arrogant rogue that he was, he'd startled the daylights out of her and caused her heart to race by asking her to dance.

And he had been devilishly brash, overconfident, and way too clever about it, too! Imagine him saying he wasn't asking her to marry him. What kind of man said a thing like that to a young lady? Especially one he'd never been properly introduced to. Katherine sighed again. Obviously the kind of man who made her stomach tighten, her breath quicken, and her heartbeat race.

His thick, shiny brown hair was surprisingly long for the current style. It had been neatly pulled back in a queue and tied with a thin strip of leather. Younger gentlemen seldom wore queues anymore. But it had made him look rather dashing. Exceptionally daring. And way too dangerous for her sensibilities.

Katherine knew very little about the Earl of Greyhawke other than that he'd left London after his wife died and hadn't returned, as far as she knew, until tonight. She'd never given the man any thought. She'd never had reason to because he hadn't been in London since her debut. If she had thought about him, she would have expected him to be older since most of the eligible gentlemen who had been married were much older than the earl. And even though he'd surprised her greatly with his request that she dance with him, he was easily the most intriguing gentleman she'd met since her making her first appearance in Society.

She was drawn to the strength she'd sensed inside him, and his tenacity, too. He wasn't tentative or awkward when talking to her, as were some of the gentlemen who had tried to win her favor over the last couple of years. What had impressed her most about the earl was that he hadn't treated her as if she were a delicate flower that might fall apart petal by petal if he said the wrong thing to her. But perhaps that was because he obviously didn't know she held a cane.

Dared she add the captivating earl to her list of possible husbands? Her stomach tightened at the thought. But she'd better not. Especially since he'd asked her to dance. He'd been so eager to join the quadrille, no doubt he enjoyed the pastime very much. She'd already decided to mark off all the gentlemen who loved to dance, and it was best she stay with that plan.

"There you are," Madeline Dormer said, sweeping up from behind Katherine, taking hold of her elbow, guiding her out of the dance floor traffic and over to a nearby wall. "Wasn't that fine-looking gentleman you were talking to just now the mysterious Earl of Greyhawke? Of course it was. I don't know why I'm asking something that I already know the answer to."

"Is he mysterious?" Katherine asked.

"Oh my, yes, he is," Melba Tiploft answered Katherine as she came up beside Madeline and joined them. "This is the first time he's been in London in over two years. Two long years, I might add. How did you manage to merit a conversation with the beast, my dear?"

"Don't be dull, Melba," Madeline said. "She's the duke's niece and this is his dinner party. That's how she managed."

"The beast?" Katherine queried Melba. "Lord Greyhawke?"

"Don't you know?" Melba questioned, her pale blue eyes showing surprise. "I thought everyone had heard."

"Remember, she's led a sheltered life," Madeline said.

"No, I haven't," Katherine argued. Even though she knew it to be true, she didn't like hearing anyone say it.

"My dear friend, if you don't know why he is called the beast, you have. But I'm happy to enlighten you. For a time after he left London he was referred to as the beast because he was so distraught after his wife died trying to have their child that he destroyed the inside of his house. Isn't that right, Madeline?"

"That's what all the gossip columns said, so it must have been true. At least, most people agree there is always some truth in what the scandal sheets say. I mean, they don't make up their news." Madeline's eyes turned dreamy and her voice softened. "I can't imagine what it must be like to love someone that much, can you?"

Katherine's heartbeat slowed. She could. But then maybe that was because she understood uncontrollable grief. She'd loved her family that much. After they were killed and only she was left alive, there were times she felt like destroying everything in sight, too.

But to her friends she simply whispered, "No, I hadn't heard that about him."

"Oh, Katherine," Penny Marchfield said as she sidled up beside the much taller and buxom Madeline to form a line of females in front of Katherine. "Every young lady in this room had her eyes on the Earl of Greyhawke the minute he stepped through the doorway. I've never heard such whispering as was going on after he appeared. And who should be the first young lady he talks to? You! Didn't you just want to melt into a puddle?"

"When did you meet him?" Melba continued with the conversation, her eyes filled with mocked accusation. "And why didn't you tell us you had met him?"

"How could you keep from telling us, is what I want to know?" Penny exclaimed.

"But never mind that," Melba added quickly. "You must tell us all about him. And right now."

"Indeed you shall," Madeline echoed. "We won't let you go anywhere until we've heard all. I'm sure the duke approves of him, yes? I mean, he must. He's an earl!"

Penny sighed softly. "He looks just the way I imagined a rake of the highest order to look. Tall, broad shoulders, and too dangerous for words. I think he would make all the angels in heaven swoon if he walked by them, don't you?"

"Angels are men, Penny," Melba corrected tightly.

Penny huffed and jerked her hands to her slim hips. "They are not. Not all of them. Not the ones I'm talking about, anyway."

"Never mind that, you two," Madeline said. "Tell us, Katherine, what did you talk about for so long?"

Katherine's gaze had darted from one young lady to the other as each had a say and asked questions about her conversation with the earl without giving her time to respond to any of them. At thirty, Madeline was the tallest and oldest of all the ladies in the Wilted Tea Society, a group that she'd started three years ago. It wasn't a large group, and the only criterion was that you couldn't be betrothed or married. But it seemed few young ladies wanted to belong to a gathering that called themselves wilted tea.

Katherine, like all the current members, found humor

in the name and enjoyed their weekly gatherings for tea, friendship, and the latest gossip. Each week they were given a sewing project to work on and bring back to the next meeting. When the group formed, Madeline had insisted they couldn't meet just for their own enjoyment but must do something worthwhile for less fortunate people, too. So the ladies embroidered handkerchiefs or knitted shawls, mittens, or caps and once a week took them to an orphanage. Katherine had joined her first Season because of this. If not for having been born into a wealthy family, she could have been sent to an orphanage after her parents were killed.

Contrary to what most people thought, the ladies in the group hadn't given up on their dreams of one day meeting a handsome prince, falling in love, and making a match. It was just that they were getting older and still unwed. Madeline had asked her to join. And Katherine soon found she had more in common with the slightly older ladies than the ones who, like her, were making their debut into Society.

"Well?" Madeline said. "Don't just continue to stand there mute. What did the earl have to say?"

Katherine didn't want to tell them what she and Lord Greyhawke had talked about. It was private, but it was also clear she wouldn't leave the barricade they had formed in front of her until she gave them something to chew on.

"We didn't talk very long," she said, stalling for time so she could come up with something credible to say that wouldn't be too far from the truth.

"Ha!" Penny exclaimed as her dark eyes widened.

"I was counting the seconds. It must have been at least ten minutes."

"Don't be ridiculous," Katherine told the petite lady with the shock of wild cinnamon-colored hair that she had tried to tame with pins, combs, and flowers. "It couldn't have been more than five, if even that long."

"Just tell us what he wanted," Melba insisted.

"Nothing," Katherine said with a shake of her head, feeling a prick of guilt about the prevarication. He had wanted something. *To dance with her!*

"What did he say?" Madeline asked again.

"Not much. It was just a simple conversation. We talked about the quadrille that was taking place." Perhaps that stretched the truth a bit, too, but at this point she really wanted to settle this with as little fanfare as possible.

"Did he by chance mention me?" Penny asked expectantly. "I was on the dance floor."

"No, I'm sorry, Penny. We didn't talk about anyone specifically, but how lively the dancing was."

"And?" Melba prompted, eagerly making a motion with her hands for Katherine to say more and to say it more quickly.

"And, well, let's see . . . we talked about miracles."

"Miracles?" all three ladies exclaimed in astonishment at the same time.

"You asked me and I'm telling you," Katherine said, beginning to feel defensive.

"That's the most preposterous thing you've said," Melba squeaked.

"It's true," Katherine insisted.

"What kind of miracles?" inquired the smallest of the three young ladies.

"Who cares what kind, Penny?" Madeline said irritably. "It doesn't matter about that. Katherine isn't telling us anything that's worth hearing. I have to admit, I was hoping for something a little more interesting than that."

"I was hoping for something salacious or at least something bordering on scandalous," Melba blurted out, and suddenly all four ladies were laughing.

"It wasn't any of those things and all of you know it," Katherine offered when their laughing subsided.

"Let's be serious," Penny said. "Did he say whether he would be staying in London now and attending the Season?"

"Or if he's looking to make a match?" Melba questioned.

"Did he ask to call on you?"

"Or ask you to go for a ride in the park with him?"

Katherine gasped at the turn of the questions. "No, no, nothing like that, ladies. My goodness. We had just met. He wasn't going to be telling me what his plans are."

"Just tell us something he said," Madeline argued.

"I'm sorry, perhaps one of you can get more information out of him. I'm afraid I failed miserably, but I—" Katherine stopped and smiled gratefully when she heard a faint *ding-a-ling*. "Oh, there's the bell for dinner. I hope each of you is paired with an acceptable dinner partner. You all know that Auntie Lee will not accept any input from me no matter how hard I try. Now, I really must go. Uncle Willard will be waiting for me," she said, holding firmly to her cane and hastily pushing her way between Melba and Penny without apology. "You know how perturbed he gets if I'm late to join him."

"I was just coming to rescue you," Aunt Leola said, easing up beside Katherine as she cleared the female blockade. "I could see your friends were wearing you to a frazzle."

"Very much so."

"They were quizzing you about the earl. Am I right?"

Katherine looked over at her tall, thin aunt, who always held her chin lifted in a regal tilt. "Yes, Auntie." Katherine slowed her pace and added, "And I know you don't ever ask a question that you don't already know the answer to."

"Thank you, dearie." Auntie Lee's eyes sparkled and she preened. "Of course you're right, too. And you will be just as perceptive as I am one day, mark my words."

Katherine thought of how she'd botched her conversation with Lord Greyhawke. "I shall count on that, Auntie, for I fear I haven't developed that trait yet."

Lady Leola, as most people called Katherine's aunt, was lovely for her near sixty years, with wide-set eyes almost as green as Katherine's. Her father's sister had never been extravagant with her clothing, jewelry, or lifestyle. She'd never needed to be. She carried herself as if she were the most beautiful and most important person in the room, no matter how she was dressed or where she went. And Katherine knew that was how her Aunt Leola felt.

"So what did you tell your fluttering and chattering friends about the earl?"

"Nothing."

"Perfect," Auntie Lee said, giving Katherine another smile. "Ah, there's Viscount Treadfield. I must give him the disappointing news that I couldn't seat him beside the duke this evening because His Grace needs to talk to the lord mayor about a matter that will soon be coming up for a vote in Parliament. It's not true, of course, but I can't have anyone thinking they can tell me where they intend to sit at the duke's dinner table. See you inside, dearie."

Aunt Leola peeled away from Katherine as easily as she'd glided up beside her moments ago. Katherine shook her head, smiled, and kept walking.

Since the age of seven, Katherine had lived quietly with her elderly uncle the Duke of Quillsbury; his brother, her Uncle Willard; and their widowed sister, her Aunt Leola. Very quietly. Katherine had seldom had anyone her age to play with when she was young. On rare occasions, distant family members or friends would visit her uncle in whichever of his many houses they might be residing at the time, and they would bring children. But that didn't happen often.

For a long time after she went to live with her uncle, she found herself wanting to scream for no other reason than to hear some noise. Her aunt and uncles were quiet. The servants, tutors, and her maid were all quiet. Even the old clock that stood in the vestibule of the aged manor house chimed so softly that she couldn't hear it unless she was standing in front of it.

Before the accident, Katherine had lived with her parents and three older siblings. Their house was never quiet until after bedtime and seldom then. Even at night, if she awakened, she might hear one of her siblings talking in their sleep or her governess snoring. But since the accident, there were too many nights to count when she lay awake in her bed wishing that she could hear the sounds of her sisters' and her brother's laughter and their voices just one more time.

So even though she couldn't dance, would never dance, she loved coming to the parties and balls and watching others twirl and swirl so effortlessly around the dance floor. She embraced the packed rooms of people hustling and bustling about. The loud music, boisterous laughter, and hum of chatter invigorated her and reminded her that her goal was to marry and have many children laughing, playing, and running throughout the house. The only thing that had kept Katherine from that goal so far was finding a man she wanted to father the half-dozen children she intended to have. And she was working on a list of possible gentlemen so that she could accomplish that goal and keep her promise to her uncle Quillsbury that she would be betrothed by the end of the Season.

A glance toward the tall, arched double doors that led into the long, narrow dining room showed her uncle Willard waiting patiently for her. Lord Willard's gray hair was thinning at his crown, and deep lines fanned the edges of his eyes, but he hadn't lost his straight spine or noble, distinguished presence. He was several inches shorter and more slight of build than his elder brother the duke and much more cantankerous of late. The older he got, the more snappish he became. He'd spent most of his adult life in the military and was a stickler for discipline, expecting everyone to follow his command. Since she was a child, he'd been able to scold her with just a look, so she'd learned early never to be late for dinner.

She'd seldom seen Uncle Willard when she'd first come to live at the duke's house. She'd spent most of her time in bed recovering from her injuries, and he was often gone on an assignment for the military. When she was older, she realized Uncle Willard actually enjoyed having her in the house when he was there, to read to him, play chess with him, or on rare occasions play the pianoforte for him in the evenings after dinner.

Whenever they had conversations, he never rebuked her for speaking her mind, and she never failed to be honest with him about whatever matter they might be discussing at the time. He had a brilliant mind, and many were the times she would have loved to engage him in discussions about his work as a military officer, politics, or even science. But he would have none of that. He thought such topics too unsavory for her. Literature, poetry, and music were the only safe subjects of conversation for young ladies as far as he was concerned.

Katherine was fairly certain the reason Uncle Willard had become so ornery over the past couple of years was that he'd begun to lose his hearing. It was almost impossible to carry on an extended conversation with him, which was also one of the reasons she always sat beside him at formal dinners. With her, he didn't have to talk if he didn't want to. He disliked trying to make conversation with anyone other than family in a room teeming with chatter, clinking glasses, and tinkling silverware.

Uncle Willard greeted her with a smile, no doubt

because she was prompt, and she smiled, too, as she reached over and gave his clean-shaven cheek a kiss.

Waiting until he could see her lips move, she said, "Good evening, Uncle. Have you enjoyed the party so far?"

"Yes, my dear," he expressed much too loudly. "It's been quiet." He paused and winked at her, then continued, "And somewhat pleasant. I've been able to avoid hearing anyone I didn't want to talk to, but I haven't heard a word of what was said to me from the ones I wanted to talk to. You'd think everyone would know by now that I can't hear a bloody word they say and they'd speak up."

Katherine knew everyone spoke very loudly to him, even though he didn't know it. She was sad for him because his hearing loss continued to worsen and no doctor had been able to help him.

"I don't think anyone realizes it, Uncle."

"Well, they should. And how about you?" he asked. "How has your evening been?"

Without hesitation she answered, "Lovely as usual," and caught sight of Madeline staring at her as she passed by to enter the dining room.

"I saw you talking to the new Earl of Greyhawke, my dear. What did you think of him?"

She supposed with a dinner party that had only thirty guests, everyone would see everything that happened. Still, for some reason she wished no one had witnessed her conversation with Lord Greyhawke. Everyone wanted to ask her about him, and though she didn't really understand why, she was reluctant to share her conversation with the earl.

Guests were filing past them and entering the dining room. She would have to talk loudly for Uncle Willard, and she didn't want anyone passing by to hear what she had to say, so she answered, "Perhaps we should talk about that tomorrow, Uncle. I think most everyone has been seated in the dining room."

He looked around and nodded. "Very well." He reached over and gently pinched her cheek affectionately. "That's what we'll do."

His brief squeeze wasn't her favorite show of fondness. She had always expected that one day he would understand that at twenty she was too old to have her cheek tweaked, but he was still doing it. She now had little hope he would ever stop. And she loved him too much to ever suggest it to him.

Uncle Willard extended his elbow. Katherine slipped her hand around the crook of his arm and he escorted her into the ornately decorated room. Tall, gilt-framed mirrors bracketed by brass candle sconces hung on each of the four walls. Two long, rectangular tables covered in fine white Irish linen had been set with the best crystal, china, and silver one could buy. The sides of both tables had fifteen small, armless chairs fitted tightly together. The duke always sat at the head of one table and Uncle Willard the other. Since both their wives had died, the places at the end of the tables were always left vacant.

Her uncle pulled out her chair and then turned to see Mrs. Isadora Henshawe waiting for him to help her be seated, too. Katherine heard him expel a low, exasperated sigh before greeting the lady. Mrs. Henshawe was a master at talking, and she seldom stopped for a breath. Uncle Willard would have to pretend he was having a lovely conversation with the lady by smiling, nodding, and occasionally shaking his head. Katherine doubted she would notice that he couldn't hear.

Katherine picked up her napkin while guests continued to file into the room to find their seats. She'd been dining at the duke's dinner parties for more than two years and long ago stopped wondering whom Aunt Leola would seat to her right. Katherine knew Uncle Willard wanted to be quiet and expected her to talk to whoever it was and not him.

Lady Leola handled all social events for the duke, including seating arrangements, and she wouldn't accept suggestions from anyone. Auntie Lee also knew that Mrs. Henshawe would talk from the moment she sat down to the moment she left. It wouldn't bother the widow at all that Uncle Willard wouldn't be able to hear a word she said. She was quite happy to talk, if only to herself. He would be miserable, and she would be delighted.

Tomorrow at the breakfast table, Auntie Lee would listen quietly to Uncle Willard's politely spoken words about her seating arrangements and then do exactly what she wanted to do at the next party. Katherine had seen very little change in the duke's household the twelve years she had lived in it.

Katherine propped the handle of her plain wooden cane against the table to her right, where it would be easy for her to grasp if she needed to excuse herself to the retiring room, and then began taking off her gloves. A shadow slowly fell across the table beside her, and her hands stilled. Her dinner partner for the evening had arrived.

Somehow before she looked up, before she thought

about glancing over at the place card, she knew the gentleman who had been seated beside her for the evening was the intriguing Earl of Greyhawke.

A shivery feeling skittered up Katherine's back, and her heart started its wild, erratic beating again.

Chapter 7

A heavy heart bears not a nimble tongue.
—Love's Labour's Lost, *act 5, scene 2*

Slowly, Katherine turned to her right and looked up. The first thing she saw was a tapered waist and a wide chest that filled out a white shirt outlined by a beige quilted waistcoat. Her gaze continued upward, past straight, broad shoulders to a beautifully tied neckcloth and on to a slightly square chin. She paused briefly at the wide masculine lips before skimming past a narrow nose and high cheekbones that led her vision to those intriguing brandy-colored eyes that had held her spellbound earlier in the evening.

Katherine's fast-beating heart felt as if it stumbled in her chest. A tingling sensation rippled across her breast and then floated slowly and deliciously all the way down to her toes. A teasing warmth settled low in her abdomen. There was no use trying to deny the potent power of his masculinity. She'd never been so intensely aware of a man and found she couldn't look away from the eyes that seemed to have the capacity to see into the depths of her soul.

The Earl of Greyhawke was tall and powerfully built, but nothing about him looked like a beast. Nothing about him seemed scary, yet she sensed he was a danger to her sensibilities.

"Good evening, Miss Wright," he said, pulling out his chair. "We meet again."

The Earl of Greyhawke smiled down at her as he bent to fit his tall, muscular frame into the small chair. As he did, he accidentally knocked the table, sending her cane clattering to the floor. She immediately reached down to collect it, and while she was coming up, the back of her head bumped his chin as he was reaching down to pick up the cane.

"Ouch," she whispered.

"Ugh," he grunted.

And together they both whispered, "My apologies."

She looked around to see if her uncle or anyone else might have seen or heard their mishap, but there was so much chatter and scraping of chairs as others seated themselves that no one seemed to have noticed her head bumping the earl.

Lord Greyhawke carefully seated himself and rubbed his chin. "Never let it be said you are soft in the head, Miss Wright."

A tremor of a smile threatened Katherine's lips. She couldn't help wondering if their meetings were destined to be a series of debacles. "And never let it be said that you can't take one on the chin."

She once again placed the cane against the table between her and the earl. Something about it being there made her feel as if it were a shield to protect her from her growing attraction to him.

"You do know our conversation earlier this evening would have been more congenial for both of us if you had simply told me you had injured your leg and couldn't dance."

Katherine drew in a breath and settled her hands in her lap as she looked at the earl. The lines in his forehead and around the edges of his mouth and eyes had tightened a bit. Judging from his expression, she sensed he was a little piqued at her. For some wickedly good reason, it pleased her that she'd managed to get under his skin as he had hers. She had already surmised that he was not the kind of man anyone could easily get the best of, no matter the situation.

"I seldom do anything the easy way, my lord."

"So I learned the hard way. I will keep that bit of information in the forefront of my mind for the rest of the evening," he said, more under his breath than to her as he unfolded his napkin with a shake before laying it across his lap.

Katherine had no qualms about placing the blame for their miscommunication squarely on his shoulders, where it rightly belonged. In a lighthearted tone she said, "I do have to admit that I was rather stunned you couldn't see the very obvious cane in my hand."

He relaxed against the back of the too-small chair and folded his arms across his chest in a comfortable manner that was far too informal for a dinner party at a duke's house. "How could I when I couldn't take my eyes off your beautiful face?"

Katherine's brows drew together in disbelief, and

then she relaxed and laughed lightly. "And I see I will have to keep in mind that you have no borders when it comes to flattery."

"I only rely on it when it's deserved, Miss Wright."

"For some reason, I find I'm disinclined to believe that, my lord."

"It's the truth." One corner of his mouth lifted in an attractive half grin. "So rather than enlighten me as to your predicament, you decided to just limp away and leave me feeling about two feet tall rather than just tell me you *couldn't* dance?"

Limp away?

No, he was more than piqued. He thought she'd duped him in some way, and he was downright annoyed. She decided to savor the moment. Clearly, he was accustomed to being in control of every situation and getting his own way. If he was uncomfortable, it served him right for missing what was before his disarming eyes. Besides, she was sure he was exaggerating; she couldn't imagine a man of his size feeling just two feet tall, no matter the circumstance.

Feigning concern, she said, "Two feet tall? Did you, my lord?"

"I did and you know it," he grumbled lightly, and picked up the glass of wine sitting in front of him. "Why didn't you just tell me?"

She smiled sweetly to let him know she wasn't in the least bothered by him and also to let him know it didn't upset her that he was frustrated with her. "Should I have held up my cane and said, 'Look at this, my lord'?" she asked.

"Yes," he answered. "Or a simple 'I've hurt my foot' would have helped immensely."

The temptation to needle him more was too great. She might as well keep the advantage while she had it. "I kept saying to myself, This man is obviously intelligent. He's an earl. Surely he will soon figure out why I am declining his offer to dance."

He opened his mouth to respond, but a servant bent between them and ladled a vegetable broth into her soup bowl and then the earl's.

After the servant moved on, she added, "And for your information, my lord, I don't limp."

He placed his glass back on the table. Amusement finally settled into his features. "Really?"

"Yes," she insisted, though why she'd said such an outrageous and untrue thing, she had no idea. She used a cane! Of course she had a limp. But that didn't mean she wanted to admit it to him. "I'm positive."

"Hobble?" he asked cautiously.

It was too late to back down now. Katherine shook her head. "Nor do I shuffle, stagger, or stumble."

"In that case, pardon me, Miss Wright. I should have said your 'unusual gait.' Is that better?"

"Much," she said pleasantly, thinking maybe it was all right that she'd made such a ridiculous statement after all. This was the liveliest conversation she could remember ever having. "And I'll thank you to remember that."

"I'm not likely to forget anytime soon."

Feeling pleased with herself for holding her own and successfully matching wits with the handsome earl,

Katherine lifted her spoon and tasted the soup. It was hot and delicious, as usual.

From the corner of her eye, she noticed Lord Greyhawke hadn't picked up his spoon. He was probably trying to come up with a way to get even with her. *Let him try,* she thought.

She glanced over at him. "You really should taste your soup, my lord, or next you'll be saying it's my fault that it's cold."

He chuckled, picked up his spoon, and then turned his attention to the guest on his right. The beautiful but elderly Dowager Countess of Littlehaven had asked him a question.

Katherine quietly ate her soup while Mrs. Henshawe and Lady Littlehaven kept both her dinner partners busy. Katherine's uncle Quillsbury was famous for his sumptuous five-course dinners, which included excellent wines and ports and didn't take hours to be served. Having been a pampered duke for all his adult life, he had little patience for things that didn't go his way. He wanted each course served as soon after the other as possible. Extra staff was always brought in to make sure everything went smoothly when he had a dinner party. He wanted the dining and fellowship of others, but he no longer wanted to sit around the dinner table for hours and listen to endless chatter. His guests also appreciated his attention to that detail.

The soup bowls were gathered, and shortly thereafter a small plate of pickled beets and sweetened figs was set before her. Mrs. Henshawe, who was seated directly in front of Katherine, had managed to garner the earl's attention away from the countess. He was politely listening to a story she was telling about a time when she traveled to Scotland and was set upon by highwaymen. The earl would alternate between looking at the lady and eating his beets and figs.

After the plates were cleared away and Mrs. Henshawe paused to take a breath, the earl turned to Katherine and said, "I must say, Miss Wright, that course reminded me of you."

Candlelight sparked in his eyes, and she felt warmth emanating from him, even though his words perplexed her. Many gentlemen had commented in various ways on her beauty, her gown, and her hair, but no one had ever mentioned food.

She wrinkled her nose at his suggestion. "I'm not sure I've ever been compared to food, my lord. In what way do you mean?"

"It was beautiful to look at, as are you. One bite would be as sweet as you are. The next would be vinegary, as you can be when you don't like what I say. Occasionally I would get a little taste of both at the same time, and that was when it was most delectable, as are you."

Katherine looked into his eyes and knew that he wasn't just flattering her. He meant what he was saying. He enjoyed the fact that she had no qualms about taking him to task and that her tartness had not bothered him. The underlying meaning of his words spread over her like a fire-warmed blanket on a cold night and rushed heated color to her cheeks.

To counter the way she suddenly felt, she laughed softly and said, "Your compliments never stop, do they, my lord. Still, I'm glad to know you are enjoying the food."

"I'm quite pleased with the food and the company, Miss Wright."

And so was she.

Katherine picked up her wine, sipped, and thought on what he'd said while the servant cleared away their plates.

"What happened to your leg?" Lord Greyhawke asked as the servant moved on.

Katherine replaced her glass, picked up the starched white napkin, and dabbed at one corner of her mouth. "An accident," she said, not allowing her gaze to meet his.

"What kind?"

"Carriage," she said, fixing her gaze on the flickering flame of the candle in front of her.

"Was it recently?"

"No."

Suddenly, she was the one who was uncomfortable. She knew people wondered about her injury. It was natural to be curious, but the earl was the first person in quite some time to be brave enough to query her about it. Once again reminding her he was not a gentleman she could take lightly in any conversation.

"Was it a long time ago?"

"Yes."

"Were you a child?"

"Yes."

"How old were you?"

"Seven."

"Your answers are short," he said in a sympathetic tone.

She remained quiet, staring at the light glimmering off the wineglass.

"And you aren't looking at me," he added in a low tone. "Does it still upset you to talk about it?"

"Yes," she answered truthfully.

How could it not?

Her entire family was killed. Her father. Her mother and the baby she was expecting. Her two older sisters and her brother. All gone from her life in an instant.

"It's been over twelve years now," she said. "I know it should no longer bother me, but there are times I remember every detail of it as clearly as if it had been yesterday, and I just have to banish them from my mind."

"I can understand that," he said softly. "How did it happen?"

Before she could answer, a servant placed a piece of baked white fish surrounded by five delicate oysters in front of her. The connection she'd momentarily felt with him was broken. He was probing but gentle. For an instant, she'd actually wanted to answer his question.

Katherine inhaled deeply and then turned to look at him, wondering why she had opened up to him and said anything at all. She never spoke about the accident or her family to anyone. Long ago, she'd discovered that if she didn't talk about her family, if she didn't try to remember them, it didn't hurt so badly.

"Lord Greyhawke," she said, adding more censure to her voice than she had intended, "do you want me asking personal questions about your past?"

His brows flew up defensively and he shifted in the chair. Even though he was obviously taken aback by her question, he answered calmly, "No, I can't say I do."

"And neither do I want you asking me." She picked up her fork and cut into the steaming fish.

"I get the distinct impression that you enjoy giving me information a little at a time."

"You would be wrong."

They ate in silence for a short time, but finally he said, "You think I was intruding and prying?"

"Prying?" she repeated. She saw no cruelty or eagerness for gossip in his expression; still, she buffered her words by saying, "Perhaps. Or maybe you're just as curious as the next person as to why an otherwise very strong and healthy young lady must use a cane to walk."

"You certainly haven't let it undermine your self-confidence."

Just as she was getting ready to tell herself the earl was an arrogant man, caring only about what he wanted and not worth her time, he surprised her. This time by giving her guarded approval. She remained quiet but gave him a hint of a smile before lifting a forkful of the fish into her mouth.

"Was it broken?" Lord Greyhawke asked, scooping two oysters onto his fork.

Twice. She could have told him, but she didn't like to talk about her injury. When she'd finally healed after the second break, she'd never again let her leg hamper her daily life except for the fact that she couldn't run, or skip, or dance like other young ladies. And, well, she had to take her time going up or down the stairs, too. But with the aid of her trusty cane, she could walk. She could even carry a cup of tea from the buffet to the breakfast table without spilling a drop.

She swallowed and turned to face him with an incredulous stare. "Did I not just say I don't want to talk about my past?"

"That was when we were discussing the accident," he answered innocently. "I was talking about your leg just now."

He was unbelievable. "They are one and the same and you know it. Or almost, anyway. You are quite incorrigible."

"I'm interested," he corrected.

In me or my injury? she started to ask, then thought better of it before the provoking words tumbled from her lips and instead returned her attention to her food. The scent of poached fish rose from the plate, and she thought, *Two more courses and then I will be free of the persistent earl with his probing questions.*

For a short time they ate in silence. She asked her uncle if he was enjoying his dinner. He smiled and nodded. The earl talked to the countess and Mrs. Henshawe again. The empty plates were removed and replaced with a thick slice of venison smothered in a dark onion gravy. After her first bite, she watched Lord Greyhawke cut into his meat with gusto. She liked the strength she saw in his hands as he worked his knife and fork and that he had such a healthy appetite.

She had hardly eaten three bites before his plate was clean. She'd never seen either of her uncles or any other gentleman enjoy a carving of meat as much as the earl seemed to.

She laid her knife and fork aside and said, "You ate as if you were starving, my lord."

He wiped his mouth and smiled sheepishly. "For food like that, Miss Wright, I was. That was the best meal I've had since I left London over two years ago. I hope you will pardon my lack of manners."

"I don't know why, but I rather liked watching you enjoy your food so much."

He looked down at her plate. "You've hardly touched yours."

"It's usually the case, I'm afraid. By the time I've had the soup, vegetable, fruit, and fish, I have little room for the main course of the evening and dessert."

He nodded. "And what is the dessert tonight?" he asked.

"Bread-and-fig pudding."

"I'll look forward to it."

She looked down at her plate and without thinking asked, "Would you like to finish mine?"

His brows rose in anticipation. "Would it be acceptable to switch plates at your uncle's dinner party?"

She pursed her lips. "No, of course not. I don't even know why I offered. It was such a strange thing for me to do."

Lord Greyhawke looked around the table. "Everyone is engaged in conversation," he said, a hint of mischief lacing his tone. "I don't think anyone would see us."

As far as Katherine knew, she had never disgraced herself at her uncle's table, but before she had the good sense to rescind her initial offer to the earl, she answered, "Then let's do it."

They lifted their plates at the same time. She took hold of his plate first, he released it, and all went well with the exchange; but when he grasped her plate, his fingers landed on top of hers. They both froze with the plate held between them. At his touch, Katherine's pulse quickened, her breasts tightened, and her skin tingled. The unexpected warmth of his hand on hers filled her with a breathless fluttering in her throat. She tried to look away from him, but it was as if something held her spellbound and looking into his fathomless gaze.

She sensed he was as surprised as she by whatever it was that happened between them from their accidental touch. Finally, he slipped the plate out of her grasp, letting his fingers slide lazily down hers as he did.

When she looked up, she saw that Mrs. Henshawe stared openmouthed and wide-eyed at her. A quick glance at her uncle told the same story. And she had no doubt that if she looked at the Dowager Countess of Littlehaven, she would see the same horror-stricken expression at such unacceptable social behavior.

Trying to hide the flush creeping into her cheeks, Katherine picked up her napkin and gently coughed into it while Lord Greyhawke did the sensible thing and settled for a drink of his wine. But their condemnation from the onlookers was not the reason Katherine's cheeks were burning. It was the realization of what had just happened between her and the earl. What she'd seen in Lord Greyhawke's eyes was his desire for her, and what she'd felt from his touch was her desire for him.

What in heaven's name was she going to do? She was attracted to the earl they called the beast.

Chapter 8

And weighest thy words before thou
givest them breath.
—Othello, *act 3, scene 3*

"Good night," Katherine called, and waved to Penny as she climbed into the carriage.

"Was that the last of our guests?" Aunt Leola asked as she and Katherine stood at the bottom of the front steps.

"Ours, yes," Katherine said, looking across the street. "Uncle Quillsbury's, no. I count three carriages waiting and probably one or two more that we can't see from here because of the hedge."

"No doubt the duke will be ready for bed and shoo them all out within an hour, but we won't worry about him. Let's go inside and you can tell me all about your evening sitting beside the infamous Earl of Greyhawke. You know, I only heard this morning that he was back in London. I have no idea how long he's been here, but I rushed an invitation over to his house, never expecting him to respond to such a late request. To my surprise, he immediately sent back a note accepting."

Probably because he was starving for a hearty meal.

"Luckily, I was able to squeeze in one more chair," her aunt said, and then paused before adding, "Right beside you."

"Why did you seat him beside me?"

"It was the easiest way to avoid upsetting my entire seating arrangements, of course. It would have been a nightmare of shuffling back and forth at the last minute if I'd tried to move anyone else." She purposefully paused. "I'm thinking now perhaps I should have."

"Why is that?" Katherine asked casually, though she was sure she knew the reason. She'd seen Lady Littlehaven bending her aunt's ear with a prolonged conversation.

Her aunt looked at her with piercing green eyes. "Did you really exchange dinner plates with the earl?"

Katherine would bet her pin money that the Dowager Countess of Littlehaven was the one who'd spilled the tattle. Still, she asked, "Which one told you? Lady Littlehaven or Mrs. Henshawe?"

"Both."

Oh dear!

There was nothing to do but admit to the breach in manners. "I'm sorry, Auntie. I know I shouldn't have done it, but all I can say is that I offered the food to Lord Greyhawke before I thought about the consequences."

"That is obvious, my dear. I did my best to smooth over your peccadillo by assuring them you saw a chip in the china and you simply couldn't let an earl eat off a dinner plate that had been damaged. Why, the broken piece could have been in his food. Imagine what would have happened if he'd bitten down on it!"

Katherine laughed. "Auntie, how did you get so clever?"

"With age, my dear. There are not many things that haven't passed by me at least once or twice. But I'm baffled as to why you would do such a thing. He had his own food."

Her aunt was not only clever, she was curious. Katherine shifted her weight from her good leg to her cane. She didn't want to be asked more questions about Lord Greyhawke. She had already been set upon by Melba, Madeline, and Penny twice tonight about the earl, and other ladies who stayed for coffee, too. Plus there was constant chatter in the drawing room about him and all the possible reasons he might have returned to Town after such a long absence. Most of the ladies were certain he'd come to London looking for a countess. Katherine had once again successfully dodged having to give any of them information about her discussions with the earl.

Lady Leola would not be so easy to evade.

"He had already finished his dinner and he still looked hungry," she said, deciding the truth was the best answer.

Her aunt looked aghast. "Hungry? That's preposterous. How does anyone look hungry?"

"Aunt Lee, I'm sorry. It's done. Over. All I can do is ask that you forgive me."

"Of course. That is not the issue here." She reached up and patted Katherine's cheek affectionately. "Knowing Lady Littlehaven as I do, I fear this incident will end up in the scandal sheets. And the duke will be asking me why you can get your name in gossip columns but not on a marriage license."

Auntie Lee looked so stricken that Katherine felt truly repentant for her antics at the dinner table. But how could she explain that even though she knew it was wrong, she'd wanted to do it for the earl?

"I will just have to tell Uncle Quillsbury that gossip is part of finding the right man to make a match."

"That will not satisfy the duke, my dear. Now, let's go in. My feet are getting cold."

"Auntie, may I stay out here for a little while? I know it's chilly, but look how big and bright and beautiful the moon is tonight. There isn't a cloud in the sky to shadow it. I promise I won't stay too long."

Auntie Lee didn't look up at the sky. She studied Katherine's face a bit more closely than Katherine would have liked. "Something tells me you want to stand out here in the quiet of the evening, look at that romantic moon, and think about Lord Greyhawke. Am I right?"

"He's like no one I've ever met before," Katherine admitted without fear of reprisal or teasing.

"That's saying a lot, my dear, considering you've been in Society for more than two years now and have met every eligible bachelor in the ton and most of the Italian counts who are visiting London, too. I must confess, it never crossed my mind when I seated the earl beside you that he might be the first gentleman to prick that hard shell of yours."

Did she have a hard shell? Yes, she'd rebuffed all the gentlemen who'd shown interest in her in the past, but she couldn't do that anymore. She'd promised the duke she would make a match by the end of the Season.

"Or that you might find favor with the man," her aunt continued.

Katherine was willing to admit to being interested in the earl. And once again, she wondered if she should add him to her list of prospects, even if he enjoyed dancing.

"The earl is very handsome and intriguing."

"Indeed he is."

"How well do you know him?"

"We've met, of course, but I don't know him."

"Did you hear gossip about him after he left London?" Katherine asked cautiously.

"Of course, my dear. We all did and we all understood." She paused. "All right, stay out here and dream your dreams, enjoy your flights of fancy. I hope the real earl will measure up to whatever your imagination conjures tonight. Don't stay out too long."

"Thank you, Auntie. I won't."

While her aunt turned away and went inside, Katherine clutched her velvet wrap tighter at the base of her throat and walked a short distance down the stone pathway to get out from under the harsh glare of the lamp beside the door. She was thankful for the few minutes alone in the cold air. Perhaps she needed to clear her head concerning the earl.

After her unexpected brush with Lord Greyhawke's hand, she'd had little to say to anyone. Thankfully, Mrs. Henshawe and Lady Littlehaven chose not to say anything to her about the breach in etiquette and carried the conversation through their buttery dessert and until Uncle Quillsbury signaled dinner was over.

Everyone knew what to do without being told. Gentlemen were to join the duke in his book room for brandy and the latest business and political gossip. The ladies joined Katherine and her aunt in the drawing room for coffee, port, and the latest Society chatter from the gossipmongers. And the main topic among the ladies had been Lord Greyhawke.

After the drinks had been poured, Katherine had been set upon by her friends to divulge her dinner conversation with the handsome earl. She managed to foil their attempts once again by insisting Lord Greyhawke spent most of the time talking to Lady Littlehaven and Mrs. Henshawe. Later, when Penny and Madeline cornered Mrs. Henshawe, they had to agree with Katherine. Once the lady had started talking, she talked only about herself and not the earl at all.

Katherine was definitely conflicted about him. It was odd. Though she hardly knew anything about him, she felt she knew him well. He created an uncommon mixture of feelings and emotions inside her. In the space of one evening and two separate meetings, he had stunned her, complimented her, and confused her. He'd made her laugh, made her remember, and made her want to know more about the thrilling, swirling sensations that swept through her when his hand touched hers.

Too, there was that unfamiliar fear that she couldn't quite shake. Just because she thought the earl had felt all the wonderful things that filled her didn't mean that he had felt the same things she had.

The front door opened and Katherine looked behind her. Her heart lurched and then began the enticing fluttering she always felt when she first saw Lord Greyhawke. He was walking out, swinging his cloak over his shoulders as he went. Looking at him from a distance, she could tell what a tall, magnificent, powerfully built man he was.

He didn't see her standing halfway down the stone path until he placed his hat on his head and started down the steps. His footfalls slowed and he removed the hat that she'd just watched him don.

His gaze swept up and down her face. Katherine felt an unfamiliar sensation in her breasts, her lower stomach, and between her legs as his stride shortened the distance between them.

Chapter 9

This is the third time; I hope good luck lies in odd numbers.
—The Merry Wives of Windsor, *act 5, scene 1*

"Miss Wright, is everything all right?" the earl asked.

"Yes, of course," she answered, automatically tightening her hand on her cane. "Why do you ask?"

"Maybe because it's well after midnight and you are standing outside alone." He stopped in front of her and pretended to look all around the area with a gleam of amusement in his eyes. "You are alone, aren't you?"

"Obviously, not anymore. You are here. And yes, everything is perfectly fine. It's just that it's such a lovely night, I wanted to enjoy looking at the sky before I retired for the evening."

He stuffed his gloves into the pocket of his coat. "You should have brought a heavier wrap if you were going to do that. It's more than chilly out tonight."

She looked down at her black velvet shawl, which she held together with one gloved hand at the base of her throat. Her gown was thin, and her dainty shoes were not made for outside wear. Her toes and nose were already cold, but she'd let them go numb before she'd admit that to the handsome earl.

"It's nippy, but not freezing. Besides, I didn't plan to be out long. Auntie Lee just went back inside, and I feel quite safe standing a mere twelve paces from my front door. I've no doubt that should I be accosted by an errant footpad, there are several carriage drivers who would hear my screams and come running to my aid." She hesitated and teased him with a suspicious expression. "So if you have any intentions of accosting me, my lord, you'd best dash them right now."

Lord Greyhawke chuckled. "You will have no need of dozing drivers to aid you tonight, Miss Wright. I am many things, but not a fool. I have no doubt you could put me in my place should I try to force you to do anything against your will."

"In any case, I would try."

He took a step closer to her. "Then perhaps I should test your fortitude, Miss Wright."

A smile touched the corners of her mouth. "I am woefully inadequate to match wits or challenges with you, my lord."

"There's not one sliver of truth to what you just said, but I appreciate your effort to try to make me think it's so. No matter the subject of our discussion, you are a worthy opponent."

His voice had been husky, low, and filled with compelling warmth. And again she wondered if he was feeling the connection to her that she felt to him.

"So our paths cross for the third time tonight," she said.

He nodded once. "Do you think perhaps there's something to that old saying 'Third time is lucky'?"

She shrugged. "Perhaps for you, but I'm afraid my luck is about as nonexistent as forthcoming miracles."

"I thought the same until I looked up and saw you standing out here in front of me."

"I suppose it's easy to see someone three different times at a small dinner party, my lord."

"Small? Only you and your uncle would consider thirty people a small gathering for dinner."

A sound somewhere between a laugh and a sigh passed her lips. "Dukes have a way of doing even small things on a grand scale. Were you not enjoying yourself? Gentlemen don't usually leave Uncle Quillsbury's book room so early."

His gaze left her face and he looked up at the night sky. She had the feeling he was remembering something, so she remained quiet.

Finally his gaze found hers and he said, "There was a time I indulged in spirits until I couldn't drink anymore. Those days are behind me now. And I find I sleep better if I refrain from too much brandy at night. It was better that I take my leave."

She was pleasantly amazed and heartened that he'd decided to give her a glimpse into his past.

"I'm much the same way," she said as casually as he'd spoken. "If I drink more than one glass of champagne in an evening I usually get a headache, and I don't sleep well either."

"You know that's because all those bubbles you drink go straight to your brain and start popping."

She shook her head at his silly comment and loosened

the tight clutch she had on her shawl. "I can't believe you said that without smiling. It's so unscientific it's grossly outrageous and you know it. You will not make me believe that's true, so don't think about trying."

He laughed for a moment, too, and then said, "All right." He glanced down at the hat in his hands before fastening his gaze on hers once again. "We'll change the subject and talk about something more serious. You looked wistful when I saw you standing near the dance floor tonight. What were you thinking about?"

She mouthed a silent *Oh* before saying, "Wistful? I'm not sure that's true."

"I'm sure it is."

"Well, you are wrong. I'm not given to sentimental flights of fancy in that way."

"Then tell me what you were thinking."

Tell him what she was thinking? Not in a million years. She couldn't tell him that she had a list of prospective husbands and she was looking at the gentlemen who were dancing, trying to decide who enjoyed the pastime and who didn't.

"No, I will not tell you," she said, and then gave a soft laugh. "You just don't give up, do you?"

"It wasn't threatening."

"Maybe not to you."

"It was a simple question."

"It was a personal question, my lord," she argued playfully. "After all we said previously about private in-quiries, you have no compunction about asking me what I'm thinking. You have no qualms asking anything that crosses your mind, do you?"

"None whatsoever," he admitted without arrogance,

humor, or guilt. "That is how you learn things you want to know, Miss Wright. And I want to get to know you."

"All right, then, my lord," she said, feeling emboldened by his foray into the out-of-bounds abyss. She lifted her chin and her shoulders. "Fair is fair, as they say. If I answer one personal question for you, you must answer one for me. Agreed?"

She instantly felt a change in him. Doubt flashed across his handsome features. He wavered. She hadn't expected that. He'd been so forceful in wanting to know about her, she thought he'd jump at the chance to quiz her no matter the price. Though she didn't mind that he wanted to think about her proposal before accepting her terms. If he agreed, fine. If he didn't, maybe he'd stop meddling into her past since he was so unwilling to give up a little of his own.

His gaze remained hard and fast on hers. "That's a hard bargain to accept, Miss Wright."

She stared back at him without flinching. "Take it or leave it. It matters not to me whether you are willing to make a sacrifice for what you want to know about me."

She smiled confidently, happy with her tactic to show him no mercy. He certainly didn't seem to be willing to show any to her.

He took so long to answer her, she was sure he was going to back away, but suddenly he said, "So it's a challenge after all?"

"If you choose to look at it that way. I think of it as simply sharing a little about ourselves with each other."

He frowned. "Sharing? There aren't many things that I would be willing to share, Miss Wright. "

She sucked in a short chuckle, hoping to appear

indifferent to his answer. "That has become quite obvious, my lord, and I completely understand your hesitancy." But she remained firm. "Your call, but if you don't ante up, then neither shall I."

He nodded slightly. "In that case, Miss Wright, ladies first. What's your question for me?"

He was constantly surprising her. "I'm impressed you want me to go first. Is it because you are a gentleman, or is it you have no fear that I won't keep my part of the bargain?"

She waited in silence for his reply. He seemed to sear her with his dark, penetrating stare. She was ready to give up getting an answer when he said quietly, "I'm not concerned about you keeping your promise at all. I'm worried whether or not I will keep my promise and answer what you ask of me if you go first."

Chapter 10

I'll smother thee with kisses.
—Venus and Adonis, *18.*

At that moment, Katherine knew the lightheartedness of their conversation was at an end. And until that moment, she'd had no thought as to what she would ask. But from somewhere deep inside herself, she found her query. "So then, I'll go first. Tell me, why do they call you the beast?"

His brows shot up. "The beast? That's news to me. I didn't know anyone did."

That admission startled her. She had just assumed he'd know about the gossip that had swirled around the ton after his wife's death.

A crisp wind blew a loose strand of hair across her cheek. And she realized she had grown not colder but warmer since the earl arrived. She dropped her hold on her shawl and brushed the hair behind her ear.

She met his gaze without flinching, but her voice softened as she said, "Rumor has it that you destroyed the inside of your house the night your wife and babe died. Is that true?"

His eyes remained calm and steady, but she knew her question troubled him when she saw that he swallowed hard. She was sure at that moment he was wishing he hadn't made the pact with her. For an instant she thought about telling him not to answer, to forget about her challenge to him that they both should divulge a part of their past. But the words never emerged from her throat.

"That's the second question you've asked, Miss Wright," he said in a low voice.

With that she knew taking her words back would gain her nothing. She had to follow through with what she had started. "You had no answer for the first."

He looked down at his hat and twirled it a couple of times in his hands before saying, "You know how to get the most out of a question. All right, the answer to your second is, yes."

She inhaled sharply, realizing she'd expected him to deny the gossip about him.

"My turn," he said, not giving her much time to recover from his confession. "Have you ever tried to dance?"

She moistened her lips, and the cold air dried them immediately. "That question is way too easy to answer, my lord. No."

"Would you like to try?"

To dance?

She hedged. "That's two questions."

"You asked two," he reminded her.

She had. It wasn't his fault he didn't know that London's ton had nicknamed him the beast. Swallowing her concern, she said, "All right, no. Wait. I mean yes, of course, yes, I'd like to try, but isn't it obvious why I can't?"

There was a glow of something in his eyes that she hadn't seen in them before. She wasn't sure, but it looked like anticipation or maybe hope.

The earl stepped closer and bent his head toward hers. "I believe I can teach you."

"What?"

Was he teasing her? Mocking her? Maybe he was a beast. Didn't he know how vulnerable she was when it came to her injury? But how could he? He didn't know that since she'd fallen down the stairs when she was nine years old and reinjured her leg, she hadn't taken a step without her cane. She couldn't.

A cold, hard chill shook her body and she gathered her shawl about her neck once more. "No." She leaned heavily on her cane and backed away from him. "You have no right to even suggest you could do that."

"Maybe not a quadrille, but I could teach you to waltz. A slow one. I would hold you firmly but properly, and gently guide you."

"I said no. Now, excuse me. It's late, I should go inside."

Lord Greyhawke took hold of her upper arm when she tried to pass him and stopped her from leaving. His hand was firm, warm, possessive. "I know I can teach you, Miss Wright. Right here, right now on your front lawn, if you will let me."

She moved as if to pull her arm out of his grasp, but he held her tighter, letting her know he was in control and she would go nowhere until he was ready to release her.

The very thought of his proposal caused her stomach to twist into a knot. "No," she whispered above the roaring in her ears.

The earl held out his other hand to her. "Trust me," he said in a persuasive tone.

Trust him?

"Give me the cane," he said again.

His confidence, his audacity, amazed her. Moonlight shadowed his handsome face, but her eyes searched his for a reason for his preposterous claim that he could teach her to dance. She struggled to free herself again.

"Why are you doing this? Let go of me. You're being cruel for no reason. You know I can't dance."

"I don't know that, and if you haven't tried, neither do you. You have a choice to make, Miss Wright. You can either give me the cane or I'm going to kiss you."

Katherine stopped struggling and stared at him in disbelief. Her senses whirled at the very idea of a kiss from the man. "We are practically strangers."

"You don't seem like a stranger to me." He looked down at his hands on her arms. "You don't feel unfamiliar beneath my grasp."

For a long moment, their gazes held. She wasn't sure what he was doing to her, but she agreed. He didn't appear a stranger to her either. "You wouldn't."

Lord Greyhawke leaned his face close to hers. "Of course I would, Miss Wright. I've been wanting to kiss you all night."

He wanted to kiss her?

Katherine's hand tightened on the handle of the cane. Her breath seemed to collect and pool in her throat.

"You'd rather I kiss you than give up your walking stick."

Would she? Tension such as she had never experienced before swirled and sparked between them.

Silently she digested what he said as a tingling awareness gripped her. She hoped the turmoil she was feeling inside didn't show in her eyes or on her face. From the moment she'd first looked up and seen him standing in front of her, there had been an inexplicable, unrelenting attraction between them.

Finally, she drew in a long, uneven breath and said, "I'm not afraid of a kiss, my lord."

Continuing to watch her carefully, he said, "So you've been kissed before?"

Her chin lifted defiantly. "No, but the thought of it doesn't trouble me. I've always expected to be kissed one day." But she had never expected to dance.

"Afraid to dance but not frightened to be kissed by a man they call the beast? That makes you very intriguing, Miss Wright."

He moved his face so close to hers, Katherine thought for sure he was going to kiss her. Shivers of dread and anticipation coursed through her and mingled together so rapidly that she didn't know which emotion would be the victor.

Instead of placing his lips on hers, he hesitated and said, "How can I refuse such a tempting invitation?"

Tightness bound her chest, and for a fleeting second she felt she was close to swooning for the first time in her life. Her knees were quivering, but not from the cold or from standing for so long. Was he or wasn't he going to kiss her?

And did she want him to or didn't she? All she really knew was that she'd never met a gentleman who stirred her senses the way Lord Greyhawke had.

She took in a shaky breath and managed to say, "That wasn't an invitation."

His lips hovered so close to hers, it was as if she could already feel them. Anticipation had won.

"It was. You are seducing me and I accept that. What I haven't decided is whether or not you know you're doing it."

Lord Greyhawke threw his hat toward the front gate and with one fluid motion he circled her waist with his hands, lifted her off the ground, and caught her up against his chest as his lips came down on hers with firm, mounting pressure. It was a powerful sensation. Katherine swallowed a small, shivery gasp and closed her eyes as his lips molded impatiently, eagerly, to hers.

Time seemed to be suspended as his mouth moved over hers with an ardor that startled her at first. It was as if he were starving and only the taste of her lips would satisfy him. Caught up in the shelter of his embrace, she felt safer and more whole than she'd ever felt in her life. The warmth of his body and strength in his arms seemed to sink into her soul and nourish her. Spirals of wonderful sensations curled tightly in her abdomen and then seemed to shoot through her body as she surrendered to the first stirrings of passion that had awakened within her. Katherine relaxed and concentrated on the pleasure soaring within her.

His lips left hers and he kissed her cheek, under her eye, and down to the corner of her mouth before returning and melting his lips to the contours of hers once more. As they kissed, the movement of his lips upon hers became more languorous and less frantic. It was as if he treasured what he was doing and how he was feeling.

The thrills that swept through her were shattering all she had ever imagined a kiss would be. Thoughts, dreams, and wishes were no comparison to a real kiss delivered passionately by a real man. Their kiss gathered intensity. Katherine felt as if she had been waiting for this experience all her life, and she welcomed it with open arms and open mind to explore it all.

Lord Greyhawke lifted his head a little and looked down into her eyes. "What do you think of your first kiss?"

She moistened her lips and inhaled a deep, shaky breath. "That I expected it to be softer and shorter. Much like when Papa used to kiss my forehead or my cheek."

He chuckled, and then in a reassuring tone he said, "Miss Wright, a gentleman's kiss to a lady is not supposed to be chaste like a father's buss to his daughter."

"I think I understand that now, and I'm wondering why I've never allowed any of the gentlemen who've wanted to kiss me to do it. Surely I've been missing many opportunities to experience these wonderful feelings it causes deep inside me."

He gave her a rueful grin. "That's not the answer I expected from you, but do not think that every man will produce the same response in you that my kiss did."

She eyed him curiously and watched shadows of moonlight play across his handsome features. "Why not?" she asked.

"I'll just say that every man kisses differently."

"How do you know this?"

His lips twitched with a little humor, and so did hers. Katherine could tell he was considering how to answer her question, so she playfully goaded him by adding, "Have you kissed many men?"

The earl laughed. It was an easy, natural sound that was pleasing to her ears.

"I have kissed no men, but since no two ladies kiss alike, I will assume it's safe to think no two men do either."

"And have you kissed many ladies?"

His gaze feathered down her face and back up to her eyes. "Enough."

Katherine stared into his golden-brown eyes that were moments before seducing her and said, "I like the way you kiss."

"I'm glad to hear you say that. I liked your kisses, too. Immensely. Perhaps we should do it again."

"That would be lovely, but dangerous. We are standing out in the open on my front lawn."

"It won't be the first time I've done something dangerous. And for reasons I don't begin to understand and have no desire to contemplate, I am of a mind to tempt fate one more time tonight and kiss you again."

His words tempted her and eased her fears. "I think I would like that, too, my lord."

The earl bent his head to hers and sought her mouth once again. Katherine knew what to expect and began to kiss him back. She dropped her cane and wound both arms around his neck, pulling him closer, urging him to kiss her harder. And he did. She skimmed her hands along the width of his shoulders and down the breadth of his back.

He trembled beneath her searching hands. His arms tightened around her possessively, pressing her breasts against the firmness of his powerful chest as if he were trying to bind her to him.

"Open your mouth," he whispered against her lips. "Let me inside to taste you."

She followed his instructions without hesitation, and his tongue flicked across the inner surface of her lips and around the corners of her mouth, surprising her. Shivers of exquisite pleasure soared through her. She had never experienced anything as wonderful as being held tightly in Lord Greyhawke's arms and kissing him.

She wanted to taste him, too, so she eased her tongue forward and slowly at first, until she heard him moan softly. That spurred her to respond to his kisses with the same aggressive eagerness he exhibited, and their tongues swirled and played.

Katherine knew she was being seduced, but she didn't care. She was enjoying every moment of it. She answered every gasp, every moan, and every breath that fell from his lips as they kissed long, deep, and savoring. He slanted his lips over hers again and again. She welcomed the feel of him, the smell and taste of him to all her senses.

"Am I doing it right?" she questioned breathlessly.

"Perfect," he answered, kissing his way down her chin to her neck and around behind her ear.

Her breath trembled in her throat, but she managed to whisper, "Are—are you feeling the same unexplainable things I am feeling?"

"Oh, yes," he murmured on a shaky gasp. "And probably many more than you are enjoying right now."

A wanting for more grew low in her abdomen. She had no idea that two people could create such long, delicious, and wondrous feelings of delight by their lips and bodies touching and coming together so intimately. Now she knew the meaning of all the love poems she'd ever read. What she was experiencing with Lord Greyhawke was the reason they had all been written. She felt as if she could go on kissing him forever.

"Someone's coming," he whispered, lifting his lips from hers.

Katherine hadn't heard anything but heavy breathing. The earl quickly stood her on her feet and stepped away from her.

Katherine looked down and realized she was standing without the aid of her cane. Suddenly her legs buckled and she fell to the ground on her bottom.

She gasped.

Lord Greyhawke swore.

He quickly bent and slid one arm under her knees and the other around her shoulders. Her arms circled his neck and he lifted her off the damp ground.

"Are you hurt anywhere?" he asked, looking down the length of her body with a quiet intensity.

"No, no, I'm fine," Katherine answered, fighting the desire to snuggle deeper into his warm, strong, protective embrace once again.

"What happened?"

"I couldn't stand. I didn't have my cane."

Katherine heard the front door open and male voices talking and laughing that suddenly went silent. She felt the muscles in the earl's arms jerk and flex with tension. Concern clouded his features. She twisted her head around and saw the duke, Uncle Willard, and three other gentlemen standing in the doorway gawking at her and the earl.

"Damnation!" His Grace exclaimed. "What on God's green earth is going on out here?"

By the expression on Uncle Quillsbury's face and the controlled shake to his voice, Katherine doubted whether she or the earl could say anything that would appease her two uncles.

Chapter 11

I have set my life upon a cast,
And I will stand the hazard of the die.
   —Richard III, *act 5, scene 4*

Adam was still trying to figure out what had happened to make Miss Wright fall when the front door swung open and he was staring into the angry eyes of the Duke of Quillsbury and his equally disturbed brother, Lord Willard. In fact, all the men seemed to be glaring at him as if he were a scoundrel of the highest order.

Not that he blamed any of them for the outrage they were showing. He was exactly what they thought him to be, a rake who had just taken advantage of an inno-cent young lady because he couldn't restrain his desire for her. There was no use in trying to deny his guilt when he held the lovely but damning evidence in his arms. He'd known someone was about to open the door. He'd heard them coming, but there was nothing he could do. He couldn't leave Miss Wright sitting on the dew-wet ground. Picking her up was the only option.

If he found himself caught in a parson's mousetrap,

it was he who had set the trap. What would he do if the duke insisted her reputation had been ruined and demanded Adam marry her? He couldn't. He could never marry again.

Prodded by the silence that seemed to be stretching, Adam said, "Your Grace, I can explain."

"Then you'd best get to it quickly," the duke said.

"Let me handle this, my lord," Miss Wright whispered so no one but Adam would hear. "I know my uncles well."

"You are not the one he wants to hear from right now," Adam said just as softly.

"Be that as it may, I will speak first," she insisted, and then looked over at her uncle and said, "Uncle Quillsbury, there is no reason for you to be so serious sounding or for anyone to be alarmed."

"Really, my dear?" he said sternly, stepping down onto the stoop. "If that is the case, would you mind telling me why Lord Greyhawke is cradling you in his arms as if he were about to ravish you?"

Oh, yes. He knew.

"I'm sorry, Uncle. I know it appears that way to you, but it isn't what it seems. Surely you know that if the earl was going to accost a young lady, it wouldn't be on her front lawn beneath a glaring porch lamp with five carriage drivers across the street looking on."

Adam glanced down at Miss Wright again and was very tempted to smile. He couldn't believe she'd just said he wouldn't do exactly what he'd just done. And she'd sounded damned convincing, too. She had courage in spades. He would grant her that.

"I thought it would be quite clear that I had fallen,"

Miss Wright continued. "Lord Greyhawke was on his way to his carriage and saw me sitting on the ground. He picked me up and was bringing me inside when you opened the door."

Adam watched both her uncles' expressions instantly turn from anger to concern.

"Then by all the saints why are you standing out there in the cold with her, Lord Greyhawke? Bring her inside. The rest of you gentlemen step aside and let him pass. Better yet, go on home. There's nothing for you to do here other than gawk and be in the way."

"You amaze me, Miss Wright. Where did you learn to be so evasive?" Adam whispered as he tightened his hold on her and headed toward the door.

"Was I?" she responded.

"The best I've come across." His foot landed on the first step. "For a moment you even had me believing I hadn't kissed you."

Miss Wright chuckled softly and slipped her arms around his neck. He was glad she wasn't concerned about the predicament they were in, but he sure as hell was.

Adam bounded up the three steps with her. He didn't make eye contact with any of the onlookers as they parted at the doorway and allowed him entrance, but the mumbled murmurings he heard as soon as his back was to them worried Adam. Suddenly he had the feeling that not one of the three gentlemen had believed Miss Wright's story, even if it appeared, for the time being, that her uncles had.

Lord Willard's long strides led the way down the corridor to the drawing room. From behind him, Adam heard the duke calling for his sister, Lady Leola, to come belowstairs.

Adam entered the drawing room and gently set Miss Wright on the wide-striped settee. He felt the tingling warmth of her gentle arms slide from around his neck and down his arms. Once again, he wanted to feel her soft, pliant lips beneath his.

A shiver of desire shuddered through him, and Adam was reminded that he wanted her. His every response to her all evening had surprised him.

Lord Willard quickly brushed him aside and knelt in front of her while the duke settled his tall, lanky frame beside her on the small sofa.

"Where are you hurt, my dear?" His Grace asked.

Miss Wright smiled lovingly and shook her head. "I'm not hurt, Uncles," she assured them. "Please don't worry. I don't know why, but all of a sudden, I was feeling quite breathless and light-headed. I was unsure of my footing, lost my balance, and fell. As simple as that. The ground was quite soft, so there is no need for concern."

Light-headed? Unsure of herself? Off balance and breathless?

Had his kisses made her feel that way?

No, Adam thought. He didn't want to think about that possibility, and he certainly didn't want to think about the way her touch and her kisses made him feel, either. That was heading into dangerous territory he didn't want to venture into.

"What's wrong?" Lady Leola exclaimed as she came rushing into the room, belting her flowing brown velvet robe tightly about her waist. A long, thin length of braided gray hair hung past her shoulders. Her concerned gaze darted from Adam to her brothers, then back to Miss Wright.

"Oh, Auntie, I wish they hadn't called for you to come down. It wasn't necessary. I am fine."

"But what's happened?" She knelt in front of her niece and beside Lord Willard and took both of Miss Wright's hands in hers.

Adam was a little amazed that Miss Wright's uncles and aunt were so concerned about her fall. Most guardians would have been more concerned that she was in his arms. Adam found that odd.

"I was outside exactly where you left me and I fell. Lord Greyhawke saw me, picked me up, and brought me inside."

Miss Wright certainly had a way with words. Everything she said was true. It just wasn't the whole truth. Somehow she had managed to give only the bare bones of what had happened between the two of them without sharing the wealth of passions and feelings that had passed between them.

Lady Leola looked up at Adam with questioning eyes before returning her attention back to Miss Wright. "You fell outside? You poor dear. Where is your cane?"

Adam wondered how Miss Katherine Wright became as strong as she was considering how her aunt and uncles coddled her. It was clear to him she hadn't been harmed by the fall.

"I must have dropped it." She looked around her and then up at Adam. "I don't see it anywhere, so I guess it's still outside."

"I'll get it, Lady Leola," Adam said, "while you see if she's injured." He glanced at Miss Wright. She glanced at him, and suddenly he had the feeling a bond had been forged between them that he was going to have a devil of a time trying to shake. He then turned and headed for the front of the house.

Adam stepped outside and inhaled the cold air into his lungs. His first thought was that he shouldn't have kissed her. His second was that he shouldn't have kissed her so deeply, so hungrily. And his third thought was why were her uncles more worried about the fall than the possibility that she'd been ravished by a man some called the beast?

It was inevitable he would kiss Miss Wright when he walked out the door and saw her standing on the lawn in front of him. He knew it right then. It was as if she were a gift wrapped with a soft, satin ribbon and ready for him to open and uncover the secrets of the kiss he was anxious to give and she was ready to receive.

If it had been the first time they'd met that evening, or maybe even the second, then perhaps he could have been strong enough to deny himself the pleasure of kissing her in the moonlight. But it was impossible when it was their third meeting, they were alone, and he'd wanted so desperately to do it. Fate had smiled upon him and granted him such an easy opportunity that he couldn't ignore it.

He walked over to where Miss Wright's cane was lying and picked it up. He looked it over. There were no intricate markings, paintings, or mother-of-pearl inlays on the shaft. No fancy silver or ivory handle at the top and no brass or waxed tip on the bottom. Nothing to make it stand out or say it belonged to the niece of a wealthy duke. It was a simple wooden cane with a well-worn handle.

She was probably right, though, Adam thought. He really should have kissed her softly the first time, as she'd expected. It was her first kiss, after all. But she'd already bewitched him with her clever wit and wistful expressions. He already knew he wanted to kiss her tempting lips before his hand grazed hers under the dinner plate and surprised them both. Once he knew he was going to kiss her, consequences didn't seem to matter. And the instant his lips claimed hers, he hadn't wanted to control his hunger for her. It had been too long since he'd savored such sweetness.

While he held her so close, it had taken every ounce of his power to keep from molding her incredibly soft body against the demanding hardness beneath his trousers. He truly hadn't expected desire to flame so quickly between them.

But now that he'd had his taste of her, he must stay away from her. For his good as well as hers. Miss Katherine Wright was the first lady he'd actually wanted to kiss since long before Annie's death. That made her a danger to his newly garnered yet tenuous peace of mind.

It didn't seem fair that he'd desired her the moment he saw her. Miss Wright wasn't a young lady he could trifle with. She had hurts that very possibly ran as deep as his. The thought of that tightened his chest. He couldn't let her think that he might be available to ask the duke for her hand. That life was closed for him forever. He couldn't put another woman through the pain that Annie had gone through.

And had he really offered to teach her to dance? Why

in hell's name had he said that? He knew. She'd looked wounded. He knew what it felt like to be wounded, and he wanted to help heal her. But why would he think he could do that when he was riddled with scars that wouldn't heal?

Perhaps he should just lay all the blame for the ending to the evening on Bray and Harrison. He probably never would have approached Miss Wright tonight if they had not just told him both their wives were in the family way.

Both?

At the same time?

To have favored him in his youth, fate certainly had a cruel hand when dealing with Adam now.

It wasn't that he wasn't happy for them; he was. But he didn't plan to be in London when their time was due. He had punished himself for Annie's death for two years. There was no need to continue.

Adam looked up at the bright night sky and remembered how beautiful Miss Wright was in the moonlight. He'd have to be satisfied with the fact that he was the first one to kiss her, the first to create desire in her for the touch of a man. And as for his own lusty desires, perhaps it was time he started looking for a mistress.

"Lord Greyhawke."

Swinging around, Adam saw Lord Willard standing in the open doorway. Shadowed by the glow of the harsh lamplight, for a moment his slim, erect figure seemed menacing. But then, that feeling might have washed over Adam because he had a guilty conscience. He didn't regret having kissed the duke's niece. How could he feel remorse for something that had given him the most pleasurable feeling he'd had in years? He did regret she'd been caught in his arms. He didn't want to bring any shame or blemish to her reputation.

"Did you find the cane?" Lord Willard asked.

Adam glanced down at the walking stick in his hand. "Yes," he answered, and strode up the steps.

"Thank you for coming to Katherine's rescue for us, Lord Greyhawke. The crisis is over. We'll see to Katherine from here." Lord Willard held out his hand.

Adam's gaze studied the older man's eyes as he talked. He didn't see any anger, wariness, or even suspicion that what Katherine said might not be true. That surprised him.

He nodded once and gave Miss Wright's uncle the cane. "Is she going to be all right?"

He put his hand to his ear and said, "What?"

"Is she going to be all right?" Adam said more loudly, overpronouncing his words for Lord Willard.

"We believe so but will know more in the morning."

"Would you like me to come back inside and carry her to her room for you?"

Lord Willard's shoulders flew back and he puffed out his chest. "That won't be necessary, my lord. Good night."

With that, Lord Willard closed the door, leaving Adam to turn on his heels and start toward his carriage. He stopped at the gate and picked up the hat he'd thrown down earlier. He replayed in his mind how quickly Miss Wright had fallen when he'd stood her on her feet. It was as if her legs had given way beneath her.

But why?

What was wrong with Miss Wright?

"No," he whispered firmly to himself, and settled his hat on his head.

It was none of his business what was wrong with her. In fact, the less he knew about her, the less he saw of her, the better off he was going to be. And she didn't want him to know more about her anyway. It was best he stay away from her.

Adam opened the gate and strode across the street toward his carriage. A part of him knew that would be hard. But another part of him knew that all he had to do was think of Annie and how she'd suffered because of him. That would give him all the strength he needed to deny his interest in Miss Wright.

He might not like it, but there was no use in making a bed he would never sleep in.

Chapter 12

Do you not know I am a woman? When
I think, I must speak.
—As You Like It, *act 3, scene 2*

A noise disturbed Katherine's slumber. Her lids fluttered open. A slice of bright light roused her further. She rolled over and saw her aunt Leola drawing open the blue velvet draperies, a duty usually reserved for Katherine's maid. Beautiful early spring sunshine flooded the room as her aunt tied the panels back with matching fringed sashes.

Katherine stretched and yawned before sitting up in bed and stuffing pillows behind her back for support as she did so. She supposed there were worse things than having a hip that constantly ached and a knee that wouldn't bend correctly. Such as the embarrassment of falling down on her rump in front of Lord Greyhawke. However, she got over that easily enough when the earl had lifted her into his strong arms. She had a fairly good notion that was the reason Auntie Lee was the one waking her rather than her maid.

"Good morning, Auntie."

"Oh, I do like the sound of the uplifting phrase *good morning*," Auntie Lee said, turning to greet Katherine with a cheerful voice. "I hope it is a good one for you. How's my favorite niece feeling today? Are you sore or in any pain?"

"Not at all," Katherine said confidently, and started weaving her long auburn hair into a hastily made braid. "I feel wonderful today. And how about you?"

"Lovely as can be." Her aunt picked up a serving tray from the dressing table and placed it across Katherine's lap.

Katherine looked down at the dainty teacup filled with chocolate, a slice of toast, and a serving of preserved apricots. "You haven't brought me breakfast in bed for several years now, Auntie. I'm quite suspicious of this act of kindness."

"No need to be," she answered, leaning a hip against the bed. "I haven't done it recently because I haven't needed to. You haven't fallen down in a long time."

"It's been years." Katherine smiled and shook her head. "I thought we'd settled some time ago that I was way too old to be coddled any longer."

"Don't be preposterous. You are, and I'm doing no such thing. I'm being nice and inquiring about how you feel because I'm concerned. I don't want you coming belowstairs until I know your leg is all right and not going to buckle beneath you."

"Then rest assured it is in tip-top shape and so am I, Auntie. I told you last night I didn't harm myself."

"But you haven't put any weight on it yet, dearie. You don't know if it's hurting anywhere."

"I do. I don't have a twinge," Katherine insisted.

"Hmm." Auntie Lee picked up a spoon from the tray and started spreading a generous amount of the preserves on top of Katherine's toast. "But you did fall," she said without looking at Katherine. "I mean, that is why you were in the earl's arms, isn't it?"

Katherine studied her aunt's unreadable face. So now they were getting to the heart of the reason her aunt was in her room, treating her as if she were nine years old and had broken her leg again. And it was as Katherine had suspected—the earl.

In a way, she could understand her aunt's keen interest. A young lady's reputation was about the only thing she had that truly belonged to her. And it was her aunt's duty to protect that valuable asset until Katherine was safely wed.

"Yes," Katherine said with a clear conscience in spite of the passionate kisses she had shared with the earl. And it was the truth. Just not all of it and maybe not in the correct order of things that happened. "And Lord Greyhawke picked me up. My story is not going to change."

"I didn't expect it would—but I wanted to be sure." She handed the toast to Katherine, who promptly laid it on her plate. "Did you know that Lord Greyhawke hadn't left the house when you asked to stay outside and—look at the moon?"

"No."

"But you had reason to believe he hadn't."

Hearing no real censure in her aunt's voice, Katherine picked up her chocolate and took a sip. "I had no idea who or if any gentlemen had left the house. You know

I was in the drawing room with you until we walked outside."

"I do know." She took her time and unfolded Katherine's napkin and gave it to her. "So you say it's mere coincidence that Lord Greyhawke, who sat beside you at dinner and captured your fancy when all others have failed, just happened to be the first gentleman out the front door after you fell."

Katherine stared into her aunt's eyes, which looked so much like her own. Her aunt didn't seem to be chiding her, or even questioning her, but Katherine couldn't be sure. Lady Leola was much too clever to reveal what she was actually thinking. Her facial features remained stoic, not expressing condemnation, acceptance, or even disbelief.

Still, Katherine suddenly had a feeling her aunt knew the earl had kissed her. Kissed her long, deeply, and passionately. But there was no way her aunt could, unless she'd been watching out a window.

Katherine couldn't see her very proper aunt doing such a thing.

"You aren't insinuating the earl and I arranged an assignation, are you, Auntie? I can assure you we didn't."

"I'm not implying anything, my dear," she countered pleasantly, relaxing more fully against the bed. "I'm simply asking. And you do know, of course, if you are interested in the earl, you don't have to meet him in secret. The duke will be more than happy to make a match with him for you. I'll go so far as to say he would love to."

For some reason that suggestion made Katherine's

pulse race, but she quickly insisted, "Auntie, I didn't meet him in secret. I have no plans to meet him—"

A knock sounded, and Katherine looked over to see her two uncles standing in the doorway, looking like two splendidly dressed sentinels. Both men carried themselves with all the power and privilege that had been theirs by birth.

"May we come in?" Uncle Quillsbury asked.

"Of course," Katherine said, feeling once again as if she were returning to the days of her youth, when her aunt and uncles stopped by her room each morning to check on how she was feeling before they began their day. "And before you ask, I am wonderful and was in no way harmed by the incident last night."

"That's good, my dear," Uncle Willard said.

"Still," Uncle Quillsbury added, stopping at the foot of her bed, "it might be good for you to stay right where you are for a day or two and rest. Don't you think so, Lady Leola?"

"Whatever you suggest, Your Grace."

"No," Katherine said, more loudly than she'd intended the word to come out, so she added a smile. She couldn't allow her aunt and uncles to rekindle their hovering over her every step as they had for so many years. "I will not be made an invalid again, Uncles," she continued, speaking loudly enough for Uncle Willard to hear every word. "I will rise and don my clothing and accomplish my morning duties as soon as all of you have left my room. I will keep my appointment with Viscount Rudyard and go for a ride in the park with him this afternoon as we planned."

"Does this insistence on carrying out your plans

today with Lord Rudyard mean a gentleman has finally caused you to take second notice of him?" Uncle Quillsbury asked.

Yes, one had, but it wasn't the viscount; it was Lord Greyhawke. But Lord Rudyard was on her list of possible husbands, and right now, the earl was not.

Katherine smiled at her uncle. "It means there is nothing wrong with me and no reason I shouldn't go and enjoy myself."

Uncle Quillsbury looked over at his sister. She shrugged lightly and said, "If she says she is feeling wonderful, we will have to accept that and let her do as she pleases."

"You must not fret over a little tumble, Uncle. I am not as delicate as I used to be when I first came to your household."

The duke looked down at her with serious brown eyes and clasped his hands together behind his back. He leaned toward her and said, "I will not fret at all once I have you safely wed and under the responsibility of a husband. Is that likely to happen soon?"

"The Season has just started, but I promised to be more diligent in my efforts to settle on a husband by the end of it, and I will."

"Good. Time is running out. This is your fourth Season, my dear," he added pointedly.

Katherine bristled slightly but hoped it didn't show. It was never her intention to argue or correct her uncle, because he'd always been so good to her. Still, she couldn't let the wrong information stand, so she said apologetically, "It's only my third, Uncle."

"First, third, fifth," he said, and straightened. "Doesn't

matter when you pass the first Season without a match. After that you start your journey to becoming a weed on the shelf. You have rejected a duke, a viscount, four barons, and two wealthy counts from Italy while swearing to me you must have love. I won't mention the gentlemen who weren't titled who asked for your hand, or the ones who were too old or too light in their pockets for me to even contemplate a match for you. And that doesn't take into consideration the ones that approached you directly that I never heard about because you were so disinterested you never even told me about them. I am sure there are plenty of those, too."

"No. I mean, there weren't that many, Uncle. A few, maybe."

His almond-shaped eyes narrowed to slits. "You need only settle on one. Need I remind you that being your father's only heir and my niece has made you one of the most sought-after young ladies since your debut?"

"That is because all the gentlemen are interested in me for my dowry, and none of them for love."

"You are fetching, intelligent, more educated and well-read than you should be, and you have a handsome dowry as well, so would you please tell me what there is about you not to love?"

Katherine smiled. "I have no argument against that, Your Grace."

"Nor should you."

"But if he doesn't love me, I at least want him to be strong, handsome, loyal, and love children."

"Great heaven of mercies!" the duke grumbled as his bushy eyebrows drew together so tightly, they almost touched. "That's too much to ask. There is no such man.

Or if there is, I've never met him and you're not likely to, either. But if you have somehow managed to discover this paradigm of manhood, nothing will get my old bones to moving faster than the prospect of posting the banns immediately so that I can consider my debt to your father fulfilled."

"No," she said regretfully. "I haven't found him." Though Lord Greyhawke might come close. He was strong and handsome. And if he'd been so distraught as to smash things in his house after his wife died, he must have been fiercely loyal and he must have loved her very much.

"So I thought," her uncle said. "I know you are as persnickety as that pampered Cheshire cat that eats from the Prince's dinner table, but would you reconsider all of your previous discards who found favor with you and do your best to find an acceptable gentleman to fall in love with this year, my dear, since that seems to be your main criterion? I am not getting any younger, and I'd like to see you wed before I pass from this earth."

Katherine knew Uncle Quillsbury wouldn't consider his debt paid to her father until she married. Since the afternoon she'd curtsied before the Queen, the duke had had only one goal in mind, and that was to make an acceptable match for her. The problem was that Katherine had rejected every gentleman he'd suggested and the ones who'd pursued her, too.

Her uncle was getting older and more cantankerous by the day. Both her uncles were. She knew the duke was eager to see her married. Her only issue with him was that he didn't seem to care whether she was happily wed as long as she was properly wed.

"You know I've already promised I will, and I won't let you down," she said. She was seriously trying to consider some of the gentlemen who had shown interest in her in the past, but she wasn't close to making a decision. Still, she tamped down her worries about that and said, "I'm committed to being betrothed by the end of the Season."

"Then that is all I ask," he said, and turned and walked out. Uncle Willard, who hadn't spoken a word during her exchange with the duke, and probably hadn't heard much of what they'd said, followed quietly behind him.

Katherine suddenly felt wretched. She hated disappointing the duke. And it wasn't as though she didn't want to marry. Of course she did. Even more so now that she knew the thrills of kissing. And she hoped married people did a lot of kissing.

"I shall go, too, and leave you to your thoughts and your toast," Aunt Leola said. "I'll send your maid up in a little while and then I'll see you belowstairs later today."

"Thank you for bringing in the tray, Auntie. I didn't mean to seem as if I didn't appreciate your kindness."

"I know. I wish it weren't so that a young lady had no goal in life other than finding a husband. Sometimes it doesn't seem right that getting married should be her only purpose. But that is how it is, and I don't see it changing. I think I probably said some of the same things to the duke you said to him just now when he arranged my marriage more than thirty-five years ago."

"Did you love your husband?"

"Of course not. But I respected him. I honored him and in turn he was very good to me."

"And it mattered not about love because you had the love of your children?" she asked, hoping her aunt would confirm her reasoning.

"Always. Those are the things that matter. A lifetime can truly be a long time. So when you do choose, my dear, choose wisely." She smiled, turned, and left the room.

Choose wisely.

That was what she was trying to do, but time was so short. The Season was already under way.

Groaning at her weakness, Katherine picked up her cold chocolate and sipped the sweetened drink. She would already be married if any of the gentlemen the duke had mentioned had stirred and disturbed her senses and her sensibilities the way Lord Greyhawke had last night. She had no idea what she'd been missing by never having been kissed, but she couldn't say she'd ever wanted any of the other gentlemen to kiss her. It had been different with the earl. Allowing him to kiss her had felt like the perfectly normal thing to do.

For some reason, she suddenly saw herself and Lord Greyhawke sweeping across the dance floor in the beautifully decorated Great Hall. She was twirling, skipping, and tiptoeing in time with the music. She wore a flowing, shimmering, golden-colored gown and a sparkling tiara on her head. She felt warmth, strength, and possessiveness in the earl's hands as he moved her through the steps, just as she had felt his power last night when he'd held her so tightly and kissed her so deeply. Her mind flitted from him gliding her through the intricate and fast pace of a swift quadrille to the intimate and sensual movements of the waltz.

And through it all, Katherine's legs never tired and her feet never missed a step.

She chuckled to herself and sipped from her cup again. It was lovely to imagine something so wonderful; however, dancing was only a daydream for her and would never happen in real life. Her injury set her apart from other young ladies in that regard, but it didn't keep her from having the same dreams of one day falling in love with a dashing and slightly dangerous gentleman such as the Earl of Greyhawke.

Most of the young ladies who'd made their debut with Katherine were already married. Some were holding sweet, chubby babes in their arms. And Katherine? She was one of the members of the Wilted Tea Society and still unwed.

With two Seasons behind her and another under way, hope for that elusive and magical emotion called love had faded and must be put aside. She would pay close attention to Viscount Rudyard on their afternoon ride. He was the youngest of the gentlemen she was considering and probably the most handsome, too. Except, of course, for the earl.

Lord Greyhawke? Was she considering him? Her chest tightened and her breathing grew shallow. Could she?

She wondered if what she'd heard about him saying he would never marry again was true. Was there any chance he would be interested in her, or would he, like Uncle Quillsbury, assume she was fast becoming a dried-up weed on a shelf and dismiss her outright?

Katherine didn't know. That was why she had put aside the search, the hope for love, and begun her hunt to find a gentleman who would be a good father to the many children she planned to have. And if the earl's kisses were anything to go by, she would very much enjoy getting started on that as soon as possible.

Yes, she wanted to marry and have children. Katherine loved her aunt and her uncles. They had been devoted to her from the moment she'd entered their house, but she didn't want to live the rest of her life in this very quiet, very proper house that had been her shelter for twelve years. She wanted to live in the kind of house she'd grown up in during the first seven years of her life. A house that was unruly, lively, and filled with loved ones and laughter. She wouldn't even mind arguing, crying, or yelling as long as there was noise and movement.

Katherine just didn't know where that house would be or who would be living in it with her. She had narrowed her search to Viscount Rudyard, Mr. Bailey Maycott, and Mr. Steven Norbury. They were all pursuing her, and though it wasn't a happy thought, she truly needed to settle on one of them by the end of the Season, marry, and begin her family.

She placed her cup in the saucer and leaned back against the pillows. Maybe it was her uncle reminding her of the dreaded task of deciding on a husband by the end of the Season. Perhaps it was the afterglow of her very first kiss by a handsome gentleman who made her feel very grown-up sensations, or maybe it was just that she'd stood near the dance floor with the handsome Lord Greyhawke insisting she dance with him when she knew she never would. But for some reason, she wanted to open the doors to her past and think about her family. She hadn't wanted to do that in a long time because the pain was always so great.

But now, today, in the quiet of her room, she wanted to remember her two beautiful older sisters and brother. She wanted to remember their laughter, their whispers, and even their anger at her when she would follow them around the house and beg them to play with her, or how they'd scold her for asking too many questions. She wanted to remember her mother's sweet smile, and her gentle hand brushing Katherine's hair, and her father dropping to one knee, holding out his arms for her to run to him and be caught up in his strong embrace.

Since the age of seven, she'd lived with this unusual family of uncles, aunt, and more servants than she could count. Since arriving, Katherine couldn't remember a time she wasn't surrounded by people just waiting to do something for her. But she'd always felt lonely. There were many times over the years she'd found herself yearning for the sounds of laughter, or singing, or even the cries of a mischievous child who was cross because he didn't get his way.

Yes, she'd wanted the love of a gentleman whose kisses stirred longings inside her that she didn't yet fully understand. A man who challenged her the way Lord Greyhawke had rather than cosset her the way her aunt and uncles did. But she also wanted to live in a house that was busy, loud, and not always so proper about everything. A house that was filled with boisterous life. It was past time to decide on a husband so she could start the kind of life she wanted—filled with children to give her love to. And she would name them all after her brother and her sisters, because their lives had been cut short and they'd never had the opportunity to have children of their own.

Katherine rested against the pillows with a smile on her face. Yes, she would honor her siblings in such a way. Surely her husband would grant her this small request.

But for now, she was going to close her eyes and indulge in good and happy memories from the past. Rather than run from them, as she often did, she wanted to embrace them and enjoy the love she'd felt for the family she'd lost way too early in her life.

It wouldn't be easy. There would be pain in doing so, but there would also be unspeakable joy to remember them.

Chapter 13

When remedies are past, the griefs are ended . . .
—*Othello, act 1, scene 3*

Adam placed the quill on its rest stand, pushed his chair back and propped the heels of his booted feet on the edge of his massive mahogany desk, and grumbled a few swear words to himself. He'd tried to continue to pore over the pages in the ledgers after his solicitor left, but he hadn't made much progress, and that made him irritated with himself. This work was important. He needed to understand how the Greyhawke estates worked, who worked them, and what they were worth before he made arrangements to visit them.

But it was of no use for the rest of the day. He couldn't concentrate. The numbers blurred and ran together until all he could see was the beautiful and inviting Miss Wright.

Miss Wright.

Who was so wrong for him.

He couldn't stop thinking about the way her supple body melted effortlessly against him, her soft sighs that were so pleasing to hear, or the sweet taste of her lips against his. And when he wasn't thinking about how much he wanted to hold her and kiss her again, he was wondering what it must be like for her to live in a house where everyone seemed to dote on her as if she were a delicate flower that might lose its petals if the utmost care wasn't taken.

Damnation, he couldn't even stop wondering why she used the cane in the first place. Her "unusual gait" didn't seem that bad to him. And why couldn't she have just answered a simple question? Why couldn't she have just told him what had happened to her leg? It couldn't be that difficult, could it?

Maybe that was why he couldn't get her off his mind. There were too many unanswered questions about her. Too many things for him to wonder about.

Adam leaned back farther in his chair and laced his fingers together behind his head. It was maddening to be so consumed with her that he couldn't adequately study what was right before his eyes. Why did his thoughts keep drifting back to Miss Wright?

Not yet two weeks back in London and already a young lady had caught his attention and bewitched him. Hell, it was the last thing he wanted or needed. Even before Annie, there were many young ladies who'd set out to entice him, bewitch him, or seduce him. He'd known how to avoid them all. He didn't believe Miss Wright had set out to do any of those things to him, not even to captivate him, yet she had done all of them without even trying.

"She hadn't even wanted to talk to me at first," he whispered to himself. "I had to keep insisting."

He shouldn't have kissed her. Adam rubbed his eyes, thinking that must have been the one hundredth time he'd thought that.

But if he was going to, he should have kissed her tenderly, briefly, and let that be the end of it. He shouldn't have been greedy and wanted more. He should have remembered that she was vulnerable, too. He should have respected the fact that it was her first kiss. But no, none of that mattered because of his eagerness to taste her. It had been so damned long since he'd met a lady he actually wanted to kiss that he hadn't been able to control himself and give her a proper first kiss.

Not that she'd seemed to notice or mind. He smiled to himself. No, she hadn't minded at all. He supposed he was lucky he hadn't frightened her with his ardent passion and sent her running inside to tell her uncles how he'd treated her.

Sensing his master's restlessness, Pharaoh looked up from where he lay in front of the low-burning fire and yawned. As if assuming Adam were talking to him, Pharaoh rose and ambled over to Adam's chair. He sat proudly on his haunches and stared at Adam as if he were waiting for him to say more.

And Adam did. "You know I wish I'd never kissed her," he murmured into the quiet of the room.

Pharaoh woofed low.

"I knew it was a bad idea, but I couldn't stop myself. All right, I didn't try too hard. I didn't want to. She was too tempting for me to resist anyway. I mean, she just had this way about her that drew me to her. And I might add, it didn't help that she was more than ready and willing to receive her first kiss, which I admit I was more than happy to deliver, seeing as I was eager to taste her lips anyway. So now you understand why it's all her fault I can't get her out of my mind."

Pharaoh made a quarreling sound in his throat and then licked his chops and woofed again.

"Yes," Adam agreed with a smile. "She tasted very good, but I still shouldn't have done it. She's been nothing but a menace to my peace of mind—night and day. It's damned frustrating," he said, looking down at the dog. "I don't know what's wrong with me. I just keep reliving the kiss as if I were still a schoolboy."

A movement caught Adam's and Pharaoh's attention at the same time, and they turned and looked toward the door. Dixon was standing quietly in the doorway, looking at Adam with his big brown eyes. If the lad had heard him talking to Pharaoh, he probably thought Adam was crazy.

And maybe he was. Talking to a dog couldn't be considered normal, but he'd often said things to Pharaoh when they'd lived at the cottage on the coast.

"I don't like her," Dixon said.

Adam looked hard at the boy and frowned. What was Dixon saying? He'd never even met Miss Wright.

"How can you say you don't like her? You don't know her."

"She smells bad."

"What?" Adam brought his feet down onto the wooden floor with a loud thunk. He remembered the scent of freshly washed hair and lightly perfumed skin. "I can assure you she doesn't." He stared at Dixon with focused intensity. "What the devil are you—you aren't talking about Miss Wright, are you?"

Dixon shook his head. Pharaoh walked over to Dixon and sniffed around his knees and his shoes. As usual, Dixon stood perfectly still and made no move to pet or speak to the Pyrenees.

"Mrs. Bernewelt," his young cousin said.

The governess.

Now they were getting somewhere, but Adam couldn't imagine that what Dixon was saying was true. The woman's recommendation letters had been excellent. Most of them had not only praised her efficiency, politeness, and skills, but said she was extremely well liked by all the children she had been in charge of.

"I want to go home," Dixon said defiantly as he held his arms stiffly by his side and clenched his hands into small, tight fists.

Adam let out an exasperated sigh. Why had fate forced a child upon him when he had no idea what to do with one? Adam had lived the life of a reckless youth, a daring rogue, a woefully unsuccessful husband, and a loner. None of those lives had prepared him to handle a child.

"This is your home," Adam said, and closed the book he'd left open on his desk.

"It's your home," Dixon argued, remaining as stiff as the toy soldiers he played with.

"And yours now, too," Adam insisted sternly. "You have no other home, so there will be no more of that kind of talk. I'll admit this isn't a situation that either of us wanted, but no one asked us, and it is what it is. We're both making adjustments, and we're going to make the best of it until you are off to Eton in a few years. This is your home," Adam said again for good measure.

As if bored with the lack of interesting scents on Dixon's person, Pharaoh wandered back to his favorite place to lie down and curl up in front of the low-burning fire.

Dixon remained quiet and made no move to leave the doorway.

"All right," Adam said in a tone softer than his previous one. "Tell me, how does she smell?"

"It's her hands."

"That doesn't tell me much. What specifically?"

The boy's eyes widened and he looked around the room as if he were searching for someone or something that could magically aid his thoughts on the matter.

"Fish?" Adam asked, hoping to prompt Dixon into remembering the foul odor.

He shook his head.

"Onion?"

Dixon shook his head again and still refused to offer any help as to what the scent might be.

"Vinegar? Lavender? Wine? Urine? How the devil am I supposed to know what you smell if you can't tell me?" Adam stopped and let out a long, exasperated sigh. "What am I saying?" he mumbled to himself. "I don't even want to know what you are smelling."

The lad's eyes turned glassy and his bottom lip began to tremble. Oh, hell. Adam hadn't meant to upset him. In different way, Dixon could be just as frustrating as Miss Wright.

"You've got to talk to me, Dixon. I can't read your mind or know what you are thinking just by looking at you."

Adam breathed in deeply again, rose from his chair,

and strode over to the fireplace, and picked up the poker. He jabbed at the burning wood, moving it around and making it flame once more. His ill temper was Miss Wright's fault, not Dixon's. She had him as irritable as an old blacksmith who'd just flattened his thumb with a hammer.

"My mum rubbed it on my chest one time when I was coughing," Dixon said into the quietness.

Adam turned back to him. "Some type of liniment? Camphor, maybe? That has a strong scent."

Dixon shrugged as if it might be but he was still unsure. "It's on her hands. I smell it when she buttons my coats or points to words in my books."

The old woman probably had aches in her finger joints and used the ointment to help ease the pain. If that was the cause, he couldn't fault her for trying to find some comfort.

He supposed he could speak to an apothecary about this and see if the man could give him something that would help Mrs. Bernewelt that didn't have such a powerful odor. But how in the hell would he suggest to the woman she use it? He wouldn't. He'd give it to Clark and have the butler handle it with Mrs. Bernewelt.

"It might take me a few days, but I'll look into it and see what I can do. All right?"

Dixon nodded.

Adam replaced the poker in its stand and looked out the window. The sky was a striking blue. A rare sight for a cold April afternoon.

An idea popped into his mind, and without taking time to think about it, he turned to Dixon and said,

"Why don't we take Pharaoh for a walk in Hyde Park? Want to do that?"

There was no smile, no joy, just: "Can I take my soldiers?"

Adam considered his request. "Two of them. One for each pocket. Fair enough?"

Dixon bobbed his head again.

Adam didn't know what to do to get Dixon to talk more and nod less. He supposed he'd have to depend on the schoolmasters at Eton to get him out of that habit and teach him to answer with words.

"All right, go find Mrs. Bernewelt and have her get your coat, gloves, hat, and meet me by the front door."

Perhaps a brisk walk in the cold air would be good for clearing his mind. Returning to London had not gone at all as he'd expected. He'd come with the intention of melding back into Society as a gentleman, an earl, and learning about his estates. That was damned hard to do when his mind was full of Miss Katherine Wright.

Half an hour later, Adam, Dixon, and Pharaoh entered the park alongside other pedestrian traffic and started making their way across the wide expanse of land. The walk from Mayfair had been tedious. Adam and Pharaoh had wanted to go much faster than Dixon's short legs would allow. Adam had been tempted on more than one occasion to pick him up and carry him.

Until they'd come to London, Pharaoh had never been on a leash. The dog still wasn't used to being harnessed and not free to roam wherever he wished. He pulled and strained at various times, trying to break free of Adam's firm hold so that he could scout out the bushes, door-ways, and streets unfettered.

The only thing Adam knew about little boys was what he remembered from being one. Though he didn't recall ever having a problem speaking, as Dixon seemed to have. He knew the best thing he'd liked about the large park was having a meat pie or sweetened biscuit while he enjoyed watching a puppet show, looking at jugglers toss several bottles in the air at the same time, or seeing some kind of rare animal that had been caught, caged, and put on display for anyone having a coin to see.

Adam stopped to scan the vast area before him, hop-ing to see where there might be a group of children play-ing or where a crowd had gathered, anything that might signal some kind of entertainment. All he saw was the usual milling people, standing and chatting, strolling, or sitting on a blanket, enjoying refreshments. There were riders on horseback, hackneys, curricles, and fancy painted carriages of all types and sizes, but nothing to indicate amusement for a youngster.

Though the skies were clear and sunny, there re-mained a cool nip in the air. It didn't seem to bother Dixon. He had his gloves off and his soldiers in his hands, pretending they were shooting at each other. Adam decided they needed to go deeper into the park.

They hadn't gone but a few steps when in the distance Adam saw a young lady walking with a cane coming toward him. His stomach did a slow roll. It was Miss Wright. He stopped short again. Pharaoh pulled on the leash, urging his master to keep going, but Adam held tight.

It was clear fate was not through with him. She was the last person he wanted to meet in the park. Correction, she was the last person he needed to see. With several hundred people roaming the grounds, what were the odds of him running into her in a park the size of Hyde? If he'd been looking for her, he probably couldn't have found her come hell or high water. But because he wasn't, she was walking straight toward him.

Looking beautiful.

Her long black cape flared out behind her. With every step she took, the flounces on her carriage dress fluttered like small leaves caught on a summer breeze. Her short-brimmed bonnet was made from the same fetching sprigged fabric as her dress. She held the handle of a fancy, ruffled and beribboned parasol in one hand and the handle of her cane in the other.

A moment or two later, he realized someone walked beside her. Adam glanced over at the tall, rather slim gentleman. He recognized Mr. Martin Rudyard. Adam remembered the man from the gaming tables at White's and the Heirs' Club but didn't know him well. Unlike Adam, the man was a member of the club and not a guest. He was a likable fellow who was maybe a year or two younger than Adam. Rudyard was friendly but didn't try to insert himself into anyone else's affairs.

Somehow it didn't seem right that Adam was trying to forget about her and here she was, walking straight toward him and filling him with the desire to pull her into his arms and smother her with kisses.

Fate was a fickle bird. He wished it would just make up its mind how it wanted to treat him.

There was plenty of time for Adam to divert his

course before the two reached him. And after last night, he figured that was exactly what he should do. He didn't need her consuming his thoughts any more than she already was. And she didn't need him teaching her any more about the ways of kissing.

It would be the best thing for both of them if he turned away so they wouldn't meet.

Now.

But Adam still had just enough rogue in him not to want to do what was right, but to do what he wanted.

Chapter 14

Our doubts are traitors
And make us lose the good we oft might win
By fearing to attempt.
  —Measure for Measure, *act 1, scene 4*

His peace of mind be damned for the moment.

The closer she came, the more Adam wanted to stay and see her. She looked so incredibly fresh and lovely, he had to resist the impulse to rush and greet her with a kiss.

Adam knew the second Miss Wright looked up and saw him standing directly in her pathway. Her eyes widened and brightened. She smiled at him. His lower stomach tightened and a slow throb started in his loins. Obviously she wasn't angry with him about their late night kisses.

He watched her glance stray briefly to Pharaoh and then over to Dixon, who stood by his side, completely engrossed in whatever war was going on between the two soldiers in his hands.

"Pharaoh, sit." The dog immediately obeyed and settled on his haunches by Adam's legs. Adam wound the

excess length of the leash around his hand so Pharaoh
had little choice but to stay right beside him. He didn't
want the Pyrenees to frighten Miss Wright. Pharaoh had
never liked strangers and would bark and growl if they
came too close to Adam.

"Stay, Pharaoh," he added firmly, and took off his hat
as Miss Wright and Mr. Rudyard stopped in front of
him.

"Good afternoon, Miss Wright."

"My lord," she answered, giving him a curtsy.

"Mr. Rudyard," he said, noticing that the man stood
so close to Miss Wright that if she moved a fraction
of an inch, her parasol would knock his top hat off his
head.

Rudyard bowed and said graciously, "My lord, it's
now Viscount Rudyard." And that was when Adam
noticed that the dandy carried a cane. Not to help him
walk, as in Miss Wright's case, but as an accessory to
his clothing. The ornate brass handle was hooked over
his forearm. The shaft was a highly polished wood that
looked as if it could be ebony. There was a fancy, three-
inch brass tip on the bottom. Perhaps Miss Wright didn't
think it was insensitive of him to carry such an adorn-
ment in her presence, but Adam did.

"My apologies, my lord," Adam said tightly, and
in turn gave the man an appropriate bow for his title.
"I hadn't heard about your father."

"No offense taken," Rudyard said, seeming oblivious
to Adam's irritation. "I know you haven't been in London long. In fact, it was only just last night that I heard
you'd returned. Though I see you have been in Town
long enough to have met Miss Wright."

Though his words weren't challenging and his manner was mild, something in Rudyard's tone bothered Adam. Or maybe it was just the fact that the viscount happened to be with Miss Wright that bothered Adam.

"Yes," Miss Wright offered when Adam didn't immediately respond. "He was at the duke's dinner party."

"Ah, I see," the viscount said, looking up at Adam before shifting his attention back to his companion. "No one ever declines an invitation to the duke's house for dinner, do they, Miss Wright?"

"I should hope not," she answered pleasantly.

"I suppose the balls and festivities of the Season brought you back to London, Lord Greyhawke?"

"I've had other things to address," Adam responded, and then looked over at Miss Wright, saying, "You seem to be walking well today. Is your leg all right?"

"Yes, thank you, my lord, all is well."

Her gaze stayed on his and he said, "That's good to hear," and he wondered if, like him, she was remembering the passionate kisses they shared just before she had fallen. And he wondered if, like him, she was wishing for more of those kisses right now.

The spring chill had added a lovely blush to her ivory cheeks, and her lips were such a tempting shade of pink. Adam had a devil of a time keeping his gaze from straying to them. She was downright fetching with the dainty parasol resting on her shoulder and framing her as if she were a portrait.

Adam cleared his throat and said, "May I present my cousin Master Dixon Greyhawke."

Clutching his soldiers, Dixon properly greeted the viscount and Miss Wright. Rudyard tipped his hat and nodded to Dixon, but Miss Wright bent down to meet him on his eye level and said, "I'm happy to make your acquaintance, Master Dixon. You are a fine-looking young man and with such pleasant manners. How old are you?"

"Five," he said, trying to hold up all his fingers and thumb without dropping his soldier.

"Only five? You are very tall for your age. I would have guessed you to be much older."

Dixon's chest puffed out. He twisted around, looked up at Adam, and smiled. A short, quiet laugh of disbelief blew from his throat. Dixon had been with Adam for at least six weeks, and in all that time he'd never once seen the child smile. Now, after mere seconds in Miss Wright's presence, she had him grinning from ear to ear. How did she do it?

She straightened and looked down at Pharaoh as she closed her parasol and tucked it under her arm. "What is your friend's name, Lord Greyhawke?"

"Pharaoh."

"A ruler. An apt name for him. He's very tall and handsome and has the look of a long regal heritage, don't you think?"

Before Adam realized what she was going to do, she extended her hand to the Pyrenees. Fearful Pharaoh might snap at her, Adam reached out to stop her, but he was too late. But rather than nip at her as Adam expected, Pharaoh sniffed her gloved hand as if she were a longtime friend. Adam grunted another short laugh. Even Pharaoh had been immediately seduced by Miss Wright's charms. Now she had enchanted his entire family.

She rubbed Pharaoh's head and said to him, "I'm overcome with envy, Your Highness. I've always wished I had golden-blond hair the color of yours. But, alas, I was destined to have very dark auburn hair just like my mother. No doubt you are the color of your mother, too."

Adam liked the way Miss Wright looked at Pharaoh, the way she gently rubbed him and talked to the Pyrenees. Adam liked the softness of her voice and her calm demeanor as she soothed and petted the dog. Adam could tell Pharaoh liked her, too.

While she patted Pharaoh's shoulder, her gaze caught Adam's with a questioning expression. "I feel something," she said. "Are those scars beneath his hair?"

"He was being abused when I found him. I'm surprised he didn't snap at you when you reached out to him. It usually takes a while for him to trust anyone."

"Well, no one can blame him for that. I'd be wary of strangers, too, if I had been mistreated by anyone."

"You are much too beautiful for anyone to ever contemplate ill-treating you, Miss Wright," Lord Rudyard said possessively, inserting himself back into the conversation. "And we really should be going. So, if you'll excuse us, my lord . . ."

Letting the viscount have the last word didn't sit well with Adam, so he said, "I was hoping to find a puppet show or maybe a juggler to entertain Dixon for a few minutes. Did you pass by anything going on in the park that might hold the interest of a youngster?"

"No," the viscount said, seeming to study on the question before answering. "I'm afraid not. Though we didn't go very far into the park. I didn't want to take a long walk for fear it would be too tiring for Miss Wright, you understand."

At Rudyard's comment, Miss Wright glanced over at Adam and softly bit down on her bottom lip. He had the feeling she didn't appreciate the viscount's inference that she couldn't walk for an extended time because she used a cane. Adam didn't blame her. He didn't appreciate the implication either.

"I had hoped to find a vendor," the slim man continued. "I wanted to buy Miss Wright a sweet scone or fruit tart, something delicious to please her. But we didn't find one."

"I can help you with that, my lord," Adam said. "There's one over by the east gate. We passed it coming in."

"Kind of you to mention that, but I really don't want to exhaust Miss Wright by making her walk that far after we've already had quite a trek this afternoon."

"I don't think you should," Adam agreed. "I would be happy to stay here with her while you go pick out something for her to enjoy on the ride back to her home."

Clearly perturbed, the viscount adjusted the position of the cane on his forearm as his eyes darted from Adam to Miss Wright. "Well, I suppose I could. Would you like me to do that for you?"

"No, no, of course not," she said with a concerned expression on her lovely face. "Why should you do all that extra walking for me when it's not on our way to your carriage? Absolutely not. It's far too much trouble, and I won't hear of it."

Rudyard shifted his stance. "Nonsense," he said. "It's not any trouble at all. It's settled. I wanted to buy you something sweet before we left, so I shall go. No bother at all." He gave Adam a determined look. "Thank you, my lord."

"Happy to mention it to you, Lord Rudyard," Adam said, pulling his coin purse from his coat pocket. "Would you mind if Dixon went with you? I'm sure he'd like to pick out a refreshment, too, since there doesn't seem to be any entertainment in the park this afternoon. Right, Dixon?"

The lad looked up at him and nodded.

"Ah, well . . . ," the viscount hedged as he looked at Dixon. Finally, he said, "Of course I don't mind." Lord Rudyard squared his shoulders and added, "And please, put your coins away, Lord Greyhawke, I'll take care of this for the boy. Leave it all to me."

"Thank you, my lord. That's very kind of you. I'll remember and return the favor."

"That won't be necessary, I assure you. Come along, Master Dixon." He glanced at Miss Wright and smiled. "I won't be gone long."

The viscount didn't know how slowly Dixon walked, Adam thought, but he'd find out.

"Did you send Lord Rudyard away on purpose, my lord?" Miss Wright asked when the unlikely duo was far enough away that they couldn't hear her speak.

"Would it bother you if I did?"

She tilted her head back. "I asked first and you didn't answer my question."

"Ah, so we are back to the same kind of conversation we had before, are we not? All right, because I can be a gentleman from time to time, I will make up for my earlier error and answer your question first. Of course

I sent him away on purpose. How else was I to have a few moments alone with you?" Adam's gaze swept slowly up and down her face. "Now, does it bother you that I did?"

"Not in the least," she answered, searching his face, too. "Tell me, is your cousin visiting with you or does he live in London?"

Two ladies and a gentleman strode past them as she spoke. Adam tipped his hat to them before answering, "Dixon lives with me. I am his guardian and he is my heir."

"Oh, I see. I had no idea. You must like children, Lord Greyhawke, to be responsible for someone so young."

"I had very little choice in the matter. He was orphaned."

Her smile faded and her eyes clouded. "Yes, that does make a difference. I'm sorry to hear that for him. It's sad for someone so young to lose his parents."

Adam swore silently to himself. He realized he'd just been as insensitive to Miss Wright as Rudyard carrying a cane. He shouldn't have mentioned that Dixon was an orphan.

"I'm sure you know how he feels, Miss Wright," Adam said softly, trying to convey with his tone and his expression that he hadn't meant to bring up unhappy memories for her. "It couldn't have been an easy time for either one of you."

"I've found that life goes on, and so will he." She reached down and rubbed the top of Pharaoh's head again but didn't speak.

"No doubt your uncles and aunt have done much

better caring for you than I have for Dixon," Adam said, remembering his earlier conversation with his cousin.

"I'm not sure I would agree with that. I fear they have coddled me unnecessarily and for way too long."

"At least they know how to do it. I fear I don't cosset enough. I know nothing about children."

She looked up at him with a tender smile. "Most people don't until they live with them. How long has he been with you?"

"A short time. He will be under my care until he is old enough to go away to school."

"I'm sure you are doing all you need to do. He seems happy." She stopped rubbing Pharaoh and he woofed at her. She laughed and patted him again. "Oh, you are a greedy ruler when it comes to affection, aren't you?" she said to the dog.

Adam had never seen Pharaoh take to anyone as fast as he had to Miss Wright. But then Adam had never taken to anyone as he had Miss Wright, either.

"I'm puzzled about something."

"What?" she asked.

"Why did you fall when I stepped away from you last night?"

"I didn't have my cane," she said innocently, and continued to give Pharaoh her attention.

Something didn't seem to fit. Adam looked at Miss Wright. From what he could see of her feet beneath the tail of her skirt, both legs were firmly planted on the ground, equally sharing her weight.

"You seem to be standing with very little support from your cane right now. And I watched you as you approached a few minutes ago. You're walking well. Do you never walk without your cane?"

She straightened and reopened her parasol. "No."

Adam lifted his hand and tipped his hat to two elderly gentlemen and a lady who were passing by and then waited until they were a distance away before he said, "You don't ever walk without your cane? Not even in the privacy of your bedchamber?"

"No," she said again, and stepped back from him and Pharaoh. "I always use my cane."

"Why?"

Her brows drew together. She seemed confused by his question for a moment. "I'm not supposed to. After I fell down the stairs, the doctors, my uncles, my aunt, everyone said I must never stand or walk without it again, and I haven't."

"When did that fall happen?"

"A couple of years after the accident." Her gaze looked past him, as if she were drawing something from the depths of her memory. "I remember my leg was finally healing. I was able to walk a little without any help. One day I was at the top of the stairs." She paused and twirled the handle of her parasol in her hand and shook her head. "I don't really remember how, exactly, but I fell down the stairs and reinjured my leg. I don't know if I tripped, or my leg gave way beneath me or what happened, but I haven't walked without the cane since."

"Would you like to try?"

At that moment, she tilted her head so that the brim of her hat couldn't shield her face from the sun. Adam was struck by her softness and beauty. Once again he thought about how much he enjoyed being with her and how stimulating it was talking to her, how much he wanted to pull her close and kiss her again.

"What? No." She laughed lightly. "I told you I can't. I've been told by everyone not to. I don't know why you are obsessed about the problem with my leg, but you need to think of something else to talk about."

Adam considered her words. He supposed it was natural for her aunt and uncles to treat her so delicately. She was the only survivor of her family. And then in her uncle's house, she fell and injured herself again. He could see how they would insist she use the cane so that it wouldn't happen again. But Adam wasn't ready to give up on her.

"I think you could walk without any aid," he said.

"Thank you for telling me that," she said dryly.

"I'm serious. How do you know you can't if you haven't tried?" Pharaoh strained to sniff around Miss Wright's feet, so Adam unwound the leash to give the dog a little more freedom. "And, I believe I can teach you to dance, Miss Wright."

Making no effort to hide her incredulous expression, she said, "I refuse to have that conversation again with you, my lord."

"Meet me tonight in your uncle's garden and I'll teach you."

"What? Do you realize you are suggesting I meet you in secret?"

"That's exactly what I'm suggesting." An easy, natural smile came to his lips. "We met on his front lawn at his dinner party last night."

"That was by accident," she reminded him. "We didn't plan it and we won't plan anything of the kind."

He had learned a little more about her, but not nearly enough. Everything about her intrigued him. And he knew he couldn't push her too hard about learning to dance. But if he eased her into the idea, maybe she would trust him enough to give it a try.

It was odd to him, but he supposed if someone told you long enough and often enough that you couldn't do something, in time you would believe what you'd been told.

"All right, I accept your answer of no—for now. Tell me, is Viscount Rudyard one of the gentlemen who have tried to kiss you?"

Her beautiful mouth made the shape of an *O* of surprise. "I'm not commenting about that either."

Satisfied, he said, "You don't have to now. What you said gives me my answer."

She gazed at him with her dazzling green eyes. He could tell he had perturbed her.

"It does no such thing," she insisted.

One corner of his mouth tilted up in a half grin and he folded his arms across his chest. "I think it does, and you saying otherwise won't make me change my mind."

"Oh, I should have never told you that other gentlemen had wanted to kiss me."

"Why?"

"Because I answered another of your probing, personal questions and now you will be constantly asking me about the gentlemen when it is none of your concern. It was my misfortune that you caught me at a weak moment."

"I told you. I'm interested. In you. I want to know

about your injury, and about the accident. What your life was like before you came to live with your uncle. I want to know who has tried to kiss you."

Her gaze swept back to his. "Those are all personal questions, my lord. Are you prepared to answer other personal questions for me if I answer yours?"

"You drive a hard bargain, Miss Wright."

"And you, sir, are downright meddlesome at times."

Adam frowned. "I have been called a lot of things in my life, but never meddlesome. But all right, I will put myself at risk once again."

"You at risk?" She titled her head back and laughed heartily. "I don't see that ever happening."

"Only for you. Ask me something personal."

"All right, let me think. Ah, I know. All the young ladies want to know if you have come to London to make a match."

"No. What part of your leg is injured?"

"My hip and my knee. So why did you come back to London if not to look for a wife?"

"To meet with my solicitors and learn more about the estates that are now entrusted to my care as the Earl of Greyhawke. How many gentlemen have tried to kiss you?"

She looked puzzled for a moment, then pursed her lips before saying, "I really don't know."

Adam was skeptical of her answer, so he pressed her. "Two, four, six, or eight?"

"At least that many. Maybe more."

That raised his eyebrows a little higher.

"How many more?"

Frustrated, she said, "I haven't kept count, my lord.

This is my third Season, and as my uncle keeps reminding me, I have rejected the offers and affections of almost every eligible gentleman in London."

And she had let only him kiss her. Adam smiled. That pleased him.

"Do you plan to marry again?" she asked.

That question surprised Adam, too. He hesitated briefly and then said, "No. Did Rudyard try to kiss you?"

"Yes." Her gaze held tightly on his. "Why won't you consider marrying again?"

Adam hesitated when he realized that for a second he'd actually thought about telling her the reasons he never wanted to marry again. He had never wanted to reveal that much of himself to anyone, and thankfully he didn't have to decide at this moment.

"Here you are, Miss Wright," the viscount said with a satisfied smile as he hurried up beside her. "I couldn't decide which sweet cake to purchase for you, so I bought the whole basket. And I hope you don't mind, my lord, but I couldn't get one for her and not get the same for Dixon."

Adam looked down and grunted ruefully. Dixon held a small basket in one hand and a half-eaten tart in the other. Crumbs had collected from one side of his mouth to the other cheek and down the front of his coat. Pharaoh smelled the treats and nudged Dixon's basket with his nose. The lad turned the basket away from the Pyrenees but then in a show of kindness gave the dog his half-eaten tart. In one bite Pharaoh swallowed it and woofed for more.

"I don't mind at all," Adam said.

"Good. Well, we must get back to the carriage now, if you'll excuse us, Lord Greyhawke."

Adam tipped his hat to them. "I enjoyed our discussion, Miss Wright."

Her gaze zeroed in on his for only a second as she said, "It was enlightening for me." She glanced down at the overstuffed basket of sweets and then back to the viscount and smiled. "These look delicious, Lord Rudyard. I shall have one as soon as I'm settled into the carriage. And thank you for getting enough for me to share."

Rudyard beamed at her pleasure.

Miss Wright pulled a sweet cake from the basket and held it out to Pharaoh. "Here you are, Your Majesty."

Once again the Pyrenees gulped down the pastry, barked his thanks, and woofed for more.

"I think you've had enough," Adam said.

Miss Wright's gaze caught his once more before she turned away.

Adam felt a knot in his stomach as they left. Rudyard had been a tip-top gentleman about the predicament Adam had forced on him. He recalled that Rudyard was good at billiards and most card games, too. Adam couldn't remember him ever betting too heavily. He wouldn't waste Miss Wright's fortune. Since Adam couldn't contemplate pursuing her, the man would probably be a suitable match for her.

That didn't mean he had to like it.

"She smells nice," Dixon said.

Adam swallowed hard. "That she does."

Chapter 15

O Opportunity, thy guilt is great!
—The Rape of Lucrece, *876*

The ladies could do a lot of knitting and embroidery in two hours. A lot of discussing books, music, poetry, and their favorite topic: gentlemen. With some of them, the more they talked, the faster their fingers and hands worked, and that was always good for the orphanage basket.

Katherine settled into the straight-backed chair and glanced around the drawing room. She looked forward to the afternoons it was her time to host the Wilted Tea Society. With more than twenty young ladies in the group, it didn't come around to her often, but whenever it did, she enjoyed it immensely. She loved the sounds of the chatter, laughter, and clinking of delicate teacups hitting saucers sounding throughout the usually quiet house.

Tea and scones had been served and devoured, and now all the ladies had found a comfortable place to sit.

Madeline and Penny were on Katherine's left. Barbara, Jane, and Agatha sat on the settee in front of her, and Rosemarie, Darlene, and Fern were seated to her right. The group was smaller than usual, which was normal for their meetings during the Season. On any given week, there were always three or four young ladies who missed their regular Tuesday afternoon assemblies in favor of accepting an invitation to a card party or a garden social or, if they were lucky enough, a ride in the park with a handsome gentleman.

Every time they met, each lady was to bring an item of clothing as well as whatever she had made for the orphanage that week. Katherine had started today's basket by depositing the three children's scarves she'd knitted during the week, a small woolen cape, and a chocolate-colored shawl.

She had checked the basket she'd left by the door before she sat down and had been pleased with the contents. The ladies had been generous with their donations today. By the time she convinced Aunt Leola and her two uncles to pilfer their wardrobes again for cast-offs to be added, she would have an overflowing basket to take to the orphanage later in the week.

Since Madeline had been the one to start the group, she'd always insisted that any young lady who wanted to tell them about what had happened to her since the last time they met must have the opportunity to do so. Madeline considered it a good way to get the group talking together about the latest gossip and gentlemen, which were the two topics most of them were interested in hearing about anyway.

Penny went first, excited to tell them all about her ride

in the park with Mr. Hugo Underwood. It was easy to tell the gentleman had made quite the impression on her. There was a rosy glow to her cheeks and an unusual sparkle in her eyes.

Then she went on to tell whom she'd danced with at the balls of the past week and which interesting gentlemen she had been presented to—including, at the Duke of Quillsbury's dinner party, the Earl of Greyhawke. Much to Katherine's consternation, Penny added that she had not been lucky enough to talk with the earl at any length, as Katherine had, and that perhaps Katherine might want to enlighten the ladies as to what she and the earl had had to say to each other. Especially since they had conversed for a very long time.

That statement, of course, prompted Madeline to ask Katherine to expand on what Penny had said. Tired of the troublesome questions directed at her about His Lordship, Katherine decided to turn the tables on them and ask a few questions of her own.

"I'm glad you mentioned that, Penny," she said to the redhead. "As it happens, I haven't seen Lord Greyhawke at any of the parties except for my uncle's. Am I just missing him? Has anyone else seen him at a gathering since that night?"

Katherine was careful how she'd worded that last question. She had seen Lord Greyhawke, of course, but it was at the park, not at a party. She had looked for him every night, hoping he would make an appearance so she could talk with him again and maybe somehow find a way to kiss him again.

The question brought low murmurings around the room.

"I haven't seen him either," Madeline concurred. "That's rather odd, isn't it? We can only assume the reason he came back to London for the Season was to make a match. I mean, what other reason could there be? And how can he settle on a lady and make a match if he's not attending the parties to meet us and dance with us?"

"I know the rumor was that after his wife died, he said he'd never marry again," Barbara said.

"Who could blame him?"

"But that was before he became an earl," Fern added quickly to what Madeline said.

"Yes, surely he will want to marry now," Penny said thoughtfully. "He'll need an heir to inherit the title."

Darlene laughed. "But you are now interested in Mr. Underwood, aren't you, Penny?"

"She's interested in any gentleman who is interested in her," Barbara said with a smirk.

"As we all are," Madeline reminded them.

Katherine remained quiet and let the ladies talk and enjoy themselves. She also made note of the fact that Dixon must not be common knowledge around Town. The earl had said his cousin was his heir. Surely if any of the ladies had known about him, they would have spoken up. Katherine smiled. Or maybe, like her, there were some other ladies keeping quiet about what they might know about the mysterious Lord Greyhawke.

And that thought caused Katherine to take a hard look at the faces of each lady in the room. Had the earl kissed any of them? And if he had, had he kissed them with the same passion he'd kissed her?

"Then I'll just have to find out where he is hiding and

remind him that I'm young, strong, and available to bear his heirs," Agatha said.

Several of the ladies laughed, and the conversation continued on the light side, with most of them taking aim at the missing earl.

Katherine was not about to tell them she'd asked the earl that very question about why he'd come to London and he'd said he hadn't come back to make a match. It wasn't up to her to disappoint them and take away the hope that they just might be the one for him. Like the other ladies, she'd found herself wishing that he had returned in need of a wife, because Katherine was in need of a husband.

After they'd said what they wanted concerning Lord Greyhawke, Barbara was the next to talk. She was relishing spreading a little gossip about her brother. She'd overheard him telling one of his friends about an un-named young lady rubbing her foot up and down his leg at a card party. While all listened, Katherine heard voices coming from the front of the house. She set her knitting aside so she could see who had come in when Melba Tiploft bounded into the drawing room. Her eyes were large and her face was flushed with excitement.

"I am sorry to interrupt, ladies," she said breathlessly.

Katherine immediately noticed that she was not holding her sewing satchel in her gloved hand, but a sheet of newsprint. To Katherine, that did not bode well.

"Melba, what held you up?" Madeline said in a scolding tone. "You're very late."

"I know," Melba answered, looking as though she were the cat that had just eaten the fattest bird in the nest. "I have a very good reason. I was feeling poorly this morning and decided I wouldn't come out this afternoon but stay home and rest. I wanted to feel wonderful for tonight's parties. And it's a good thing I did." She held up the paper. "This came while I was resting and my maid brought it up to me. After I read it, I threw off my robe and rushed to get dressed. I hurried to get over here before all of you left."

"What is it?" Madeline asked.

"It must be the gossip column," Barbara suggested.

"Who is it about?" Agatha asked in an excited voice, rubbing her hands together hopefully.

"Oh, I do hope there's something in there about me," Penny said, laying her knitting aside. "I've always wanted to be written about in the gossip columns."

"Then perhaps you should do something scandalously outrageous for once in your life so that someone will want to write about you," Madeline suggested sweetly.

Everyone laughed.

Including Penny, who added, "I would, but I can't find a gentleman willing to put me in a compromising situation. They are all afraid they will be caught in a parson's mousetrap."

"And they would be," Fern boasted.

"Ladies," Melba said in an exasperated voice. "Perhaps I should just get on with it and read this."

"Go ahead," Darlene said. "But please don't try to sound like an actress on a stage. You really don't do that well."

"Ah!" Melba objected. "I have never tried to read like an actress in my life."

"You do it every time you read a poem to us," Darlene insisted.

"I wouldn't," Melba insisted.

"Ladies, this is not the time for idle bickering," Madeline declared. "Let's settle down and let her read however she wishes. We just want to know what it says. Shall we?"

"And it is about someone in this room—but no, Penny, not you," Melba said. "Now, do the rest of you want me to read this or not?"

"Yes," several of the ladies said.

Melba remained standing right beside Katherine, unfolded the paper, and began to read:

The new Earl of Greyhawke has returned to London and is setting off more fireworks than you can see at Vauxhall Gardens on a dark night. The first and only sighting of him so far this Season, as best determined at this writing, has been at a dinner party given by the Duke of Quillsbury. It is on good authority of the recounting of events which are written here that the duke's niece was seen in the earl's arms before the night was over.

A low, slow, collective gasp sounded around the room, and every eye fixed on Katherine.

Melba stopped reading and held up her hand to silence the room. When everyone's attention centered on her again, she continued.

But as shocking as that may be to the dear readers of this column, there is an even bigger indis-

cretion that needs to be reported here today. It has been confirmed by more than one that while at the duke's table, his niece and the earl, who were dinner partners, exchanged dinner plates.

Melba finished with a deep intake of breath and a satisfied smile on her face. "Now, Katherine," she said as she folded the newsprint dramatically, "you must tell us what you have to say for yourself about this."

"Did he really pick you up in his arms?" Penny asked.

"What I want to know is what it felt like to be lifted up in those strong masculine arms," Madeline said.

"Did you see him coming and fall on purpose so he'd be obliged to help you?" Darlene wanted to know.

"Say something," Barbara insisted.

Katherine gave the ladies an uncertain smile and looked specifically at Penny. "Do you still want to be in the gossip columns?"

It took another hour, which seemed like four, and no small amount of double talk by Katherine to satisfy the Wilted Tea ladies that the story, as told in the column, had been exaggerated by enormous proportions. She had no idea if any of them believed her in the end, but all eventually, though slowly, bade her farewell and took their leave.

After the door shut behind the last member, Katherine hobbled up the stairs to her aunt's room. The door was open. Her aunt sat at her desk with her back to Katherine. This was not a conversation she wanted to have.

Swallowing past the tightness in her throat, Katherine knocked and said, "Auntie, may I come in?"

Lady Leola turned a blank face to Katherine. "Of

course. And yes, I've seen it. I expected it. I'm just surprised it's taken so long for it to come out in the open."

Katherine's shoulders drooped and she leaned heavily on her cane as she entered the room. "Has the duke read it?"

"Not yet, but he will. He and Lord Willard left this morning for Kent. Said they'd be back in a couple of days. You know how restless the duke gets if he stays in one place too long."

Katherine remembered well. When she was younger, they often moved from one manor house to another, then back to London for a few weeks before retracing their steps to the country. He'd tell her that as long as he kept moving, he wouldn't get old.

"I'm sure this gossip will make him unhappy."

"Yes, but it won't last. He gets over things easily and quickly. Being a duke, he's always had so many things on his mind to deal with that if he didn't take care of a problem and then forget about it and move on, he would never get anything done. He is not a worrywart. After he reads it when he returns, the only thing he will want to know is whether I have taken care of the problem. Which I shall do."

Katherine wasn't unhappy her uncle Quillsbury was gone. She'd just been hounded unmercifully by her friends, and now she had to get through the same discussion with her aunt. She was glad there would be a reprieve before she had to go through this with her uncles.

She let out a sigh. "It's just that they made it sound so much worse than it actually was."

"That is why it's called scandal, my dear," her aunt said calmly, and laid her quill aside.

Katherine appreciated that she never heard any condemnation in her aunt's voice. "What should we do now?"

"Nothing."

Katherine bristled. She didn't like that idea. She didn't want to just give up and let the gossips have their say without fighting back. Living the rest of her life with her aunt and two uncles was not how she envisioned spending her future.

"Nothing," she repeated. "So this is it? I won't go to any more of the parties? I'm to be shunned by all of Society?"

"Heavens have mercy, Katherine!" Her aunt rose in astonishment and walked over to her. "Of course you won't. You are a Wright. Whether or not you are always right, you will hold your head and shoulders high and act as though you are. The duke would never allow a niece of his to be shunned, even if she were caught in bed with a man and with neither of them wearing a stitch of clothing! The best way to put a rumor to rest is to ignore it. That is what we shall do."

"Good," Katherine said, feeling somewhat better. "I didn't like the idea of just giving up."

"Wrights never give up." The corners of her aunt's thin lips turned up in a grin. "We would never do that. Nor will we give it any merit by referencing it or crying foul and furiously denying it."

"That would only fuel the fire," Katherine surmised.

"Precisely. We will attend all the parties this evening,

and tomorrow evening, and the evening after that, and all the others until there are no more parties to attend. We shall act as if you have been slandered and vilified, but we are above the tawdry efforts of the gossipmongers. We will show them all that you have done nothing wrong, and you have nothing to hide from anyone. Are you up to that?"

"Absolutely," Katherine agreed.

"Wonderful. We will simply act as if nothing is amiss." She paused. "Which really there isn't, right?"

Katherine looked at her aunt but remained quiet. Something was very much amiss, but she didn't know what she could do about it.

She couldn't very well admit to her aunt that Lord Greyhawke had kissed her and that she desperately wanted to see him again. When she'd seen him at the park, all she could think of was how wonderful it would be if he could kiss her again. If he held her close and kissed her as he had that marvelous night in front of her house.

But the earl wasn't cooperating.

Lord Greyhawke refused to come to the parties, so neither she nor any of the other ladies could see him, talk to him, and get to know him. Katherine knew she was supposed to be looking for a husband, a man who would give her strong, healthy children to love and care for. But the only man she could think about was the one who'd said he wasn't going to marry again. The man who'd obviously loved his wife so much that he became a beast and smashed the furniture in his house when she and his babe had died.

Perhaps that was one of the reasons she'd been so

attracted to him. He was unattainable. But he also challenged her. He was the only man who didn't seem to pander to her limp as much as her aunt and uncles did. He wasn't bothered by it, either. In fact, just the opposite was true. He thought he could help her learn to walk without her cane.

And to dance!

Could he?

Could she?

After all these years, should she defy the commands of her aunt, uncles, and all the physicians who'd looked at her leg and throw down her cane and try to live without it?

Lord Greyhawke made her think and say and do things that no other man had come close to even tempting her do. But what was she to do with all these pent-up feelings of dancing and womanly desires that he'd stirred up inside her if he wouldn't come to the balls and parties and make himself available?

Chapter 16

You are not wood, you are not stones, but men.
—Julius Caesar, *act 3, scene 2*

It was the most nondescript building on London's most fashionable street. The Heirs' Club. It didn't have the notoriety, the membership, or the reputation of the older, prestigious White's, but it had an exclusivity that neither White's nor any other gentleman's club could boast. No gentleman could join unless he was titled or an heir to a title.

Adam stood on the pavement in front of the door to the famed club, waiting, as he always had, for his friend Bray to arrive and gain him entrance, but this would be the last time. In all his years of coming to the club, Adam never thought he'd be a member. With Bray, he'd never needed to be. After today, he would be a member and could come and go as he wished.

While in his twenties, when he was often a guest at the club, Adam was third or maybe fourth in line for the title of Earl of Greyhawke. Inheriting it wasn't something that ever crossed his mind. And even now, it wasn't that he wanted or even needed to join, but Bray and Harrison wouldn't rest until he did.

The Duke of Drakestone had always been his voucher past the stiff-lipped attendant who guarded the door as if the king's diamond-encrusted scepter were held inside. Unlike Adam and Harrison, Bray had been born an heir. Though his admittance into the elite club hadn't been easy for him to come by when he came of age. And Adam and Harrison were the main reasons.

The three of them had met at Eton. All were tall, strong, and capable of most anything for their young age, and they had done plenty that was foolish and often dangerous, too. They excelled at whatever they did and seldom had to put in the same amount of study time as most of the other boys at the school, which left the trio with time and an eagerness to do the things they enjoyed. That usually meant getting into trouble with the headmaster and Bray's stern father, who had been a hard taskmaster.

Years ago, the three of them had almost caused a rift in the membership at the Heirs' Club. Some of the oldest members didn't want Bray to join because they knew he'd invite Adam and Harrison to join him there—often. Which he did. With little chance of Adam and Harrison ever being an heir, at the time, most of the members didn't want the well-known troublemakers in their quiet, respectable club.

No surprise to any of them, Bray's father, who was a powerful duke himself at the time, had remained silent on the matter, but Bray had an older friend who'd stood

up for him, and the disgruntled members had been
forced to back down. So even though Adam, Harrison,
and Bray had enjoyed their raucous game of cards com-
plete with ribald jokes, loud, salacious songs, and an
abundance of fine brandy when they were at the stilted
Heirs' Club, they'd managed to stay just under the
threshold of getting kicked out onto the street and told
never to return.

The brisk wind whipped around Adam's neck and he
lifted his collar, wondering how long he'd been waiting
for his friends. Either he was early or they were late.

He tipped his hat to a couple of older ladies who
walked by. He shifted his weight and looked up and
down the street. No sign of Harrison or Bray. The door
to the club opened and he nodded to the gentleman who
walked out as he passed.

"Lord Greyhawke."

Adam looked up to see the old attendant, who'd managed the door ever since he'd been coming to the club
with Bray, smiling at him. The man had never had a
pleasant expression for him.

"No need to stand out in the cold. Come on in and
have a drink while you wait. I'll tell the duke you're
inside."

That was a big change. Adam had never been allowed
entrance before Bray arrived. But then, he'd never been
an earl when visiting the club, either.

He handed off his coat, hat, and gloves to the man
and then made his way to the taproom. From another
part of the club, he heard the sound of billiard balls
smacking together, followed by muted laughter. Someone was either very good with a cue stick and getting the

accolades he deserved, or he was very bad and getting punished with laughter.

Adam smiled to himself and followed the direction of the hum of chatter down the corridor and into the taproom. He couldn't help notice that several of the patrons looked up at him and the room slowly fell silent as he entered. Their reaction didn't surprise him. No doubt the members still considered him the wild youth he was a few years ago and, as always, every time he entered they wondered if this would be the time he disturbed the peace and quiet of their respectable club.

Except for the Duke of Quillsbury's dinner party, he hadn't been to a public gathering since arriving in London. Though it wasn't that he hadn't thought about attending the evening parties. He'd even wanted to when he'd first arrived. What he hadn't expected was to gaze into sparkling green eyes and be mesmerized by a young lady who refused to dance with him.

Ever since that first look, his feelings for Miss Katherine Wright had taken root, and against all his efforts they were deepening. There was something about her that gave him a warm, contented feeling when he thought of her. And after his stint on the cold northern coast, it was damn hard to deny himself someone as intoxicatingly sweet as Miss Wright.

Adam asked for ale as he passed the bar and picked out a table in the far corner to sit down. He hoped Bray and Harrison arrived soon. He didn't want to have time to sit and think. When he did, it was usually Miss Wright he was thinking about.

He'd been tempted to attend the parties the last couple of nights just so he could see her. It had been difficult, but he'd managed to resist the enticement to go. Seeing her in the park had convinced him he needed to keep his distance. Knowing that he wanted to see her made him realize he didn't need to see her. And that was the very reason he was declining all invitations. He hadn't come to London looking for a young lady to bewitch him with her charms, and she was very close to doing that.

"Who am I trying to fool?" he whispered. She wasn't close to bewitching him. She had. All he thought about when he looked at Miss Wright was that he wanted to make her his. But that could never happen.

After spending his days trying to make sense out of ledgers and documents, he'd been filling his nights reading the history of the Greyhawke legacy. Since he was never supposed to be the earl, he hadn't been schooled on the extensiveness of the entailed property or what the first Earl of Greyhawke had done to receive the peerage from the king.

Another thing Adam wouldn't allow himself to think about was his two best friends' wives being in the family way. He was happy for them. Bray and Harrison needed sons; they deserved sons. But their wives' upcoming time wasn't something he wanted to hear about.

He was also spending more time with Dixon each evening, teaching him how to play chess. The lad seemed to have a keen aptitude for strategy, which kept the pastime from being boring. Reading and the games had kept him occupied so he wouldn't change his mind and go to the balls.

As soon as the server set his tankard down, Adam saw Bray walk in.

"I know I'm late," Bray said after they had greeted each other and he had taken the chair opposite Adam. "I thought Harrison would be here by now, too."

"I just arrived myself. For the first time, the attendant at the door offered to let me come inside rather than have me wait outside for you. Perhaps that's why I feel like everyone is looking rather strangely at me today."

"I don't think any of the members of the Heirs' Club would be happy to hear one of the staff had left an earl outside in the cold. But it could be that others are looking at you for another reason."

"Do they still believe that our presence is going to somehow tarnish this sacred club?"

"That is probably a good bet, too, but that isn't what I'm talking about either. Did you read *The Times* today?"

"No," Adam said on a laugh. "I'm still trying to get through years of account books and documentation, trying to familiarize myself with the Greyhawke estates and businesses and how they work." Bray looked a bit serious, so Adam added, "Why?"

"I take it, then, you haven't seen the scandal sheets or any of the gossip columns today?"

Damnation, Adam didn't even want to think about that. He had a feeling he knew what Bray was talking about. He grabbed his tankard by the handle and took a drink, then replaced it on the table before saying, "If I had time to read the news, the latest tittle-tattle wouldn't be the first section I'd go to. I can assume by the expression on your face that I'm mentioned in at least one of them."

"All of them, actually, according to Louisa. I took her word for it. And you weren't mentioned alone."

That confirmed Adam's fear. He shifted in his chair. "I expected as much. What did they say?"

Bray motioned to the server for a drink. "That after most everyone had left the Duke of Quillsbury's dinner party, you were caught holding Miss Wright in your arms."

"Hellfire," he whispered.

"So it's true?"

"Yes, it's true," Adam said, swearing again under his breath. "But I was carrying her because she had fallen. I had picked her up."

Bray remained silent, his features stoic.

"You don't believe me?"

"No, no, I do," Bray said, leaning back in his chair as the server placed a tankard of ale in front of him. "If you say it, I believe it. You have no reason to lie to me."

"She uses a cane, you know."

"Everyone knows," Bray said dryly.

"I assume her walking is unsteady at times. The truth is, I don't know why she fell. Maybe it was because she was on uneven ground."

"So she was outside when she fell?"

"Yes."

"With you?" Bray asked.

"At the time. Yes. And just so you know, her uncles were quite pleased I picked her up and carried her into the house. Unfortunately, her uncles weren't the only ones who saw me do that. Three other gentlemen were also there."

"Obviously one of them decided to talk about it."

Adam leaned over the table. "If I knew which one, I'd—"

"Do nothing," Bray cut him off. "That would only stir up more gossip for the two of you, and it sounds as if you have more than you can handle for now."

"More? Why do you say that?"

"One of the scandal sheets wrote something outlandish about you and Miss Wright exchanging dinner plates at the duke's table. What kind of madness will the gossipmongers come up with next?" Bray paused. "You didn't, did you? . . . You did."

"It's a long story and best told when we're old and gray and have nothing better to talk about. That is not important, but she really fell." And he was still trying to figure out why, when by all he could tell from watching her, she could probably walk without that cane if she tried.

Adam took a long drink from his tankard. He wondered how Miss Wright was handling this debacle. She was the strongest young lady he could remember ever meeting, but no young lady would be immune to the horrors of having gossip spread about her.

"I believe you, but why did she fall?" Bray asked.

"I don't know. And that is the truth. Was there anything else written?" Adam asked cautiously.

"Wasn't that enough?" Bray's eyes narrowed. "What else could there be? Wait a minute. You didn't kiss her, did you?"

Oh, yes!

Adam remained silent.

"Tell me you didn't kiss her. And at the duke's house. . . . You did. You probably kissed her right under his nose."

"On her front lawn," Adam said, knowing there was no use denying it to Bray. They had been friends too long to try to hide anything from him. "I'm surprised that wasn't mentioned. Somehow they seemed to have heard everything else."

"If you kissed her on her front lawn, you can probably expect to see that in the scandal sheets tomorrow."

Adam didn't even want to consider that possibility.

"Were you trying to leg shackle yourself?"

"No," Adam insisted.

"Were you trying to ruin her reputation?" Bray pressed him again.

Adam stiffened. "You know better than to even suggest that. I wanted to kiss her, so I did. That is all there is to it. A simple kiss."

Maybe it wasn't so simple.

"Perhaps you should have at least waited until the second or third time you saw her before you kissed her."

Waited? He wished he hadn't done it at all.

He couldn't explain it, but Adam felt as if it were the third time he'd seen her. They'd had three separate meetings and conversations over the course of the evening. And by the third, he felt as though he'd always known her, that they had been waiting for the right time to kiss.

"What are you going to do?"

Adam studied over Bray's question. "There is nothing for me to do. The truth is, she fell. I picked her up. Her uncles believe that. She can weather this," he continued, but he wasn't sure if he was trying to convince himself or Bray. "Her uncles were happy I was carrying her, and I suspect His Grace can quiet the ton if he so chooses."

"And what about next time?"

"What?"

"You know what I mean. What about the next time you kiss her? And don't try to tell me that you have decided you are no longer interested in her."

Oh, there was interest all right. All he was thinking right now was that he wanted to see her and make sure she was all right. He wanted to know that she was handling the gossip the way she handled her "unusual gait," with strength that said, *This will not defeat me.* She didn't appear to be the kind of young lady who would hide from Society at the first sign of gossip.

But he couldn't be sure.

And no matter how much he wanted to see her, he couldn't. He was as involved in her life as he wanted to get. There was something about her that had touched him deep in his soul the moment he saw her standing by the dance floor, and that hadn't lessened. If anything, it had grown stronger. He must keep his distance from her, stay focused on the work he was doing with his solicitors, and then leave London and start touring his estates just as he had planned.

Whenever he was with her, he felt good. Happy, even. He wanted to get close to her, touch her hand, her cheek, just touch her. Feeling those things could only take him places with her he didn't want to go. He couldn't let himself become a part of whatever concerned her.

The hell of it was that Miss Wright was wrong for him.

"Here comes Harrison," Bray said.

Adam leaned back in his chair and winced inside. No doubt he'd have to go through the entire conversation again. Sometimes having best friends was a damned nuisance.

He drained the tankard and motioned for another drink.

Chapter 17

'Tis not so deep as a well, nor so wide as a church door; but 'tis enough, 'twill serve.
—Romeo and Juliet, *act 3, scene 1*

Katherine, her maid, and her driver climbed the six steps that led to the front door of the large building that housed the small Potts Orphanage. They had been there three times before when it was Katherine's turn to collect the clothing articles from the Wilted Tea ladies, so they knew the routine.

There was no use grasping the heavy iron door knocker because no one would answer it. The house was left unlocked during the day. If you had business inside, you simply went in and looked around until you found someone who could help you. Thankfully, they already knew where to deposit the clothing in the drafty old structure.

The foyer was an empty, sizable square room that had several corridors leading off it. The long corridors were mostly empty rooms, too. She remembered walking down three of them before she found someone to talk to the first time they visited. Mrs. Potts had told Katherine that she could fill the rooms with children if only she had the money and staff to do so.

As they passed one of the corridors, Katherine heard a voice that caused her to stop and look down the passageway. Her heart started beating a little faster. The man sounded just like the Earl of Greyhawke.

But why would he be at an orphanage?

Her maid and driver stopped, too. "No," she told them. "You two go ahead and deliver the baskets. I will either catch up with you in a few minutes or meet you back at the front door."

She stared down the wide corridor. The voices seemed to be coming from about the third door down. It probably wasn't him, Katherine tried to convince herself. But she had to be sure. And even if it wasn't His Lordship, she wanted to see the man who sounded so much like the elusive earl.

Slowly and with soft footsteps, she turned and tiptoed down the corridor. She didn't know why she was walking so softly or slowly. It wasn't as if she planned to eavesdrop on the conversation and didn't want anyone to know she was there. She simply wanted to get closer and see who was in that room. Cautiously, she took a few more steps, then stopped when she saw the man was backing out of the doorway, talking to someone.

"Yes, Mrs. Potts. I would appreciate that. I look forward to hearing from you on the matter."

He turned and stopped in his tracks when he saw her standing in the middle of the corridor not a dozen paces in front of him. Her skin prickled with anticipation. He held his black greatcoat over his arm and his hat in his

hand. Katherine had never seen him look more dash-
ingly handsome in fawn-colored riding breeches with
shiny black knee-high boots and a camel-colored waistcoat and coat. And as certain as she knew her name, by
his expression, Katherine knew that Lord Greyhawke
was glad to see her. And by the racing of her pulse, she
knew she was glad to see him, too.

"Miss Wright," he said, striding in eagerness toward
her. "What are you doing here?"

She gave him a ladylike shrug. "I was going to ask
you the same question."

"Ladies first," he answered, stopping a respectable
distance from her.

"I was dropping off some things the Wilted Tea Society collected for the children who live here."

"Thank goodness," he said, an easy smile coming to
his lips. "When I first saw you, I thought you might be
a mirage."

"Do you see me as unreal or unattainable, my
lord?"

His brandy-colored eyes met her stare for stare. "Perhaps. When I look at you as I am now." He paused. The
corners of his mouth lifted devilishly. "But when I realized you were actually standing in front of me and you
were not an illusion, I wondered about the possibility
that Miss Wright might be following me."

Her eyebrows lifted a little and so did her chin. She
made no effort to hide her amusement as she casually
folded her gloved hands together in front of her. "And
why would you suspect that, my lord?"

"It's simple. I take a walk in the park and it just so
happens I see you taking a walk in the park. I come to

the orphanage and you come to the orphanage. Do you see why I might think this?"

She chuckled softly. "Yes, but you have it wrong. It must be you who is following me. You never told me why you are here, and I freely confessed my mission."

"You're right," he admitted. "I didn't. This is where Dixon was first left after his mother died. When he was found and brought to me on the coast, I was told some of his things had remained here. I came to ask about them for him."

Her smile faded. "I hope they had them."

"Yes. Thankfully. Mrs. Potts has them safely stored away in the attic. I made arrangements with her to have them picked up tomorrow."

"That's a kind thing for you to do, my lord. I'm sure he'll appreciate having all his possessions with him."

"It's the right thing to do, Miss Wright. I told Dixon I was coming to look into claiming his possessions. He said he wanted to come with me, but when we arrived, he refused to get out of the carriage."

Her eyes softened. "Do you suppose he thought you might leave him here?"

"That could be it, I guess. But why didn't he just tell me he didn't want to come?"

"Maybe because he is five years old and not yet a young man who knows what he wants or what he can handle."

"I think that could very well be true, Miss Wright. So it's true. There is actually a society called Wilted Tea?"

She laughed a little. "Indeed there is. We know that

not everyone sees the humor in our name, as do those of us who belong to the group. But yes, as odd as it sounds, that is what we call our little society."

"You wouldn't want to know the names of some of the groups that I belonged to when I was a younger man, and I wouldn't tell you if by chance you did."

"I've heard that gentlemen enjoy their secret societies."

"We do, and it's best that I not talk about them in front of a lady."

"Why is that?"

His expression questioned her. "Is that a personal inquiry from you, Miss Wright?"

"If it is, I'm glad I was the first one to ask this time. It's usually you who ventures headlong where only angels go."

"It's difficult to be a gentleman at all times, Miss Wright. It seems that at your uncle's dinner party we aroused suspicions in a few people as to the real reason you were in my arms."

"Unfortunately, that is so."

His eyes and lips softened. "I didn't want that to happen. Has the gossip been bad for you?"

"You could have called on me to find out."

His expression changed to one of uncertainty, and she wondered if he felt she'd been too forward.

"You're right. I could have. I wanted to. It's just—"

"Nothing for you to worry about, my lord," she interrupted, taking him off the hook she had just placed him on. "My aunt cleverly convinced everyone that I exchanged dinner plates with you because yours had a chip in it, and the duke has convinced everyone you were my savior that night by lifting his injured niece off the ground and rushing her into the house before she could catch consumption."

He grimaced. "You're right. I should have stopped by to see you. The reasons I didn't are purely selfish ones."

"You've been busy, I know."

"You are not going to let me get off that easy, are you?"

"You chose not to call on me."

"I didn't because I know that you, Miss Wright, are wrong for me. It's best I stay away from you."

Katherine's breath caught in her lungs. Did that mean he had been as affected by their kisses as she had? Did it mean that when he looked at her, he felt the same wonderful feelings she felt when she looked at him? And if he did, was the problem that he felt he was betraying the memory of his beloved wife?

Her gaze held fast to his. "Is that why I haven't even seen you at any of the balls or parties?"

"I told you I didn't come to London to attend the Season, that it's mainly for those who want to be on the marriage mart."

"Yet you came to my uncle's for dinner."

"Yes, but when we met, I realized that was a mistake. I shouldn't have gone."

"Because we kissed?"

He stepped closer to her, keeping his intense gaze on hers. "No, not because of it, but because of the way we kissed, because of the way it felt." He stopped. "I came to London for business reasons, and as soon as I've accomplished them, I will be leaving."

His words felt like a stab to her heart, and she took a step back. "Oh, I didn't know you would be leaving."

"Yes," he said on a sharp intake of breath. "And you will be continuing to get to know and measure Lord Rudyard and other gentlemen who are pursuing you in your quest for a husband."

"Yes, of course I will," she agreed, feeling an odd sense of rejection. "I told you I promised my uncle I would settle on a husband by the end of the Season. I won't go back on my word."

"It's a shame he's put a time restraint on you about that."

"He is past ready for me to be some other man's responsibility. He feels he must fulfill his duty to my father and see me properly wed. I am holding up his fulfilling that obligation." She paused and let her gaze gently, slowly, sweep up and down his face. "I will settle on someone. I must. But I want you to know I will never forget our kiss. And I am pleased that my first kiss came from you."

Lord Greyhawke swore. He reached over and opened the door to his left and looked around. Then, without saying a word, he grabbed her wrist and gently pulled her inside with him.

Chapter 18

Men that hazard all
Do it in hope of fair advantages.
—The Merchant of Venice, *act 2, scene 7*

Despite reason and common sense, Adam shut them inside and backed Katherine against the door. They remained quiet for a moment, gazing into each other's eyes. They both knew he shouldn't have done it, but neither of them was going to do anything to correct it.

Just looking at her caused Adam's lower stomach to tighten and a surge of desire to catch between his legs.

Thank God she hadn't screamed or resisted him when he'd seized her wrist and pulled her with him into the empty room. This was probably the worst idea he'd ever had, except perhaps for kissing her on her front lawn, but Adam could no longer bear not touching her, and this cold chamber gave them privacy.

He had tried to stay away from her. By the holy saints, he'd tried. And he'd actually been good about doing it, for him, anyway, forcing himself not to go to the places she might be: the dinner parties, the balls, the opera, and all the other social gatherings he'd had every intention of enjoying when he'd first arrived in London. But that was when he'd thought that after living in isolation for so long, he'd be able to dance, banter, and enjoy a lively social Season with delightful young ladies who would be no danger to his heart.

Miss Wright had shattered that idea his very first night out.

But what was he to do when fate kept seeing to it that their paths crossed?

And now at an orphanage, of all places!

Fate wasn't fickle after all. It was a menace, creating trouble for him at every turn, knowing he desired Katherine Wright more than he had ever desired another woman, and knowing that he was no saint.

Katherine's beautiful, sparkling green eyes smiled at him as he gazed down into their depths. He breathed a sigh of relief. She wasn't frightened or angry with him for forcing her to come with him. Hope flared inside him that maybe she had wanted this time alone with him as much as he'd wanted to be alone with her.

He caressed her soft cheek with his fingertips, letting them slowly trace the outline of her gorgeous lips. His fingers continued to travel down her face to where the ribbon of her bonnet was tied under her chin. He pulled on the end of it and the bow unraveled. With a steady hand, he untied the sash that held her short velvet cape together, letting it slide off her shoulders, drop to the floor, and pool at the back of her feet.

The neckline of her pale gray dress was just low enough that he could see the gentle billow of her breasts. How glorious it would be if he could completely disrobe her. But that would be far too foolish. Instead, he reached down and kissed each firm swell, then enjoyed hearing the sharp intake of her breath. Adam lifted his head but kept his face very close to hers. He placed his middle finger at the hollow of her throat and let it rest. There he found the telltale sign of her wildly beating pulse and knew excitement was building inside her, too.

Dropping his coat and hat to the floor, he moved in close to her. "I want to kiss you," he said huskily and with more feeling than he thought he was capable of.

"I want you to," she answered breathlessly.

Adam bent his head and nuzzled the warm skin of her cheek, letting his nose travel over to her ear. He inhaled the exhilarating scent of fresh-washed hair and would have loved to rip her bonnet off and push his hands into her shiny auburn tresses. For a moment, he kept his nose buried at her temple and indulged himself in that small fantasy as he breathed deeply, drinking in her tempting womanly fragrance. He then let his lips travel to the crook of her neck as he reached down beside her and searched the area around the doorknob.

"There's no key," he said when he looked up at her. "I can't lock the door."

"Does that bother you?" she asked.

"I'm thinking about the scandal it would cause if someone came in and caught us in here alone together."

A twinkle caught in her eyes. "Would it irreparably damage your reputation if we were, my lord?"

Adam laughed lightly at her clever answer. He boxed her in by flattening his hands on the door near her shoulders and leaning in so close to her that his legs touched her skirts and his chest grazed her breasts. She was just too tempting to resist.

"My reputation was ruined long before I met you, Miss Wright who is so wrong for me. You are still an innocent. You are the one I'm worried about and you know it."

Amusement twitched the corners of her lips and she relaxed more fully against the door. "That is so. Still, I will do my best to protect you from anyone who tries to come into this room."

He grinned. "You think you're that strong?"

She nodded and said with a teasing smile, "But I hope no one puts me to the test."

"So do I, Katherine." A flash of surprise spread across her lovely face. "You don't mind if I call you Katherine when we are alone as we are now, do you?"

"No, of course not. Though it would pain my uncles to hear me say it, I rather like not being so formal all the time."

"As do I. You can call me Adam."

"All right, Adam. Perhaps you'd like to tell me if there is a reason you pulled me into this room."

His breath hitched. "Are you trying to tell me you're tired of waiting and you want me to get on with this and kiss you?"

"That is exactly what I'm waiting for you to do," she said softly.

Slowly, so as not to startle her, he reached down and slid his hand over hers, engulfing it with gentle pressure, and took hold of her cane. "You won't need this."

A wrinkle formed in her brow and her gloved hand clenched around the handle.

"Let go. You can trust me, Katherine. I will hold you up."

She hesitated a second or two longer and then gradually, finger by finger, let go of the cane, but she kept her gaze on it as Adam leaned it against the door beside her.

Adam knew what it cost her to put her faith in him, and he gave her a tender smile. He lifted her chin with his fingers, bent his head, and slanted his lips over hers in a slow, tender kiss. A very chaste and proper kiss. Then he raised his head and looked into her eyes again. She remained still except for the heavy rise and fall of her chest.

"Now, that is the proper way I should have kissed you for the first time," he said.

Her gaze raked over his like hot coals. "Perhaps for the first time," she answered, and then moistened her lips. "That was very nice and fatherly, my lord, but I like it better when you kiss me this way."

She rose on her toes, wound her arms around his neck, and placed her lips against his in a hard, demanding kiss. Her attempt was awkward at first, but Adam instantly got her meaning and started helping to show her how to kiss. She was letting him know she had no use for his chaste, proper kisses. And that sent a slow spreading of delicious warmth sizzling through him.

He circled her small waist and pulled her soft, pliant body into his arms, hugging her tightly against him. She felt as good and right in his arms as she had the last time he'd kissed her. *No, better,* he thought as hot, throbbing desire for her jolted through him.

Adam accepted her eager kisses with a deep, unfed

hunger gnawing at him. Without prompting, she parted her lips and leaned sensually into him. Impatient to taste her sweetness once again, he slipped his tongue inside her mouth, sweeping it from side to side, plundering its depths. Their raspy, uneven breaths mingled and melted together.

"Oh, yes," he whispered on a gasping breath. "I like this much better, too."

There was no hint of shyness as she surveyed his back and shoulders with her hands, running them down to his waist and back up and over his shoulders again. He liked the feel of her slender feminine arms cupping him and her exploring hands kneading his muscles as she pressed him closer to her with soft, urgent, relentless movement.

His lips left hers, and he kissed his way down the long sweep of her neck. At the hollow of her throat, his tongue came out and tasted her heated skin before going lower and leaving a trail of moisture down to her cleavage. She moaned in delight and arched her back, giving him better access to her throat and chest.

Taking full advantage of her generous response, he slid his hand up her midriff to cup her breast. Her pillow-soft swell filled his palm and sent more heat shooting directly to his manhood. He was gentle, slow, giving her time to adjust to his advancement or tell him no. When she acquiesced with a soft moan of pleasure, he let his hand linger on her breast, satisfying them both.

The fabric of her dress was thin. His fingers searched for her nipple hidden beneath the fabric of her dress and undergarments. With little effort, he located the tight bud and gently tugged on it, making it tighten and grow harder under his gentle touch.

A tremor shook her body and she gasped again with pleasure. Her soft sounds of enjoyment and passion spurred Adam to go further to pleasing them both. Fondling her breasts helped ease the longing he'd had to enjoy and relish making love to a woman he truly desired. And knowing she was loving all the heady sensations he aroused in her gave him immense satisfaction, too.

His lips moved back up to hers once again, and she took them hungrily, intensely, just the way a lover should. Their need for each other grew quickly, sharply. Placing his hands on her waist, he pressed her gently against the door once again and fitted himself against her soft womanhood, sending heat like a fire scorching through his veins.

Her gasp was instant and uneven, but she didn't push him away. Slowly, not wanting to alarm her or rush her, he continued his onslaught of kisses and caresses. Cautiously, he snaked his arm between her and the door and cupped her buttocks in his palm, pressing her even closer and harder to the throbbing member beneath his trousers.

She gasped with pleasure and thrust her hips to meet his, surrendering her body to him. A burning heat surged through his loins and a longing filled his heart. He knew he'd desired her the moment he saw her, but he'd never expected to want her so desperately that his body trembled with need at her welcoming response to his touch. An eagerness to completely possess her seared inside him, overwhelming him with the need for only her.

He swallowed down a moan of pleasure. "You don't know what you are doing me," he whispered against her lips.

"I would hope the same thing you are doing to me," she answered, gulping for breath.

"It is a powerful aphrodisiac to know that you are feeling what I am."

"My senses are reeling, my body is trembling, and I feel as if my skin is melting."

He smiled against her lips and kissed her again. He was nearing the end of his endurance. His longing to possess her grew frantic. He was desperate for her, and she was willing. Swiftly, he pulled up her skirt, took hold of her injured leg, and pulled it up. His hand landed on the warmth of her bare thigh between her stocking and drawers, making him grow harder. He pulled up her leg higher, holding it with his hip, and slipped his hand around to her firm, round buttocks. He cupped her cheek and pressed her against his throbbing ache while his lips devoured hers.

His body tensed and tightened at the gratifying feeling. The sensation was so heavenly, so intoxicating, that Adam wanted to forget all his fears of what could happen and just melt into her.

Aching with wanting, he let go of her buttocks and moved his hand around to her lower stomach and slowly let his hand slide down and cup her womanhood.

Her breath quickened. Her chest heaved as a tremor shook her body. Adam trembled, too. She was as aroused as he was.

But sane reasoning infiltrated his senses and told him he must stop before it was too late.

There would be no going back. If he took her and satisfied them both right now, he'd have to marry her. Even during his wild days, he'd always been a man of honor. He wouldn't ruin innocents. And he could easily marry Katherine. Already he felt he was her captive. What he couldn't do was take the chance he might leave her with a child.

Slowly, painfully, Adam's body went still. He sucked in a deep, agonizing breath and laid his forehead on the crest of her shoulder. The hand that bunched her skirt and held her leg squeezed tight as his body fought with his mind. His mind insisting he couldn't go through with this no matter how desperately he wanted her and his body telling him he must have release now, the consequences be damned.

"No, don't stop," she whispered into his ear, cupping his head to her shoulder.

As soon as he caught his breath, he rasped, "I didn't come here to seduce you."

"I know. I am not afraid of what we are doing."

She was eager for his touch, and that made his wanting her all the more difficult. He raised his head and looked deeply into her eyes. "But I am," he confessed reluctantly.

"Why?"

He couldn't tell her.

Her hands continued to soothe his back and shoulders. Her eyes were glazed with passion. "I want to continue. Adam, please."

He loved the sound of his name falling so delicately from her lips. The first time he'd kissed Katherine, he'd known she was innately passionate. He desperately wanted to teach her all the ways a man and woman could pleasure each other. But no matter how alluring she was, he couldn't make her his. The thought of her carrying his child frightened the hell out of him.

"Believe me, it's not that I don't want to finish what I started."

"I have no doubts, no reservations, about this."

As much as it pained him to say it, he murmured, "I have enough for both of us."

"Banish them," she argued firmly. "I am willing."

But he wasn't. The danger for her was too great.

Adam had no doubt she meant exactly what she said. It was torture having to disappoint her. She deserved the fulfillment and satisfaction his kisses and caresses were promising. He hadn't delivered on that. As a man, he had an innate reluctance to leave her wanting and unsatisfied.

Adam damned his fear, but it was real.

He understood her raw need for consummation. It wasn't easy for him, either. Human nature was a difficult thing to fight. He understood her wanting, deserving, total release from him.

He slowly lowered her leg. "I can't do this to you."

Adam started to say more but sensed her withdrawal from him at that comment and knew that it was best to leave their conversation where it was unless she added more to it. With every dram of willpower he possessed, he dropped her dress and stepped away from her.

She remained calm, leaning against the door, letting it hold her up. He reached down and grabbed her cape from the floor, then fitted it around her shoulders, securing it with the sash. She watched his hands as he then straightened her bonnet that had been knocked askew and retied the ribbon into a bow. He could tell she was in deep thought, but about what, he didn't know.

"Did I not measure up to your expectations?"

"What?" he spit out on a gasp of surprise. "Of course you did."

"Then why did you retreat from me?"

Adam frowned. "I had to. It had nothing to do with you, Katherine. I made sure you felt my need for you and how much I desired you."

"Yet you pushed me away."

"No," he argued. "I did not push you away. It was a struggle to leave your arms. I told you I didn't come to London to find a wife."

"I didn't ask you to marry me."

He grunted a laugh. "It's a good thing you didn't."

"I know how deeply you loved your wife, and I could never take her place."

"Annie." Adam was ashamed to admit even to himself that since he'd met Katherine, he'd seldom thought about the feelings he'd once had for his wife. "Not making you mine just now has nothing to do with her or how I feel about you. As soon as my work is concluded here in London, I will be leaving."

Her eyes searched his face for what seemed like forever before she asked, "How long will that be?"

"Soon."

"Then you had best get busy, Adam, if you plan to teach me to dance before you're off. That is, if you are still so certain you can do it."

Her eyes were clear, strong, and determined. Her tone was frosty, but he didn't mind. After what just happened between them, he deserved more than her wrath. She was probably being kind considering how she could have been reacting.

"Is that a challenge, Katherine?"

She jerked at the fingertips of her woolen gloves and slid off first one hand and then the other. She clasped them together and threw them down to the floor at his feet.

"Does that answer your question, my lord?"

In a huge way.

He had no problem with Katherine throwing down her gloves and issuing him a dare. But did she do so because she felt he had insulted her honor, which was the reason most gentlemen threw down the gauntlet, or was she just referencing the familiar ritual's meaning? Women didn't usually fight duels; therefore, he couldn't take her challenge lightly and further insult her.

He nodded once. "I'd say this makes the challenge official. I accept."

Adam reached down and picked up her gloves and gave them back to her.

Katherine gave him a satisfied smile. She took the gloves, grabbed her cane, then turned, opened the door, and walked out without saying another word.

She hadn't even looked to see if there was anyone in the corridor before rushing away. Oh yes, despite the smile, she was miffed at him for not following through with what he'd started, no matter his reasons. He didn't blame her. Only himself and his demons.

Maybe he should have told her he couldn't run the risk of getting her with child. That would have caused more questions than he wanted to answer. Causing one beautiful lady's death was enough. He wasn't strong enough to deny himself a few of her eager kisses and caresses when the opportunity presented itself, but that was all he could do.

When he'd pulled her into the room, he had thought only to enjoy a few short, sweet kisses that would move agonizingly slowly over her lips. He should have known that his desire for her was too great and he wouldn't be able to stop.

The honey-sweet taste of her still lingered in his mouth. Her surrendering sighs echoed in his ears, and despite all the reasons he knew he shouldn't see her again, he found himself damn glad he was going to see her again. He wanted to see her throw down that cane and dance before he left town. And oh, he wanted so much more, too, but those were thoughts he had to push to the back of his mind.

Adam was contemplating where he might find a private place he could teach Katherine to dance when he heard Pharaoh barking and Katherine calling to him.

Hellfire, that couldn't be good. He'd left the dog in the carriage with Dixon.

Chapter 19

Mischief, thou art afoot.
—Julius Caesar, *act 3, scene 2*

Leaving his coat and hat where they lay on the floor, Adam rushed out of the room, raced down the corridor, and bolted out the front door. He saw Katherine standing on the pavement, calling for Pharaoh to come to her. Dixon, with his short, spindly legs, was running after the Pyrenees, who was dragging his leash, barking like a fiend, and chasing a gray rabbit back and forth across the small expanse of lawn in front of the stately old building.

Adam whistled and then yelled, "Pharaoh! Come!" as he sped down the steps.

The dog paid him no mind. He was having too much fun racing at breakneck speed, splashing through the muddy patches of dormant grass in hopes of cornering the frightened rabbit. Pharaoh had often chased hares, squirrels, and other small animals when they lived on the coast, but this was the first opportunity he'd had to

go after an animal since they'd been in London. The
Pyrenees would not give up the pursuit easily. As far as
Adam knew, Pharaoh had never caught one of the lean,
fast hares that roamed the countryside, but he could very
well overtake the fatter, slower rabbit.

Adam needed to get close enough to grab hold of the
flapping leash and bring the excited dog under control
before something happened. He cursed under his breath
and then in a mad dash took off after Pharaoh, jumping
over a row of shrubbery and dodging a large overturned
urn in his haste to control the dog.

In seconds he caught up to Dixon and said, "Go stand
with Miss Wright. I'll get him.

"Pharaoh! Heel!" Adam called again, but the dog
kept up the chase as if certain he would capture his prey.

Adam headed diagonally across the lawn toward the
dog, hoping to head him off, but the animals were dashing so rapidly and changing direction faster than Adam
could keep up with them. He quickly skidded to a halt
and altered his course, too, going back over territory
he'd just covered.

Fleeing for his life, the rabbit changed direction again
and they were rushing across the pavement in front of
two startled, elderly gentlemen who were strolling by.
Adam flinched as the hare darted into the street with
Pharaoh hot on his trail and both were nearly run down
by a passing mail coach, but at the last moment they
sprinted out of the way, only to cut right into the path
of a milk wagon and narrowly escape death for the
second time.

"Pharaoh! Come!" Adam called sharply again as
the two dashed behind a parked carriage and then

raced back up the pavement onto the lawn of the orphanage.

Suddenly the commotion stopped abruptly. The rabbit had disappeared into a hole in the foundation of the
house that was much too small for the large dog to enter.
Pharaoh kept his nose at the entrance. He barked and
growled as he scratched the ground. Winded, Adam
ran up to the dog and reached down for the leash at
the moment Katherine called, "Pharaoh, come!" and
the Pyrenees suddenly bolted and headed straight for
Katherine and Dixon.

Adam knew what was going to happen. He took off
like a bat out of a chimney at dusk but felt as if he were
running in slow motion, getting nowhere.

"No! Pharaoh, heel!" he yelled, but the Pyrenees kept
going, loping at full speed, and plopped his big mud-
covered paws right onto Katherine's chest.

She tried to brace for him with her arms, but the force
and momentum of his sturdy body was no match for
Katherine's slight frame. Her arms flailed out beside her.
Dixon grabbed hold of her arm to help her, but his light
weight was no match for the dog's strength and force,
either. The three of them landed on the ground with a
swoosh and a thud.

Seconds later, Adam reached them and dropped to
his knees beside them. Katherine was lying on her back,
laughing, trying her best to keep the slobbering, muddy
dog from licking her face.

"Pharaoh, heel," Adam said harshly for the third time
as he grabbed the leash and jerked on it.

As if knowing his fun were finally at end, Pharaoh
obeyed and sat on his haunches and barked once. Keeping

a strong hold on the leash, Adam bent down and scooped one arm under Katherine's knees and the other around her shoulders and lifted her.

"No, I can do it," she protested, kicking her legs and pushing at Adam's chest. "I'm all right. Put me down."

His arms tightened around her. "Katherine, do I need to remind you that the last time I put you down on your feet when you didn't have your cane, you fell?"

"But I wasn't expecting it that time. I am now. Besides, people are watching. Please, put me down before we cause another scandal."

Adam looked around, and sure enough, he saw that several people had stopped to watch the chase, but none of them had hurried over to help Katherine after she was knocked down. He carefully stood her on her feet and, keeping hold of her wrist, bent and picked up her cane and held it out to her.

She took the cane and said, "I wanted to get up by myself."

"Surely you know that as a gentleman, it would have been impossible for me to stand by and watch you struggle to get to your feet without helping you."

"I suppose, but it's past time I found out just how much I can do by myself."

"I would encourage that if we were not standing on a busy street. As you have already pointed out, there are a lot of eyes looking at us right now."

Katherine turned to look at Dixon, who was brushing off his coat. "Are you all right, Master Dixon?"

He nodded.

"Thank you for trying to help me." She placed her

hand gently on his shoulder. "You were the perfect gentleman to step in and help me just now."

"I'm sorry I didn't save you," he said.

"Oh, but you did," she said, giving him a convincing smile. "You broke my fall so that I didn't hurt myself. Because of your bravery, we both remain unscathed from Pharaoh's naughty little adventure."

Dixon's chest puffed out and his eyes sparkled at her compliments.

Adam liked the reassuring way Katherine talked to Dixon. Her voice was soothing. Her words were kind and true. The flush on her cheeks and radiant smile had Adam wishing he could pull her into his arms again and hold her. She'd never been more alluring to him than she was right now, making sure the little boy was all right and making him feel good for trying to save her from the fall.

Adam's stomach tightened. She would be a loving and caring mother someday. And right now he was wishing like hell he could be the man who would one day give her those children. From the moment he saw her, he knew it would be easy to love her, if only he could allow it.

Katherine breathed in deeply and turned to Adam. "That was quite an invigorating escapade."

He grinned. "Getting slammed to the ground by a dog?"

She straightened her bonnet and laughed lightly. "He didn't mean to. He was just happy to see me. Isn't that right, Pharaoh?" She reached down and rubbed his head. He barked once.

"I think he was remembering the last time he saw you and was hoping you had another treat for him."

"I'm sorry I don't have one. Perhaps I should keep something sweet in my reticule for him."

"Maybe you haven't seen that his little stunt of jumping on you ruined your dress? There's mud from his paws all over it."

"I saw," she said, and closed her cape over the soiled dress. "It's no matter."

"You should have never given him one of your sweet cakes that day at the park. I fear you've made a friend for life."

"I can always use another friend, my lord." She looked down at the dog. "I think he would be a good companion."

"He is," Adam agreed, pleased that she liked his dog. "You know, I was just thinking it might be difficult to find a private place where I can teach you how to dance."

"Really?" She smiled playfully at him. "Are you already trying to renege on the challenge you accepted?"

His eyes narrowed. She was stunning when she teased him. "I think you know me better than that, Katherine."

"I hope so."

"I was only indicating that it might take some time for me to accomplish it."

Katherine lifted her chin. "You strike me as a man of means. I'm sure you will come up with something and that you will let me know when you have it all arranged."

"The sooner the better," he answered.

She looked at something over his shoulder. "Here comes my maid and driver out of the building. I should go, but I'll be looking forward to those lessons. Good day, my lord."

Adam watched her join the servants and get into the landau. She didn't seem to have any trouble walking or climbing into the carriage. That was good. Pharaoh could have easily injured her.

He looked down at the muddy blond Pyrenees. "Pharaoh, you were a bad dog today. London has not been good for you. Seems you left all your training on the coast."

"Are you talking to the dog again?"

Adam looked over at Dixon and said, "I am. I do and I will continue. You'll get used to it, and one day you'll probably talk to him, too."

"Does he talk back?"

"Sometimes. But what happened to you? First you said you wanted to come with me to the orphanage, and when we got here you refused to go inside. You wanted to stay in the carriage with Pharaoh. And then you both end up outside. What transpired that caused both of you to get out? And how did he run away from you?"

Dixon's eyes moved from side to side before he looked up at Adam. "He whined and scratched the door. I thought he had to go."

"Ah, I see." Adam nodded and cleared his throat. "But he was really sensing the hare. You weren't holding him very tight and he ran off without you, right?"

Dixon stared at Adam with his big brown eyes. "I didn't mean to let him go. He's strong."

Adam shrugged and patted the boy's shoulder. "Indeed he is. It's all right. There's no way you could have stopped a dog that big if he wanted to get away. Besides, there was no real harm done. Except, of course, for Miss Wright's dress, and I expect her maid can clean it."

Dixon nodded and then said, "You were gone a long time."

Was it a long time? It seemed as if he'd been with Katherine only seconds before she'd whirled on her heels and left him standing in the cold, empty room.

"It took longer than I expected."

Adam watched as Katherine's carriage pulled away from the hitching post and headed down the street.

"Are you going to give me back to the orphanage?" Dixon asked.

Adam looked down. Dixon's expression was full of concern. "No, of course not." His heart went out to the lad. "You know I went in there to ask the whereabouts of the things left to you by your mother. What made you think I was asking about returning you?"

He didn't answer.

"Look, I wouldn't let you stay here even if you wanted to, which I'm sure you don't. I told you, my home is your home, and I meant it. That's not going to change."

Adam looked back up at the large, almost empty building, and an idea swirled across his mind. "Was anyone ever mean or harsh to you while you lived there?"

"Just one. He liked to push me."

"An adult or boy?"

"Boy. He didn't like me. He thought I couldn't talk."

"Well, it's true you don't talk a lot. How about Mrs. Potts? Was she kind to you and the other children?"

He nodded. "She made him stand in the corner every time he pushed me down."

"Good for her," Adam said. "Here. Take Pharaoh and go back to the carriage. I'll join you in a few minutes."

"You're going back inside?"

Adam looked down at Dixon and saw trepidation in his young eyes. "Yes, but don't worry. This time the reason I'm going has nothing to do with you. And I won't be as long this time. I promise I'm coming back, so don't worry. All right?"

Dixon nodded.

"Good. Come on now and let's go. I'm going to help you and Pharaoh climb back into the carriage, and this time I don't want you to let him out for any reason."

Dixon looked up at Adam and gave him a smile.

Chapter 20

An ill-favored thing, sir, but mine own.
—As You Like It, *act 5, scene 4*

The ballroom of the Great Hall shimmered elegantly with hundreds of lighted candles. Katherine was always in awe of the famed building with its massive Corinthian columns, painted ceilings, and ornate fretwork and moldings. The many chandeliers and wall sconces radiated with extraordinary bright light, giving the room a breathtaking golden glimmer that scattered from corner to corner.

There were pots, urns, and containers of every size filled with flowers of every shape and color. At the end of the square room, the orchestra played a lively tune. The large dance floor was crowded with beautifully gowned ladies and finely dressed gentlemen swinging, skipping, and twirling as they moved about the floor in tempo with the music. A separate room off to one side was dedicated to tables lined with silver trays filled with such delicacies as chilled oysters, baked fowl, and stewed plums, plus all the champagne and wine one cared to drink.

Katherine stood near the entrance of the ballroom. Most of her friends and the eligible gentlemen, too, were on the floor enjoying themselves. Including Viscount Rudyard. She supposed he was the most acceptable of the gentlemen she was considering for a husband. He was titled, handsome, and eager to please her. He would probably give her strong, healthy children, too. It wasn't that she didn't hold him in high regard; she did. But he wasn't the man on her mind. Lord Greyhawke was. She didn't want to be in the viscount's arms. She wanted to be in Adam's arms, sharing kisses with him.

But that wasn't likely to happen. He'd made it clear that he was not in the market for a wife, and taking her innocence wasn't going to happen, either.

Two days had passed since she'd seen him. How long did it take to figure out a way to be alone with her?

She'd kept hoping she would see the earl walk inside the ballroom before the night was over and tell her he had a plan for them to meet and dance. The hours were passing, the evening was getting later and later, and there had been no sight of him.

She didn't know why she had thrown down her gloves at Lord Greyhawke's feet other than that, at the time, it seemed the right thing to do. She was angry with him. Not so much because he wouldn't take her innocence when she so blatantly offered it, but because he would be leaving London.

Even now, the thought of him going away and her never seeing him again caused a stabbing pain in her chest. Everything would be perfect in her life right now if—and it was a big if—seeing and being with Lord Rudyard made her feel the same way as when she was with Lord Greyhawke. She could then happily agree to marry the viscount as soon as possible and start her family. But those exciting and thrilling feelings were not there with Lord Rudyard, and she knew they never would be. He had many qualities to admire, but she didn't even have a needlepoint of desire for his touch.

Uncle Quillsbury had returned from Kent while she was at the orphanage. She'd expected to be summoned to his book room to explain herself, but that order had never come. He must have been satisfied with what Aunt Leola had to say about the gossip. Everyone else seemed to be, too.

At the parties, the first night after the scandal sheets had printed their gossip, she and her aunt had expected her to experience some measure of censure from several of the older ladies in the ton, but rather than condemn her, she had ladies coming up to her and commending her for being so observant as to see the chip in the plate before the earl had a chance to see it.

There had also been unexpected comments of pity that set Katherine's teeth on edge. Though she'd never given anyone reason to be solicitous toward her concerning her limp, some of the ladies made it clear they were, and it bumped Lord Greyhawke up a notch in their eyes because he'd helped the crippled young lady in her hour of need. If she hadn't been so annoyed by the comments, she would have laughed.

Katherine didn't want people thinking she was that frail, but in the end, she supposed it was better than speculations that she and the earl had been doing exactly what they'd been doing two days ago at the orphanage—kissing madly.

She rubbed her palm against the handle of her cane and leaned heavily on it, as she was prone to do at times. A server approached her and said, "Miss, would you care for a glass of champagne?"

Remembering Lord Greyhawke telling her that it was the champagne bubbles in her head that caused her to get a headache if she drank more than one glass made her smile. She looked at the man and shook her head.

"Begging your pardon, but I would like for the miss to take the glass and the note beside it. A gentleman paid me quite handsomely to take the risk of getting it to you without anyone's knowledge but yours."

Katherine's stomach tightened. Her mind swirled. The note must be from Lord Greyhawke. Maybe he was here and wanted her to meet him on the terrace or in the garden.

"Yes, thank you," she whispered to the man. "I believe I would care for another glass."

He lowered the tray, and she carefully picked up the note and the glass at the same time. The server left, and suddenly Uncle Quillsbury was standing in his place.

Katherine jumped and spilled the champagne down her hand and over the note. She was caught.

"Good heavens, Katherine, you aren't usually so clumsy."

Instead of reaching for the note, he reached in his pocket for a handkerchief. She realized he hadn't seen the piece of paper. She sucked in a deep, silent breath, thanked her lucky stars, and closed her fist around the message and the stem of the glass.

"Here, let me hold your champagne while you dry your hand."

"No, that's not necessary, Uncle," she said, refusing the handkerchief and holding tighter to the glass. "It was only a drop. Nothing to worry about."

"Then perhaps you should sit down. You've probably been standing too long and you've overly tired your leg."

"I'm quite fine. Tell me, where is Uncle Willard?"

"Hmm. I should have thought to tell you he went home half an hour ago. Said he couldn't stand the noise any longer." The duke gave her a rare smile.

Katherine laughed. "I don't believe he said that. You are teasing me, Uncle, and I love it."

"Of course he didn't. I'm sure he was tired of trying to hear what others were saying above the music and other chatter. Just as this will be your last Season, I'm sure it will be the last we attend as well. Concerning your aunt, I have no idea, but we brothers no longer have the fortitude to handle nights such as this for weeks at a time."

Her uncle's words pricked her heart. He was her guardian, and he felt it was his duty to escort her to the parties each evening. She became tired of the endless weeks of parties, too. Katherine pressed her palm harder onto the handle of her cane as a huge attack of guilt for not having already settled on a husband mingled with her fervent desire to be alone so she could read the note. What if right now Adam was waiting for her in the garden?

"Tell me, have you spoken with Mr. Whittenfield to-night? I saw he was here."

"Yes, earlier we had a chat, but . . ."

"But what? He's young, suitable, and well-heeled. His brother has been generous with him. He's not a gambler who gets in too deep, nor does he wallow in the bottom of his tankard."

"Thank you for reassuring me on those points, Your Grace. And you forgot to add that he's quite hand-some, too. You'll be happy to know I am considering him." At this point, she probably had to consider every eligible bachelor. "But he seems exceedingly young to me."

"He's your age, is he not?"

"I believe so. Now if you don't mind, I think I will go sit down for a while."

The quadrille that had been going on ended, emp-tying the dance floor. Katherine saw Lord Rudyard looking her way. He smiled at her as he escorted a young lady back to her chaperone. Katherine wished she could feel longing for the viscount.

"Yes, you do that," her uncle said. "I'll find your aunt and see how much longer she wants to stay. If she's ready, we'll plan to escape from this ball shortly."

Katherine had to read that note. She couldn't leave now if the note was from Adam, asking her to meet him somewhere in the garden or one of the three terraces. To the duke she said, "All right, you find Aunt Lee and see what she is thinking."

"Good evening again, Your Grace," Viscount Rudyard said as he walked up to join them. "Miss Wright, I hope I'm not intruding on a private conversation."

Katherine cringed.

"Not at all, my lord," the duke said. "In fact, you have perfect timing. I was just going to speak to someone, so I'll leave you to entertain my niece for a while, if you don't mind. I think she may want to sit down. You don't mind escorting her to a chair, do you?"

"Not all, Your Grace."

Botheration, Katherine thought as her uncle walked away. Just when she'd thought she was going to get away from her uncle, the viscount arrives.

"Should we find a place to sit, Miss Wright? I'm sure your leg is bothering you. I think you've been standing all evening."

She had been, but her leg was tired before she ever arrived at the ball. She had been practicing in her room standing and taking a few steps without her cane. It wasn't easy, but with time, she knew she would get better at it.

"Perhaps in a moment," she said, afraid that if she sat down with him, he would never leave her side so she could read her note. Time was passing and she was feeling anxious. "I'm really fine right now. His Grace worries too much about my comfort."

"He only wants to care for you, as do I," he added softly.

"That's very kind of you both, but I'm beginning to believe I am stronger than anyone thinks."

"You don't need to be strong. You need a husband to be strong for you. Now, I was wondering if I might be fortunate enough to have you agree to another ride in the park with me tomorrow afternoon or perhaps another day if it would be better."

"That's very kind of you, my lord, but I'm not certain of my schedule for the week."

The viscount's smile faded. "I understand."

Katherine looked at her uncle's retreating back and remembered her promise to him to settle on a husband. The one man she wanted, didn't want to get married.

"But no matter my schedule, my lord," Katherine added quickly. "Perhaps you can come over one afternoon and we'll have tea in Uncle Quillsbury's garden. May I send a note around to you tomorrow about a day and time?"

His eyes brightened again. "That would be lovely, Miss Wright. I would be pleased to accept."

"Good."

He took a step closer to her. "You know, I saw you watching me on the dance floor. I'm sure it bothers you when I dance with other young ladies, and I want you to know that I will not dance with any of them again once you have made a commitment to me."

"What?" Katherine hadn't been watching just him. She'd been looking at everyone and mostly at their feet. "Why would you do that? Lord Rudyard, I don't care if you dance with other young ladies. I wouldn't even if we were engaged or married. I can't dance, but I enjoy watching others have fun doing it. So no, I certainly wouldn't want you to not dance because of me."

"If you are sure."

"I am," she said, suddenly eager for him to be gone. "Now, would you be so kind as to get me a cup of punch?"

He looked at the champagne glass she held in her hand, and so did she.

"I'm afraid this has gotten warm," she added.

"Then let me take it away."

Katherine gripped the glass tighter. If she gave it to him, he would see the note in her hand; and though she was sure he wouldn't ask her what it was, she didn't want him to know she had it.

"I'd like to hold on to it until you return, if you don't mind."

He looked at her oddly, so she smiled and said, "That way no one else will approach me offering to get a drink for me."

That seemed to satisfy him. "I shall return shortly."

"Not too shortly, I hope," she murmured as soon as he was gone.

She couldn't hold her cane and the champagne and open her note all at the same time. She looked behind her for the nearest table or server so she could get rid of the glass and open the message. Neither was close by, but she did see a large urn of flowers sitting on the floor directly behind her. Maybe she could fit the glass among the flowers and have her note read and safely tucked down the sleeve of one of her gloves before the viscount returned.

With the glass teetering on the edge of the urn, Katherine had just started to open the note when she heard her name called. "Heavens to glory," she whispered, and crumpled the note in her fist once again. She turned and saw Madeline, Penny, and Melba hurrying her way. She had to be careful. While she didn't think that Lord Rudyard would inquire about the note in her hand, she was certain her friends would have no qualms about doing so if they saw it.

Angels above! Was she ever going to be able to be alone and read what the note said?

"Good evening again, ladies," she said in a lighter voice than she was feeling.

"Guess what we heard?" Penny said, resting her hands on her hips.

"You'll never guess," Melba added, shaking her head.

"No, she won't," Madeline agreed. "So I'll tell her. We heard that the Earl of Greyhawke has an heir and he is living with him."

Master Dixon.

"There is always an heir to the title, isn't there?" Katherine asked, choosing her words carefully as she wadded the note into her palm.

"Yes, but the heir is usually the title's son," Penny said. "This boy is not His Lordship's child."

"Or so we were told," Melba said, her words dripping with skepticism. "I find it very—let's just say that it's very interesting that the child is living with him."

"Who told you all this?" Katherine asked.

"Oh, we have it on quite good authority," Madeline offered.

"It was Lady Littlehaven who told us," Melba admitted without hesitation. "Her husband is a member of the Heirs' Club. I'm sure you've heard of it. Anyway, Lord Greyhawke applied for membership there a week or so ago. He had to add the child's name as the heir to the title. He told them the boy lived with him."

"She also said this is the reason he isn't coming to the parties. He already has an heir," Penny said, and then frowned. "He didn't come to London to make a match."

"That is disappointing news for those of us who would have liked to see him on the marriage mart," Madeline commented.

"It is," Katherine agreed, knowing she would very much like him to be looking for a wife. "Very disappointing for all of us, but, Penny, I saw you with Mr. Underwood tonight. Was he affectionate to you?"

Penny gave her a radiant smile. "He sought me out," she said, cooling herself with a hand-painted fan. "And he told me I look divine in this shade of pale green. Did you see us dancing? He is very light on his feet and quick with his wit as well."

"Good evening once again, ladies," Viscount Rudyard said as he joined them.

Katherine saw the cup of punch in the viscount's hand and froze. What was she going to do? If she opened her hand and took it from him, everyone would see she held a note. That wouldn't do.

While her friends and Lord Rudyard greeted each other, Katherine adjusted the paper downward and held it tightly against her palm with her last two fingers. With her other two fingers and thumb, she safely grabbed hold of the cup when Lord Rudyard extended it to her and managed to hold on to both without dropping either one.

Now her objective was to get away from the viscount and her friends as fast as she could, but moments turned into minutes and time slowly ticked by. No one made a move to leave. It was maddening to know she had a note, which she assumed was from Lord Greyhawke, and she couldn't get a moment alone to read it for her gabby friends.

Since they wouldn't leave, Katherine was going to have to. With the possibility of Lord Greyhawke waiting outside for her, she simply couldn't wait any longer.

"My lord, ladies, would you excuse me? Uncle Quillsbury was looking for Aunt Leola earlier. I need to see if I can help him find her."

"I'll go with you," Penny said.

"You'll do no such thing," Katherine said with a generous smile. "I need no help. You stand right here and talk to Lord Rudyard. I'm sure he enjoys being surrounded by so many beautiful ladies, don't you, my lord?"

"Ah, well, yes, of course," he answered. "Of course."

"Good. I'll see all of you a little later in the evening." And with that, Katherine turned and started walking away before anyone could say more and detain her further. She'd had enough of everyone delaying her. She had to know what the note said.

Katherine placed the punch on the first table she passed and then hurried behind one of the massive columns and leaned against it. She inhaled a deep breath and opened her palm. *Alone at last,* she thought with a smile. She placed her cane between her legs and started unfolding the note.

"What are you doing, Katherine?" Aunt Leola said, appearing out of nowhere.

Startled, Katherine glanced up, wincing inside.

"Here, let me help you with that. Take hold of your cane. You're going to end up falling again if you aren't careful."

Before Katherine could react, her aunt reached for the paper.

Katherine snatched it up to her bosom. "No." She swallowed hard and in a softer tone said, "I mean, I'm perfectly capable of opening a simple note, Aunt Lee."

"Of course you are, dearest. But why should you be bothered when I can do it for you? That way you can use your cane as it's supposed to be used. Now, don't be a silly goose. Let me help you." She slipped the small piece of vellum from Katherine's clutched hand and started unfolding it.

Katherine's breaths turned fast and choppy, and she felt light-headed. Her aunt was going to know that the earl was trying to make an assignation with her.

Aunt Leola's eyes narrowed as she strained to read the note in the dim light. Katherine thought she might faint before she heard her aunt say: " 'Bring items to the Potts Orphanage at half-past three tomorrow afternoon. Same room as before.' It's not signed. But of course there was no need when you know who gave you the note as a reminder about the orphanage."

Katherine let out a small gasp. Relief made her limbs weak.

"That's all it says?" she asked breathlessly, thinking surely there must be more.

Her aunt turned it over and looked on the back. "It appears so." She handed the note back to Katherine.

The earl was very clever to not sign his name. He must have known there was a possibility the note would be intercepted by someone other than her. His comment was simple and written so only she would understand its meaning.

"Did you forget to take some of the things you had collected with you when you went to the orphanage a couple of days ago?"

"There's more for me to take," she said. "I'll take care of it tomorrow, if that's all right with you."

"Of course. I'm just sorry you forgot some of it and have to go again. It's got to be a nuisance. If you aren't up to it, I'll take care of it for you, my dear."

"Auntie, please. There is nothing wrong with me." She stopped, took a deep breath, and smiled sweetly. "There hasn't been for several years now. I am perfectly fine and more than capable of doing everything for myself, if you will only let me."

She gave Katherine a curious look. "I do."

"When you brought me my toast in bed, you put the butter and jam on it for me."

"So?" she asked, seeming completely bewildered by Katherine's comment. "Oh, all right. But you know I don't mind helping those poor orphans any more than you do. I think it's a wonderful act of kindness what you and the Tea Society ladies do for them each week, and I wanted to do my part."

The steam popped out of Katherine's argument. Her aunt couldn't bring herself to say "Wilted Tea Society." "Thank you, Auntie, and I do believe they appreciate your efforts, too."

"Will you be meeting any of the other ladies there tomorrow?"

"I don't think so," she added, and felt a little guilty at the near prevarication. "I think Uncle Quillsbury is ready to go and so am I. Are you?"

Her aunt smiled. "That's the reason I was looking for you. It's time for us to go."

With her good leg, Katherine pushed away from the column. Though there was sweet relief at not getting caught with a note from Lord Greyhawke asking for a rendezvous, there was also acute disappointment that the earl wasn't waiting outside to dance with her.

Chapter 21

The web of our life is of a mingled yarn,
good and ill together.
—All's Well That Ends Well, *act 4, scene 3*

Adam strode through the front door, taking off his hat. He laid it, and the package he held, on the side table in the vestibule. It had taken much too long at the apothecary's shop, but it was a job that had to be done. He'd promised Dixon that he'd do his best to find Mrs. Bernewelt a different ointment for her hands, and he'd failed to make any effort to get that done until today.

Who would have known that there were so many different concoctions available to help one's aches and pains? And none of them smelled like flowers. The man had Adam sniffing so many different ointments, liniments, and salves that his stomach started roiling in protest. He finally had to leave it up to the shopkeeper to pick the one with the least foul scent.

It was really a small thing to do for a little boy who'd lost his parents and was suddenly thrust into a household with a stranger and his large dog, who until recently had scared the daylights out of Dixon. Adam was happy that ever since Dixon had given Pharaoh a bite of his sweet cake in the park that day, he hadn't seemed frightened by the Pyrenees anymore. And Adam hoped the new ointment would help Mrs. Bernewelt as well as make it easier for Dixon to endure when she was close. If not, there were certainly plenty more for them to try.

"Good afternoon, my lord," Clark said, coming up to him. "Let me help you with your cloak."

"I have it," Adam said, swinging the heavy woolen cover off his shoulders. Pharaoh came running up to him, seeking attention. Adam reached down and gave the Pyrenees a couple of generous pats on his back, then rubbed his head a few times. "No, Clark," Adam said when his butler reached for his hat. "No need to put my things away. I'm on my way back out again."

"But you have—"

"Whatever it is," Adam interrupted him, "I'll deal with it later. I only stopped by because I wanted to bring you this." He picked up the small package and handed it to Clark. "This is an ointment for Mrs. Bernewelt's hands."

The man looked puzzled but said, "I'll be sure she gets it."

Adam saw the blank expression on Clark's face and knew further explanation was needed. "She's not expecting it. You'll have to tell her it's from an apothecary and it will help ease the pain in her finger joints, but it doesn't have the foul odor of what she's using now. She should try this and let you know how it works. I certainly don't want her using it if it doesn't work as well."

Clark's brows rose. "You want me to tell her all that, my lord?"

Adam picked up his hat and cloak. "It matters not to me whether you tell her or if you give the message and package to the housekeeper and have her handle it. Just see to it that she gets it and that she uses it. I'd like a report back on how it's working for her."

"Yes, Your Lordship, consider it done. But I must tell you before you rush out again that Lord Thornwick is waiting for you in the book room. He asked to stay and await your return. I hope that was all right?"

Harrison?

"Of course it's all right," he said, handing his cloak and hat to Clark. "I'll go see what he wants."

Adam looked over at the tall clock standing in the corner by the door while he took off his gloves. He didn't have much time before he had to meet with Katherine. He didn't want to be late. If he wasn't already there when she arrived, he was afraid she might not wait for him. The server last night had assured him that the note had been successfully delivered to the right young lady. Adam hoped that was true. If it was, he had no doubt Katherine had the courage and cleverness to find a way to return to the orphanage.

Harrison stood in front of the window looking out when Adam walked in, saying, "Good to see you, my friend."

"You too." Harrison greeted him with a handshake. "I expected I would find you at home working with your solicitors. I was surprised when you weren't here."

"I should be." Adam knew he should ask his friend to sit down, but he really didn't have the time to be polite. "I needed a day to do some other things, so I told them not to come today."

"That's right. You've been here a few weeks now. There's a lot to learn, isn't there?"

"More than I could have ever expected," Adam said, feeling anxious to be on his way.

"But you are up to the task and no doubt probably enjoying learning about the estates more than you thought you would."

"All true," Adam admitted. He would also enjoy staying for a long visit with Harrison, but this wasn't a good time. "So tell me what brings you here? Are you on your way to the club?"

"No." Harrison smiled nervously. "I wanted to tell you that Angelina had the baby last night."

Adam felt an instant jolt to his stomach. He hadn't expected Harrison to say that. He hadn't even known it was time for the baby to be born. Now that he thought about it, he realized he'd seldom thought about the fact that his two best friends' wives were expecting babes. It was an easy thing to put out of his mind. He should have at least asked how they were doing once in a while, but he hadn't. Miss Katherine Wright was the only lady he ever thought about.

"All went well," Harrison continued when Adam didn't respond immediately. "The baby and Angelina are fine. I thought you'd want to know."

"Yes. That's good news."

"Yes, it is. You're the first person I've told."

"Thank you for letting me know." He appreciated that Harrison had wanted to do that. "I'm happy for you."

"I knew you would be."

He shook Harrison's hand and clapped him on the upper arm. "So, tell me, do you have a son or daughter?"

"Son."

Adam laughed, and he was glad it was a genuine, cheerful laugh. "What every man hopes for, yes? Congratulations, my friend. And you say everything went well with both of them?"

"I'll say. An hour after the baby was born, Angelina was sitting up in bed declaring she was starving and wanted a bowl of lamb stew."

"A healthy appetite. That's definitely a good sign that all is well. I'm glad." Adam felt he was doing a pitiful job congratulating Harrison. But hell, he didn't know what else to say other than that he was happy for him. "So what about Bray's wife? I mean, is she . . . you know?"

"No babe yet as far as I know. I'm going to see him when I leave here. I'll ask how she's doing."

Adam nodded. "You have a son. This calls for a celebration. Why don't we all meet at the Heirs' Club later for a drink? Unless, of course, you need to stay with Angelina."

"No, no, later will be fine," Harrison said. "She needs to rest. Let's say we'll meet at six and hopefully Bray can join us."

"Good," Adam said. "I'll see you there. Come on. I was just leaving, so I'll walk you to the door."

Chapter 22

Be not afraid of shadows.
—Richard III, *act 5, scene 3*

Katherine wasn't nervous about her clandestine meeting with Adam. Making the arrangements to meet him hadn't been easy, but she found it exciting. However, she had much trepidation about trying to dance.

At first she'd wondered what on earth had made her challenge the earl to teach her, as he'd claimed he could. But she knew. In the heat of the moment, she would have said or done anything to get him to stay in London a little while longer. The truth was that she didn't want him to go. The thought of never seeing him again caused an intense dull ache inside her.

There were times she gave in to darker thoughts and allowed herself to insist that life had been so unfair to her. She'd lost her family way too young. The accident and later the fall down the stairs had left her with a limp. She had lived in a good but quiet house, always longing for the sound of laughter, chatter, or even shouts of anger. Something other than the always polite, unemotional conversations between her aunt and uncles or the whispered mutterings of the servants. She never allowed those thoughts to stay and fester. Her happy nature would always return quickly.

But now, the one gentleman who stirred her senses, who challenged her at every turn, who had somehow managed to reach beneath her armor and touch her soul, was going to leave London. She didn't know if she would ever see him again after he was gone. So coming to meet him today was an easy decision for her.

Before sending her maid off to the other side of the orphanage with the basket of clothing, Katherine explained there were some things she had to take care of and she would be returning late to the carriage. Her maid was to wait and not to worry. After the woman disappeared down the corridor, Katherine headed for the room where she'd last met with the earl. The door was closed when she reached it. She inhaled deeply to steady her breathing, knocked lightly, and stepped back.

Lord Greyhawke opened the door. Katherine's heart skipped a beat and then soared at the sight of him. Blinking so her eyes could focus in the windowless room, she took in the dark trousers and white shirt that had no neckcloth or collar. The garment fit his torso like a well-worn leather glove, showing the breadth of his muscular chest and shoulders. She had no idea his waist was so narrow and his hips were so lean and slim. The legs of his dark trousers fit seamlessly into the tops of his shiny calf-high boots. He was so magnificent, he simply took her breath away.

"You look like you've seen a ghost, Katherine."

"Not a ghost, a man."

His forehead wrinkled in concern. "You don't have to do this if you don't want to, Katherine. I won't force you to do anything that makes you uncomfortable."

He continued to question her with his golden-brown eyes as she walked past him and into the room. It took several seconds for her to realize he'd taken her hesitation as reluctance. It was astonishment. She'd never seen a man so casually clothed. Assuring herself she was doing the right thing, she reached over with her free hand and quietly closed the door.

"Does that settle it for you?"

"I believe it does."

"Good. I have no doubts about being here." Her gaze swept up and down his tall, masculine frame again. "It's just that I've never seen a man without his coat on. My uncles always wear them. I have no memory of ever seeing my father without his on, either. In the summer, I've seen farmers and commoners on the streets without a coat, but never a gentleman."

"Keeping the coat, collar, and neckcloth on is the gentlemanly thing to do in front of a lady, but as you know, I have been known to be far less than a gentleman on many occasions."

"You are a very handsome man, my lord."

He smiled his appreciation for her compliment. "I was beginning to wonder if you'd gotten my note after all."

"I'm sorry I'm late. At the last minute I had to persuade my aunt she didn't want to come with me."

"I'm not surprised you managed to sway her in another direction." Adam reached down beside her and turned the key in the lock.

A faint thread of puzzlement wove through her. "You found the key?"

"No. Mrs. Potts gave it to me."

"Oh my," Katherine said, thinking that might not have been the best thing for him to do. "You asked her for it?"

"Perhaps I should explain. I told her I needed the privacy of one of her empty rooms for an afternoon. She needs money to help take care of the children who live here, so we quickly came to an equally beneficial understanding."

Katherine leaned forward. "She's knows I'm here?"

"No, and she won't. After I assured her I would do nothing other than hold a meeting in here, she had no interest in why I wanted the room. She was only interested in the donation I made to the orphanage, which will help her buy things like furniture to fill this room so she can use it, books so the children can learn, and other things that she needs."

"I see. That was very generous of you. I'm sure it pleased her. I know she's always grateful for donations."

"It was a good bargain for both of us. What she doesn't know is that I was going to do it whether or not she allowed me use of the room. Dixon said he was treated well when he lived here. Mrs. Potts was good to him. For that I'm grateful. I want to help her continue to take good care of the children who are here now and any who come in the future."

"How are Master Dixon and Pharaoh?"

"Both at home this time, I'm happy to say, so there should be no mishaps today."

"I shall miss seeing them."

He looked down at her pale buttercup-colored dress. A lazy grin lifted one corner of his mouth. "I'm glad they aren't here. You look absolutely fetching in that dress. I'd hate to see Pharaoh jump up on you and ruin it. So, shall we get started?"

Her pulse quickened. It was now or never. "Yes."

He lifted his chin a notch and looked at her. "I'm thinking maybe you should take off your cape and bonnet. It will be much easier to dance without them."

"All right." She untied the ribbon of her bonnet and sash of her cape. Adam took them from her and laid them on the floor out of the way.

"Now, let's see how well you stand without the cane." He reached for it. "May I?"

She didn't speak but allowed him to take the cane out of her hand.

While he laid the cane on top of her clothing, she stood perfectly still, waiting for whatever was going to happen next.

"Do you want to take a few steps without the cane? I'll be right here to catch you if you fall."

Katherine hesitated for only a moment before she stepped forward, first with her stiff leg and then with the other. She swayed a little but kept her balance. Adam backed up and she took another. She looked up at him, smiled, and took two more steps.

He grinned. "I think you have been fooling me about not walking without help."

She laughed lightly, almost shyly. "I admit I've been practicing in my room."

"And now you are walking without a cane."

"It's only a few steps."

"For now. It will take time, but you'll get stronger and surer of yourself the more you do it."

Her eyes searched his. She wanted to believe he was right. She'd never really thought about how much she relied on the cane until she met Adam, and now she desperately wanted to be able to walk wherever she wanted without it.

"I know, and I hope you're right."

"Let's see how much more you can do." He took her left hand and placed it on the crest of his shoulder. He then grasped her right hand in his and with his other hand pressed just above the center of her back and pulled her body close to his.

Katherine felt his warmth and his strength immediately.

"You feel relaxed in my arms. That's a good start. Some ladies feel stiff and awkward when I dance with them."

She was relaxed because she enjoyed being in his arms and it felt heavenly to be so close to him again.

"Now, the first thing you need to know is that I'm going to step forward with my left foot and you will step back with your right foot. Do you think you can do that? That's all we are going to do at first, all right?"

He looked so serious that Katherine had to laugh a little.

"Did I say something funny?" he asked ruefully.

"No, my lord."

"My name is Adam."

His gaze stayed steady on hers, and her breath hitched a little. It was so easy to think about kissing him whenever he was this close. Whenever she was looking at him. Especially whenever he looked at her with his enchanting, brandy-colored eyes.

"As you wish, my lord," she said. "Adam, I've been watching ladies and gentlemen dance for over two Seasons now. I've studied their feet more times than I can count, so although I've never waltzed, I think I know how to do it."

A grin played on his lips. "Do you now?"

"Yes," she said rather confidently.

"So you don't think I need to go over the basic steps with you before we begin?"

"No. I'm quite sure I know them and can do it."

"Well, then perhaps you don't need as much instruction as I thought and we should have no problem dancing. I'll hold you tightly like this and give you a firm frame to brace against. Do you feel it?"

Oh, yes, she felt his strength and his warmth. She smelled shaving soap and fresh-washed clothes.

"All right. I'll count to three and then we'll start. One, two, three . . ."

His very first step landed on her toe. "Ouch," she said.

Adam swore under his breath. "I'm sorry."

"No, no, it's all right," she said. "It was my fault."

"It's never the lady's fault when a man steps on her toes."

She gave him a grateful smile but said, "I didn't get my foot out of the way fast enough. Let's try it again."

Adam counted to three and moved forward and stepped on her foot again.

Apologies and excuses were mumbled a second time. Katherine insisted they try once more. They did, with the same outcome the third time.

"Oh, the devil take it!" she exclaimed, her frustration quickly mounting to more than she could bear.

"Did you just swear, Katherine?"

She grimaced. "Don't say anything."

His lips twitched with humor. "I am not one to lecture anyone about their language."

"Let's just try it again," she said in an annoyed tone. "I know I can do it."

"So do I, but you don't have to hold my hand so tightly and you don't have to try so hard. Take it easy and the steps will come. All right?"

Katherine looked at her hand clasped in his and saw that her knuckles were white. She drew in a long breath and slowly loosened her grip.

"That's better," he said. "I think you need to take a longer step back. Stretch back as far as you can and I'll take smaller steps, too."

"Yes, that should work," she answered, though her confidence was waning with each start.

Adam counted again and they made it to the third step before his foot landed on hers. Katherine mumbled something about the devil under her breath again. What had made her think, what had made her hope, that he could teach her to dance? It wasn't going to happen.

"All right," she said in an exasperated voice. "I admit it's not as easy as every lady on the dance floor makes it look."

He smiled understandingly, and her heart melted. She so wanted to learn how to dance for him, and for her.

"No, it's not, but I know you can do it. Why don't we try it my way this time and start with just walking through the basic steps before we try dancing them."

Katherine nodded, and so it went for the better part of half an hour. Hands clasped. Backs straight. Starting and stopping. Toe to toe and sometimes toe on toe.

Frustrated that it was harder than she'd thought it would be, disappointed that she wasn't doing better than she'd expected when she was trying so hard, Katherine finally stopped, dropped her hands to her sides, and said, "I can't do this. I'm never going to master this because my knee doesn't bend enough and there's a catch in my hip that won't let me step back as far as I need to."

"Never is a long time," he countered.

She let out a huffing breath and said irritably, "I know how long never is."

With his fingertips, he lifted her chin and looked deeply into her eyes. "Then don't get upset if you don't learn how to dance in thirty minutes. You have plenty of time to learn."

Not if you are leaving, she wanted to say but remained quiet.

"Look," he continued, "you are standing on your own without benefit of your cane or me for support. You didn't do that the first night we met and now you are."

"Standing still is different from walking," she said.

"Is your leg hurting?"

"A little," she admitted honestly. "More tired and aching than hurting."

"I don't want you feeling either. Let's rest for a few moments." He looked around the room and then strode over, grabbed his cloak, and spread it out in the center of the floor. "I'm sorry there isn't anything in here to sit on other than this."

"I don't mind," she said as he took hold of her hands and helped her to sit on top of his cloak.

He looked down at her and said, "I think if you work your muscles by practicing and don't depend on the cane every time you walk, one day you will be dancing. You do know the steps. You just have to learn how to adjust your weight from one leg to the other when you move."

Feeling defeated, she said, "Maybe one day I'll walk completely unaided, but you don't know what you're saying about dancing. I think I just proved you wrong."

"No one learns to dance in thirty minutes, Katherine. You're being too hard on yourself. Your injuries were healed a long time ago. The muscles and joints in your leg just need to be used."

"My aunt and uncles were being kind to me by never letting me try to dance. They knew I couldn't do it. Dancing is so beautiful and graceful and I made it look—"

Adam dropped to his knees in front of her and pressed his fingers to her lips, cutting off her words. "Don't say it," he said, softly outlining her lips with the pads of his fingers. "Because whatever you were going to say, it's not true. And I don't want to hear it."

She didn't want it to be true, but it was.

"I want to look at your leg. Do you mind?"

There was no command in his voice, but his words caused her heartbeat to skip with apprehension. Her throat suddenly felt dry and her lungs felt void of air.

"You want to see my leg?"

His cocked his head back and let his gaze waft up and down her face. "Only with your permission," he said, and then without waiting for it, he wrapped his strong, warm hand gently around her ankle and held it. "I don't want to frighten you."

Katherine's stomach tightened. Her weak leg was out straight in front of her and the other was bent underneath, helping to support it. "It's ugly and you don't want to see it," she answered, and made a move to pull her foot from his grasp. He held it firmly. The strength of his hold told her she must put up a tougher resistance before he'd let go.

A hint of a smile touched the corners of his lips and he sat on the backs of his legs. "Does it have scars on it?"

"Three," she answered. "And they are not pretty."

"There isn't anything about you that isn't pretty, Katherine. You are the most beautiful young lady I've ever seen." He carefully rested her foot on top of his knee and slipped her shoe off her stocking-clad foot. "You have gorgeous green eyes, shiny auburn tresses, and lips that are . . . well, are gorgeous, too. You are tall and slender, and from what I can tell beneath your clothing, you are beautifully shaped. I have no doubts that your scars are as pretty as the rest of you."

Katherine laughed and shook her head. "You cannot make me believe that, any more than you made me believe that champagne bubbles pop in my brain and cause me to have headaches."

"I agree that one was questionable, but not what I said about your beauty." An easy smile came to his lips. "To me you are the most beautiful lady I have ever known."

She wasn't sure she believed him, but she said, "Thank you for telling me that."

He took hold of the hem of her dress and slowly

started easing it up her leg. "Now, may I continue or are you going to stop me?"

His implication was clear. She could stop him, but she had to put forth a worthy effort. Determined not to show her fear, Katherine watched her dress rise up her leg but said nothing. To her surprise, the intimacy of what he was doing wasn't horrifying or even uncomfortable. It felt natural.

He pushed the skirt of her pale yellow dress up past her knee to about midthigh. Holding her ankle with one hand, he squeezed her leg all the way up to just past her knee and back down. His hands were large but gentle. She watched his wide, lean-muscled chest and thick arms ripple with movement beneath his shirt.

"Does it hurt when I do that?" he asked.

"No. It actually feels wonderful." *To have your hands on me,* she added silently.

"Good. I'm going to pull down your stocking."

Her gaze shot up to his and a shiver stole over her.

"Stop me whenever you want," he said quickly.

Katherine didn't want to stop him. Instead, she instinctively leaned back and placed her hands on the floor behind her. If he wanted to see her leg, she would allow it. His gentle touch had started a slow heat of yearning deep in her lower stomach, and she wanted it to continue.

Katherine wasn't prepared for the shock of pleasure that flowed through her as he rolled down her stocking to her ankle. Her stomach quivered and a teasing warmth tingled across her breasts. How could such a simple, everyday life occurrence fill her with such anticipation that more was to come?

Adam caught the calf of her leg in the palm of one hand and held her ankle in the other. With confident hands, he turned her leg to the left and right. He bent her knee as far as it would go, and then he straightened it and looked at her scars. There was a three-inch scar below her knee and two smaller ones above it.

"The scars have almost faded away," he said. "They aren't red." He ran his fingers gently over them several times. "They aren't raised or welted, but definitely the wide stitching of a physician and not the small, delicate needlework of a woman."

"Men are not usually very skillful with a needle."

"These aren't ugly. They are hardly even noticeable. I think you have a beautiful, shapely leg."

Katherine hadn't looked at them in a long time and admitted to herself that they didn't look as horrifying as they used to.

"It's true, Katherine. And I know with a little hard work, your leg will get stronger, too."

Adam's warmth, kindness, and encouragement drew her like the heat of a fire on a frigid night. In reality, she should be frightened, or appalled, or at the very least feel somewhat compromised because she was showing him her leg, letting him touch her in such an intimate way. But the only feelings she experienced were desire and wanting. His touch felt good and natural.

"Your hands are gentle," she whispered, watching his fingers massage her muscles.

"It's easy to be gentle with you."

With care, he rubbed up and down the lower part of her leg, tenderly massaging the back of her calf all the way up to the back of her knee and down again. His movements were seductive and languorous. Breathtaking sensations stirred and mounted inside her. The sensual touch of his hands heated her. The warmth curled and wove its way once again up to her breasts and teased them before spiraling down to the center of her womanhood and settling there.

She watched the bulge of his taut muscles flex and tighten beneath the fabric of his shirt. He was a powerfully built man, but his touch was tender. His hand caressed and massaged her leg, sending delicious feelings spreading throughout her body.

Adam's half-closed gaze remained on her face. The cold, hard truth was that he knew exactly how he was making her feel, but she didn't know what he was going to do about it.

She leaned forward a fraction and before she could stop herself asked, "When can we meet again?"

He continued to caress her leg. "I don't know. I'm not sure we should."

The intensity of his gaze forced her to lower her head and look away from him.

"Not because of your dancing, Katherine."

She knew he wasn't referring to her dancing. She exhaled a steadying breath. "Then why?"

"Look at me," he said.

She acquiesced.

"Because of how I feel when I'm alone with you. Because of what I want to do but can't."

She swallowed hard. "What do you want to do?"

Watching her carefully, he said, "Kiss you, of course."

Feeling fortified, she said, "I like your kisses."

He grunted a half laugh. "I like yours, too. Believe me, I do."

He reached over and placed a sweet brief kiss on her lips before resting on the backs of his legs again.

"That was like a first kiss, Adam. We are way past kissing like that, are we not?"

He let out a heavy breath. "Don't tempt me any more than you already have, Katherine."

"But I want to." Katherine scooted closer to him and wound her arms around his neck. Looking deeply into his eyes, she admitted, "I enjoy kissing you."

"I enjoy it, too." He stopped. "I should be strong enough to deny you, but there are times your powers of persuasion overcome me. Like now. When I kiss you the way you like to be kissed, it makes me want to touch you like this." He slid his hand up her midriff and caught her breast in the palm of his hand.

Katherine's stomach did a delicious somersault as bone-melting pleasure raced through her. Tingling warmth settled low in her abdomen as he fondled her breast, feeling its weight, its shape, and its firmness beneath the fabric of her dress and stays.

"I don't mind you doing that," she said, realizing her breaths were coming faster and shorter. "It's quite pleasurable."

"For me, too," he said huskily. "But when I touch you like this, it makes me want to kiss you like this." Adam wrapped his arm around her shoulders and pulled her close. His head dipped low and covered her lips with his in a long, hard, urgent kiss.

He kissed her again and again and again. She savored

every taste, every breath. She loved the feel of his lips on hers and the touch of his hand caressing and shaping her breast.

She opened her mouth and Adam's tongue swept inside with satisfying swiftness.

"Yes," she whispered as her hands dug into the fabric of his shirt, pressing him closer to her. "Kiss me like this."

They kissed deeply, hungrily, and eagerly over and over until Adam finally lifted his head and whispered breathlessly, "And when I kiss you like this, Katherine, and touch you like this, it makes me want to also do this." Cradling her back with his arms, Adam gently tumbled her onto his cloak and lowered his body on top of her.

Katherine had never felt anything more powerful than Adam's weight settling on top of her. She welcomed it. Automatically, her legs spread and he fit his lower body up against her womanhood. It was the most glorious experience. She couldn't imagine that anything could ever rival the exquisite feeling.

Adam continued to kiss her and caress her with the fierceness and passion she wanted as the hardness of his lower body pressed against her softness. At times his kisses skimmed over her cheeks and down her neck, but he'd always find his way back to her lips and ravish her mouth again. It was thrilling to know that he desired her as desperately as she desired him.

He lifted his head, gazed down into her eyes, and whispered, "And when I am on top of you like this, I want to do this."

With his strong hand, he reached up and tugged on

the neckline of her dress and undergarment, sliding them off one shoulder and halfway down her arm. With tender fingers, he pulled down on the clothing and exposed her breast.

His eyes were glazed with passion as he looked at her. "You are as beautiful as I knew you would be. Your skin is flawless. Your breast is perfectly round and inviting." He bent his head, and his mouth covered her nipple quickly, tasting her eagerly.

Katherine gasped and arched her back. Shivers of exhilaration flooded her. Her breath jumped erratically. A tremor of desire shook his body, too. He was as affected by her as she was by him. That thrilled her even more. All she could do was moan with pleasure and wrap her arms around his firm, strong shoulders. His tongue flicked and played with her breast, sending shivers of delirious tingles shooting throughout her body.

Her hands moved down his broad back and she cupped his firm buttocks, pressing him closer to her. He moaned and trembled again. His hand raked down her other breast, her rib cage, over her hip and thigh, to press her tightly against the hardness caught between his legs.

Leaving her breast moist from his tongue, he suddenly placed his hands on either side of her face and dragged his lips from hers. Breathlessly, he looked down into her eyes and said, "Can you feel how desperately I want you right now?"

"Yes," she murmured.

"But I cannot have you. Now, do you see why I don't know if we should meet again?"

"No, I don't see. Something wonderful and thrilling is happening between us. I don't want it to stop."

"It must. I fear you will drive me insane with wanting. I swear by heaven I have never wanted another woman with the intensity I want you, Katherine. Not Annie. Not anyone. But I cannot make you mine. My fear for you overrides my wanting you."

His words were so sincere, she suddenly felt close to tears. She touched his cheek. "But I don't understand. What fear?"

"There's always the possibility you could have a babe from our coming together. I can't allow that."

She stiffened and suddenly she felt cold. She reached down and pulled her dress up her shoulder and over her breast. "Because you don't want to marry me."

"I can't marry anyone." He rolled away from her and rose to his knees again. He reached out to help her sit up.

Feeling bereft, Katherine refused his outstretched hand. "I can do it by myself. Thank you."

"You need to understand that I was able to stop this time, but I fear the time will come when I won't, and that is too dangerous for you."

She could see that he was very serious about what he was saying, but she still didn't comprehend his meaning. "Why would it be dangerous?"

"That's a personal question, and we both know how you feel about them," he said. "Just take my word for it that my reasons for not marrying are good ones."

"So you will never have the warmth of a woman in your bed again?"

"You are so innocent," he whispered. "Mistresses are schooled to know how to keep from getting in the family way."

His words tore through her heart like a knife. "You have a mistress?"

"No." He shook his head. "Not at present."

"But you will have one. You would rather have a mistress than a lady who loves you."

"Katherine, I don't want to talk about mistresses with you."

Does it embarrass you?"

"No. No, it makes me angry. I want you. I want marriage and a son, not a mistress. But there are reasons I can't have you and you'll just have to take my word for that because I'll not say more."

He rose and walked over to pick up her cape, bonnet, and cane. While his back was turned, she pulled her dress and stocking into place and then, with a little effort, stood up.

Adam's expression was somber as he handed her things to her.

"Will I see you again before you leave?"

"I don't know. Katherine, you have known almost from the first night we met that I did not come to London looking to make a match."

Aching from his rejection, she said, "And I believe I've told you before that I've not asked you to marry me. Now if you don't mind unlocking the door, I'll take my leave."

Chapter 23

Men of few words are the best men.
—Henry V, *act 3, scene 2*

The bright blue sky was dusted with wispy white clouds. The air was breezy but not chilling as Katherine stood in the budding back garden, waiting for the arrival of Viscount Rudyard.

She had spent the morning practicing walking and her dance steps while thinking about Adam and all that he'd said to her after their passionate embrace. There was no figuring out what he had meant by thinking she would be in danger, other than that he wouldn't marry her even if she was in the family way.

There had to be more to what he was saying than that. Adam was a gentleman. A man of honor. He would never leave a young lady defenseless and not marry her if that happened. Katherine was as sure of that as she was of her own name.

She'd spent considerable time thinking about their maddening kisses and caresses, too. After the way their last meeting at the orphanage had ended a few days ago, she had thought seriously about giving up trying to dance and walking without the cane. If Adam wasn't going to help her anymore, why should she try to get stronger or better and more balanced on her feet? But that kind of thinking hadn't lasted long. She wanted to walk without a cane and learn to dance whether or not she ever stepped on a dance floor with Adam or anyone else.

She wouldn't quit. She wanted to do it for Adam, but she had to do it for herself. Hence, she had been practicing every morning for the past few days and some afternoons, too. Her leg was getting stronger with each day. She knew she would never glide gracefully across the dance floor as so many young ladies could, but one day, if she continued to work at it, she would be free of the cane for good and maybe be able to dance a little, too.

Katherine had come to another realization. She was in love with the Earl of Greyhawke, though it had taken her some time to realize it. She had no doubts about that now. He was the man she dreamed about, the man she longed to see, and the man she wanted to marry and live with for the rest of her life. She wanted Adam to be the father of her children. But what could she do when he claimed he didn't intend to marry again?

She would do her best to change his mind if only she could see him. There was no doubt he desired her as much as she desired him. If only there was some way she could get him to the balls and the parties in the evenings so she could see him and talk to him. If she weren't plagued with having to go everywhere with a chaperone, she would go to his house and force him to see her.

"Katherine?"

At the sound of her aunt's voice, she pulled her ruffle-trimmed pelisse tighter about her and turned toward the back door. Her aunt and Viscount Rudyard were walking down the back steps.

"I'll sit over here and read my book while the two of you have a visit," Aunt Leola said, and headed to the corner of the garden where a table and four chairs stood. "I've asked for refreshments to be served in a few minutes."

"Thank you, Auntie," Katherine said.

The viscount followed Lady Leola to the sitting area to the left side of the lawn and pulled out the chair for her before heading Katherine's way.

Lord Rudyard was a tall, handsome man and a dandy of the highest order, she thought as he walked toward her. He'd already doffed his top hat and there wasn't a sign of a crease in his dark brown hair from wearing it. His starched neckcloth was beautifully tied and showed no sign of a wrinkle or crimple anywhere on it. His brown wide-striped coat and trousers were perfectly tailored to his slim frame, and the sunlight sparkled off the shiny brass buttons on his dark red waistcoat. The silver-handled cane was missing from his arm, but he might have left it inside the house with his greatcoat and hat.

When he stopped in front of her, she curtsied and suddenly realized what it was about Lord Rudyard that bothered her. He was always splendidly dressed. He always said and did the proper things, just like her aunt and uncles. Manners and propriety were of upmost importance to him.

But it was a man who seldom said or behaved as she expected—a man who cared little for what others thought, who was willing to take off his coat and relax with her—a man who caught her up in his arms and ravished her who held her heart captive.

"Good afternoon, Lord Rudyard," she said.

"And a very good afternoon to you, Miss Wright," he returned. "You picked a perfect sunny day with a pale blue sky for our tea in the garden. I'm pleased that we have no dreary clouds to cover us today."

"So am I."

"I do worry, though," he said. "I think perhaps you should have a parasol to keep the sun off your face."

Katherine smiled and hoped it wasn't as sad as she suddenly felt. Lord Rudyard had said exactly what her aunt had said earlier when she'd started outside without her parasol. "I believe the rim of my bonnet is sufficient to take care of that, my lord. It's quite wide."

"I'm sure you know best," he conceded, and extended a small bouquet of colorful flowers to her.

She took them, carried them to her nose, and inhaled with a gentle smile. "They are lovely and fragrant. Thank you, my lord."

"I'm pleased you like them."

"Do you want to walk around the grounds or would you prefer sitting down with my aunt for a chat?"

"I would very much like to walk with you. But we'll only do it for a short time. I don't want to overtire your leg. I'm sure it pains you if you stand on it too long."

It would probably always give her some discomfort,

but recently it was mostly when she first awakened in the mornings. "No need to worry about me, my lord. I'm finding that exercising it often is actually good for my leg. Besides, it's not paining me at all right now."

"Splendid! I was hoping for a chance to talk to you alone for a few minutes."

Oh dear.

She knew it would be for the best if he mentioned marriage to her again, but still, she wished he wouldn't. It wasn't a conversation she wanted to have, because her heart longed for Lord Greyhawke.

Katherine looked down at the flowers she held in one hand and her cane in the other. She wasn't ready to give up the cane yet, but she felt even more confident that one day she would. And it would be because Lord Greyhawke had questioned her reliance on it and then had faith in her that she could walk without it.

They strolled down the stone pathway that ran beside the yew hedge on both sides of the garden. Every shrub in the knot had survived the winter. Its intricate pattern was already beautifully green. The flower gardens had been newly planted and the colorful flowers were beginning to sprout and bud. A few had already bloomed.

"I was hoping you might enlighten me as to what I might do to win your favor and encourage you to agree to accept my proposal of marriage."

"Marriage is not something to take lightly, my lord."

"I agree, but I made the proposal to your uncle more than a year ago."

She grimaced. "Was it truly that long ago?"

"Probably longer." He chuckled. "But in any case, I understand that a lady must take her time and consider cleverly about something that will affect the rest of her life. Still, I believe I have given you plenty of time so that you can't think I'm rushing you."

It was her uncle who had put a time limit on her. It wasn't that she blamed him. And she understood. Her aunt and uncles were tired of being a chaperone and guardians to a twenty-year-old lady who couldn't make up her mind whom she wanted to marry. They were tired of the Season's endless parties and balls, preferring small, quiet dinner parties like the one where she had met Lord Greyhawke.

Katherine glanced over at Lord Rudyard and wished she felt that all-consuming need to be with him that she felt whenever she was with Adam. If only she felt that desire, she would give Lord Rudyard her answer this very afternoon.

"I don't feel that you have rushed me," she told the viscount. "And in truth, I am seriously considering your proposal, my lord."

"I'm honored to hear that, Miss Wright. I know you have many other gentlemen wanting the promise of your hand. But I want you to know that none of them would take better care of you than me. I will cherish and shelter you dearly, just as your uncle has done all these years. I will treat you like the delicate flower you are."

But Katherine had no desire to be treated delicately. "I am not that fragile, my lord. I assure you, I am strong and very healthy. Now tell me, do you want to have children?"

He gave her a look of surprise. "Of course. All men want a son to carry on their name."

Adam didn't and that puzzled her. She couldn't understand his reluctance about something that was as natural as breathing for most gentlemen. Perhaps because of the death of his first wife, he was reluctant to try for a family again. She had firsthand knowledge of how devastating it was to lose all you held dear.

"And," Lord Rudyard continued, "as in my case, a son to carry on the title as well. Why do you ask? Do you fear motherhood, Miss Wright? I know that some ladies do."

"No, of course not." She laughed because he had so misunderstood her reason for asking. "I want to have children. Many children."

And she would honor her brother and her sisters by naming her children after them.

"We will have as many as you like. It matters not to me, because they will be with the nanny most of the time and not bothering us anyway."

Katherine frowned and her hand tightened on the bouquet of flowers as well as her cane. "I don't think I would ever consider my children a bother to me, my lord."

He stopped and smiled down at her. "Of course, they can be. You wouldn't know because you grew up in your uncle's house without small children around, a house with civility. I grew up in a house with three younger brothers and two younger sisters, and it was quite chaotic most of the time."

But that was the kind of life she was looking forward to.

"I remember," Lord Rudyard continued, "I always felt calm and peaceful once all the little ones were put to bed for the evening. And I was never happier than when

I was too old for my bedchamber to be in the nursery wing of the house. So no need for you to worry, Miss Wright. We will enjoy our quiet evenings by the fire, reading and playing cards. And of course we'll want to travel a few months each year as well."

A sudden breeze blew down Katherine's neck and she wrapped her pelisse tighter about her. The life the viscount described was not the kind she was dreaming about, but she remained quiet. She couldn't forget her promise to be betrothed by the end of the Season. Complaining would make her ungrateful for all her uncles and aunt had done for her. She couldn't do that. She would tell anyone that they had done what was right by her. Taking her in as a child and now supporting her through her third Season. She couldn't ask them to give her another year, but oh, how she wanted to.

"Look what we have managed to accomplish, Miss Wright."

"What's that?" she asked, thinking it must be that she was more uncertain than ever that she wanted to marry Lord Rudyard.

"We are standing behind the fountain. Do you know what that means?"

The tall, urn-shaped fountain stood near the back gate, in the center of the garden. The rim was flanked by two large cupids with their wings spread wide. The cupids appeared to be drinking water from the overflowing urn. An abundance of freshly planted flowers surrounded the base of the fountain.

Katherine shook her head. "I'm afraid I don't know what you mean."

"I can't see your aunt, can you?"

She looked around. "Not without moving."

"Good. I think this is the perfect place to steal a kiss from you. You don't mind, do you?"

Do I?

No. I want him to.

She looked into his handsome face and thought, *Yes, please kiss me. Kiss me and make me feel the soul-wrenching, delirious feelings that Lord Greyhawke made me feel when he kissed me.* She wanted the viscount to gather her in his arms and hold her so tightly that she ached. She wanted him to make her feel desired.

He reached down and kissed her briefly, softly, on the lips. It was much the same way Lord Greyhawke had kissed her when he'd said it was the way a young lady should receive her first kiss. It was pleasant enough, but certainly not earth-shattering.

Lord Rudyard looked at her and smiled. "Did that make you happy?"

She ignored his question and said, "May we share another before we continue our walk?"

His brows rose. "Indeed."

He moved to kiss her again the same way he had the first time, and she put up her hand and stopped him. He backed away. "No, don't move. This time I want you to kiss me with your arms around me. You know, holding me tightly to your chest."

At those words, he frowned. "That wouldn't be proper, Miss Wright. We can't start anticipating the wedding night." He smiled again. "I fear your uncle would throw me out of his garden by my ear if your aunt should look around and see us embracing and tattle. But I am pleased to know that you want me to hold you."

Adam had no such fears. "Of course, you're right," she said, and they started walking again.

"I hope you aren't too disappointed. You see, I believe we will be married, and I don't want to do anything to upset the duke and ruin my chances with you."

"I understand, my lord," she assured him. But she didn't. If he truly desired her the way Adam did, he would take the risk of getting caught just to hold her in his arms.

In a way, she was glad he had not taken her up on her offer. Somehow, deep inside, she knew he couldn't make her feel the way Adam had, even though life would be so much easier for her if he could.

It had been a few days since she had heard from Adam. For all she knew, he could have already left Town. An ache grabbed her stomach, and she inhaled deeply at that possibility. She couldn't bear the thought of never seeing him again.

Katherine heard the back door open and saw a servant bringing out the refreshments tray.

She sighed as they turned the corner and started up the pathway toward her aunt. The viscount was a good man, and he would be a capable father. And if she married him, maybe one day she would develop stronger feelings for him than she had at present. But as of right now, there was nothing about him that excited her senses or caused her heart to trip in her chest.

And all that left her with was a feeling of sadness and the wish that she could see Adam again.

Chapter 24

The very instant that I saw you, did
My heart fly to your service . . .
   —The Tempest, *act 3, scene 1*

Adam surprised himself sometimes, and never more so than since he'd met Katherine. He was sitting in his slowly rumbling carriage, making the block around her house for at least the tenth time, giving him plenty of time to ponder. He'd actually managed to stay away from her for several days. It hadn't been easy. It had been damned hard. Denying himself something he wanted had never been one of his strengths.

That day at the orphanage, he'd come so close to making love to her. The thought of getting her with child scared the hell out of him. He didn't trust himself where she was concerned. But after he'd watched Katherine's uncles sit down at a gaming table for a hand of cards at the Heirs' Club, he knew what he wanted to do.

She would be safe from his advances at her home—somewhat safe, anyway—unless for some reason she was alone. He could spend an hour or two with her, if—and it was a big if—fate decided to smile upon him and let him find her at home. There was always the possibility that she could be at one of the popular afternoon card parties or taking in the sights and sounds at one of the parks with Lord Rudyard or someone else.

When he'd arrived at her house, he'd seen Lord Rudyard's landau waiting in front of it. The dandy was visiting her. Adam chuckled to himself. And here he was circling her house, waiting his turn to go to her door.

His patience paid off when, in less than half an hour of his arrival, Rudyard's landau was gone.

Adam knocked on her door, and it was opened by a short, slender butler.

"Good afternoon," Adam said, removing his hat. "I'm the Earl of Greyhawke, here to see Miss Wright."

"Is she expecting you, my lord?" the spry man asked.

"Yes, she is," Adam said with all certainty that Katherine wanted to see him.

"Come in," he said. "She's in the garden. Let me show you into the drawing room and I'll let her know you are here. I believe her aunt has already retired to her chambers for the afternoon, but I'll let her know you are here."

"I ask that you please not disturb Lady Leola," Adam said, having little hope the butler would take his suggestion. Still, it was worth a try. "I won't be staying long. Why don't you show me to the garden? The afternoon is so fair, there's no need for Miss Wright to come inside for such a short time. You don't mind, do you?"

"I respect your suggestion, my lord, but think I should leave it to Miss Wright to decide that."

Sometimes Adam hated the proprieties of Society.

"All right. I'll go with you to ask her." Adam smiled and handed the man his hat, then stuffed his gloves in the pocket of his greatcoat as he followed him down the corridor to the back door.

When the butler opened the door, Adam saw Katherine standing toward the back of the garden near a large fountain, holding a teacup in one hand and her cane in the other. She looked up at him and his stomach did a slow roll. Every long, boring lap he'd made around the block waiting for the viscount to leave had been worth it for this moment alone.

Katherine looked so incredibly fresh and lovely, he wanted to grab her in his arms and swing her around. She was like a ray of sunshine on a bleak and dreary day. He remembered how she'd responded to him, how soft and passionate she'd felt beneath him when he'd been with her at the orphanage. He hungered to feel her in his arms again.

She started walking toward him.

"No need to announce me," he told the butler. "She sees me."

"But my lord," the butler said, "I really should."

Paying him no mind, Adam hurried down the steps toward Katherine.

"Lord Greyhawke," she said, meeting him halfway up the path. "This is a surprise."

"Don't tell the butler that." Adam looked back and saw that the man was going back inside the house. "I told him you were expecting me. I hope you don't mind that I came without an invitation."

"No, of course not. But after our last meeting I wasn't sure I'd see you again."

"Neither was I."

"Has there been a change in your feelings or plans since we last talked?"

"No, but that doesn't mean I didn't want to see you. To see how you're doing."

Her hopes dashed, she inhaled deeply and said, "You know I'm always happy to see you, but I—why are you here? Is something wrong?"

Yes, I was aching to see you.

"Nothing's wrong. I saw your uncles sit down to a card game at the Heirs' Club and I decided to take the chance I could see you alone for a few minutes."

"My aunt went up to her chambers to rest a few minutes ago. I'm sure Hanson will tell her you're here and she'll be down shortly."

"Then we will have to make the best of the time we have. Was Lord Rudyard here?"

Her brows raised. "Yes. He joined us for tea earlier." She walked over to the table and placed her cup on it.

Adam followed her. She was still miffed at him, and he didn't blame her. "How long did Rudyard stay?"

"I'm not sure. Perhaps an hour and a half."

"He stayed that long?" Adam asked. "You must have had a lot to talk about."

She smiled. "I guess we did."

"What kinds of things did you discuss?"

"That is a personal question, my lord, and you know what I think about personal questions."

"You enjoy his company."

It was impossible to not be affected by Adam's charm, and she couldn't hold on to her ill feelings concerning him, either. Katherine laughed and her eyes sparkled delightfully. "Did you just ask another personal question?"

"No," he admitted. "I was making a statement."

She shook her head and said, "I'm afraid the tea is cold now, but I'll have hot tea brought out."

"I didn't come for tea, Katherine."

She looked up at him and asked, "Why did you come?"

She knew, but he didn't mind her asking. "I've already told you. To see you. To see how you are doing."

"I'm well."

"Still using your cane."

She cleared her throat and lifted her chin. "When I'm not alone. But I've been practicing walking without it in my room. Besides, I'm not ready to let my aunt and uncles know I'm not using it faithfully as I used to. I know it would upset them."

"I understand. I've seen how they dote on you."

"Because they care," she said softly. "Everything they have done for me for the past twelve and a half years has been because they thought it was best. They simply want me to be safe."

"No one could doubt that," he said, and moved closer to her. "Let's dance?"

Her eyes widened and her mouth opened in silent shock. "We can't do that here in the garden."

He looked around. "Why not? We're alone. For now, anyway. It's a beautiful day. It's beautiful here. The grass, trees, and shrubs are budding and flowering. The ground is level. Show me your shoes."

She lifted her dress up to her ankles and they both looked down.

"Flat slippers," he said. "Perfect for outside dancing."

"Have you ever danced outside?"

"I can't say I have. I'm always willing to try new things. How about you, Katherine?"

She hesitated.

"Say yes," he whispered huskily.

"You know there is a good possibility we could get caught dancing in the garden."

"Yes." He took hold of her cane and laid it against the table. "And there is always the possibility we won't. Who knows how long it will take your aunt to rouse from her nap and join us in the garden?"

"You are forgetting about the servants. They are very loyal to the duke."

Sensing her unease, he said, "As they should be. But it looks as if the gardener has gone for the day, and the other servants are probably having their tea, preparing dinner or who knows what they might be doing. Enough excuses. So what do you say, Miss Katherine Wright? Do you feel like tempting fate this afternoon and dancing with me?" He held up his hands in the dancing position.

Her features relaxed and she laughed softly. "I've been tempting it ever since the night I met you. I see no reason to stop now."

Adam took her hand and embraced her. "Now show me how well you have been practicing."

He started to move forward, but he felt her stiffen and stopped. "Is there someone behind me already watching us already?"

She looked at him with wry amusement. "No. I was just

wondering why it is that whenever you touch me, I am more interested in kissing you than dancing with you."

His gaze swept up and down her face. "I feel the same way, but for now, I will have to resist the urge and so will you."

"Will you kiss me before you go?"

Her responses to him were always natural and came from her heart. "How could I not?" He swallowed hard. "That's really the reason I came over this afternoon. Now, on the count of three . . ."

And so began her lesson. The grass had not fully grown out and the ground was still hard, making it easier than Adam had anticipated to traverse back and forth across the garden. Her movements weren't fluid yet, but they weren't nearly as choppy as the last time they'd danced. He knew it wasn't easy for her to maneuver her stiff leg, but she wasn't just walking the steps, she was dancing to his whispered count of one, two, three, four. One, two, three, four.

"You have been practicing. I can tell."

"A little."

"I'd say more than a little. Do you realize I haven't—" He landed on her toe. She stumbled and they stopped.

"I'm sorry," she said.

"No. It was my fault," he admitted. "I was about to praise myself and say I haven't stepped on your toes one time, when suddenly I did."

"Perhaps I should wear boots as you do."

"Now there's an idea for us to consider."

Adam danced her down to the large fountain he'd seen at the back of the garden and stopped, thinking that would be an excellent place to pull her to him for a few quick kisses.

"I do believe we are hidden from the house right here, are we not?"

Katherine unexpectedly started laughing.

He grinned. "Do you want to share the amusement with me?"

"I see no reason I can't. I was just behind this fountain with Lord Rudyard not half an hour ago."

He should have guessed. "Were you now?"

"Yes."

Adam pulled her close to his chest and held her tightly. "Did he kiss you?"

Her eyes searched his without any guile. "Yes."

It was a personal question, but it was one she wanted him to know the answer to. And it had her desired effect on him. He was jealous as hell that the dandy's lips had touched hers.

Bending his lips close to hers, he whispered, "How?"

"Like a first kiss."

Thank God, he thought to himself. But he asked, "Did you enjoy it?"

"That's a personal question, my lord. If I answer, you'll have to answer one for me."

"We have no time for our game of questions this afternoon, Katherine. I need to kiss you now." He slanted his lips over hers in a long, passionate kiss.

Katherine responded with a sweet moan of pleasure. Though he needed no encouragement from her to continue his assault on her lips, Adam loved the way she always immediately gave in to the excitement of their kisses and abandoned herself to the moment.

She tasted of tea and smelled of sunshine. Aware of her every breath, he deepened the kiss, and she answered by instinct and parted her lips for his tongue to enter her mouth. His tongue played with hers, teased the roof of her mouth, and explored its depths with slow, sensual movements.

Desire grew quick and strong inside him. It was difficult to hold back his eagerness because his body was always hungry for her.

"Mm, I've been wanting to do this since the last time I saw you," he whispered into her mouth.

"Then why did you wait so long to come see me?"

"I need to stay away from you, Katherine. Your name may be Miss Wright, but remember you are Miss Wrong for me."

"I don't believe that, Adam."

"It's true."

"You taste good," she whispered. "You smell good. I feel so good whenever I am in your arms."

Her words thrilled him. His lips left hers, and he kissed his way down her chin, over her jawline, and down to the neckline of her pelisse. Her skin was cool against his hot mouth. His heart beat wildly and the blood rushed through his veins in a heady sensation that made him want to forget the danger he would put her in if he denied his fear and made her his.

"I've been ravenous to touch you again," he whispered as his lips traced a pattern over her eyes, her chin, and her nose with soft, feather-light kisses.

His hand moved to her breast and molded it against his palm. Her body trembled beneath his hand, and he smiled. Spirals of heat curled and tightened in the pit of his stomach and between his legs. He gloried in the luscious sensations rippling through him. His tongue sought her mouth again as his body ached to tumble her to the ground, cover her, and make her his.

Damnation, he'd give anything if she didn't feel as if she were already his. He had no rights to her, could never claim rights to her. Still, she felt as if she belonged to him. Only him.

Finally, he found the strength to let her go and step away. His breath was coming in ragged gasps as he said, "I have no boundaries when I am with you. You really should put some on me."

She caught her breath and cleared her throat. "How can I when I don't want there to be any?"

"Which is why, for the first time in my life, I have to be the one to do it." He took hold of her elbow and started walking with her toward the front of the garden. "It's not natural for a man, you know." He inclined his head toward her. "We usually depend on the young lady to keep us in line and not let us go too far."

"I suppose there is nothing about me that makes me a typical young lady."

"No, you are very special to me."

"Adam, there are things about you that I don't understand. You say you can't—"

"I know," he said, cutting off her words. "And because of that I've tried to stay away from you. You know I have. I have declined all parties and social events, and for a time it seemed as if fate were demanding we be together." He looked away for a moment and then said, "Your dancing was very good today."

She could see in his eyes that he meant it, but still

she shrugged as if his comment meant nothing as they stopped beside the table.

He picked up her cane and handed it to her. "I should go before someone comes out."

"When will I see you again? Will I see you again?"

He wished he could just tell her no. No, he couldn't see her again. But he couldn't say that. He'd been trying to tell himself that since the first night he'd met her. So far, he hadn't been able to stay away.

His eyes searched hers. "I shouldn't," he said, and he turned, bounded up the steps and into the house, and was soon out of sight.

Chapter 25

Suspicion always haunts the guilty mind.
—Henry VI, *act 5, scene 6*

The rain had been beating steadily against the window-panes in Adam's book room. Even with the fire blazing most of the day, a chilly nip lingered in the air. Adam's solicitors had sat across the desk from him for several hours, answering his questions about his various properties, businesses, and investments. But thoughts of Katherine had never left his mind.

He'd finally dismissed the solicitors half an hour ago, and now the quiet of the house was closing in on him. Once, the solitude had been welcome. Not anymore. Now it was more like a burden.

Learning about the Greyhawke entailed property and other holdings had been challenging, but he was now feeling confident that he could visit the estates and properties. He knew the status of each holding, how it was managed, and who directed it.

The lamps had been lit. Pharaoh lay near the fire, and

Dixon played quietly with his toy soldiers near the hearth. He'd been patiently waiting for Adam to play a game of chess with him.

But something was missing. Katherine. He wanted to see her sitting by the fire, stitching her embroidery, knitting scarves for orphans, or reading her book of poetry and occasionally looking up at him and smiling. He actually felt her absence.

In the two years he'd spent in isolation on the coast, silence had been all he'd wanted. He supposed he'd needed that time to himself. But now he wanted more. When Dixon had been left on his doorstep, it had given a reason and purpose to his life. Adam smiled to himself. He should find Mr. Alfred Hopscotch and thank him for bringing the boy to him.

The one part of his life that wasn't settled was Katherine. He squeezed his eyes shut. He loved her more than his own life. It was easy to admit that to himself. Thinking about her was invigorating and maddening. He had no doubt he would be good for her. Already she was walking and dancing when she hadn't even attempted to stand without her cane when he'd first met her. If only he could marry her. But he couldn't overcome the harsh blow fate had dealt him.

Pharaoh roused his head and woofed. He rose and trotted toward the doorway, but Adam called him back. "Pharaoh. Come here." The dog stopped and looked over at Adam and then back to the door. He barked again and then stared at Adam as if to say, *I hear something.*

"Answering the door is Clark's job, remember. Now, get over here beside me. Besides, it's probably just another messenger dropping off yet another invitation to a dinner or party. Whoever it is, he doesn't want you standing at the door growling at him." It seemed to Adam that he received two or three invites a day.

Clark walked into the book room and whispered to him, "The Duke of Quillsbury is here, my lord. I took the liberty of asking him to wait in the drawing room and offered him a drink. I hope that was all right."

Adam relaxed against his chair. So either the aunt or the butler had seen him kiss Katherine yesterday afternoon in the garden. Sweet hell, he had no one to blame but himself. He'd known the chance he was taking when he went to see her. He knew he wouldn't be able to keep his hands off her. Even though he hadn't stayed very long, had he sabotaged himself?

"Tell His Grace I'll be right in."

"Yes, my lord."

Adam rose and so did Pharaoh. He looked down at the dog. "No. Stay." Pharaoh quarreled with him and barked. "Yes, it will be a difficult visit, but I don't need you in there, my friend."

"Are you talking to the dog again?" Dixon asked.

"Yes." Adam didn't want the chance of Dixon wandering into the drawing room and overhearing his conversation with the duke either.

"Dixon, I'm going to close the door behind me. Stay in here with him and see he doesn't get out. I have a guest in the drawing room. Understand?"

Dixon ran over to Pharaoh and put his arms around the big dog's neck. "He won't get out this time."

Adam rubbed Pharaoh's head and then Dixon's before slipping out of the room and closing the door behind him.

"Good afternoon, Your Grace." Adam stopped and bowed before continuing on into the drawing room.

The duke rose and greeted him with a slight bow and nod. "I'm sorry for arriving without making an appointment. I hope I'm not interrupting anything too important in your afternoon, my lord."

"Not at all. My business has been concluded for the day. Please, sit down." Adam walked over to pour himself a nip of brandy and asked, "Can I add a splash to your glass?"

The duke shook his head and sat down in the wingback chair. "I suppose you know why I'm here."

No reason to make it easy on the old man, Adam thought as he settled himself in the chair opposite the formidable-looking duke. "I wouldn't presume to venture a guess."

"No, I don't suppose a clever man would ever implicate himself in anything. I now know of three instances where you've been seen with my niece in your arms."

Guilty of the three and a few more.

Adam remained pensive. He knew what the duke wanted. Hell, Adam wanted it, too.

"The first was outside my own front door, which as you know I witnessed."

"You know the reason for that incident, Your Grace."

"And thanks to Lady Leola's quick thinking, the repercussions were manageable. Besides, I only know what I was told about the evening." His gaze held firmly on Adam's. "Then there was the afternoon in front of Potts Orphanage, which Katherine has been known to frequent carrying her donations from that ridiculous

Wilted Tea Society to which she belongs, though only
God knows why."

The duke paused again and looked at Adam as if he
expected an explanation, so Adam obliged.

"It's true we were both there at the same time. Quite
by accident. No doubt Miss Wright has explained how
that incident came about."

"I've not spoken with her about it, or about my visit
to you this afternoon. Nor do I intend to."

Adam found it odd that the duke hadn't questioned
Katherine before coming to see him. He would do his
best to make sure no condemning light was shed on
Katherine.

"She was doing her charitable work, and I was there
because Dixon, my heir, lived at the orphanage until I
was located. Some of his personal things were left there
when he was brought to me. I was checking on them
for him."

"I've no doubt you both had obvious and legitimate
reasons for being there. There were several who witnessed her in your arms that afternoon, and it cost me a
tidy sum to squelch the rumors swelling from it before
they were printed."

Adam had wondered why the incident never showed
up in the scandal sheets. He'd assumed it was because
it was clear Pharaoh was the villain and he'd had to help
Katherine up off the ground.

"So you know it was my dog who created that scene
and there was nothing I could do but help Miss Wright
stand up."

"Surely I don't have to tell you that gossip and truth
are seldom cut from the same cloth."

There was a long silence. Adam swirled the brandy, but he hadn't tasted it.

"And then there was the incident yesterday in my back garden," the duke said.

Oh, yes, there was.

And for that one, Adam had no viable excuse as to why Katherine was in his arms. Maybe it was the warm sunshine on his back. The scent of freshly trimmed shrubs, the earth, and Katherine's fresh-washed hair. Just the fact that she was in his arms and dancing with him. Whatever it was, once he saw her, he knew he couldn't leave without tasting her passion for him once again.

"I'm sure if I asked, you'd tell me she tripped over a twig and you had to help her."

So the elderly duke had a sense of humor.

"I fear if she falls one more time before she is betrothed, my lord, she'll lose all the offers she currently has for her hand in marriage."

"I don't see that happening, Your Grace."

"One never knows. So is there anything you want to ask me?"

Adam's eyes narrowed. He knew exactly what the duke was getting at. And hell, yes, he'd like to offer for her hand right now, but how could he chance getting her with child? Fate had made that impossible.

He met the duke stare for stare, wanting to do what was right, what he wanted. But he said, "No."

His Grace's passive expression never changed. "So, you don't think you have damaged her reputation beyond repair and you have no responsibility to save her from further scandal and ruination?"

That was a harsh way for the duke to say it. Still, Adam remained silent.

"Our servants will talk to their servant friends about what was seen yesterday afternoon. Those friends will talk to their employers and other friends, who will talk to their friends. By the time everyone is finished dragging Katherine's name into the woods and back with a man that's been called the beast, I fear not even that besotted young Viscount Rudyard will want to wed her."

Adam grimaced. The duke was making a powerful case for marriage. Adam was tempted. There were precautions he could take, that Katherine could take, to keep her from getting with child, but that's all they were: precautions.

"If you are not a beast but a man of honor who holds dear the title Earl of Greyhawke, I implore you to do the only respectable thing for my niece and offer for her hand and save her from the torrent of gossip that is sure to follow her for years if you don't."

The duke knew how to aim directly for Adam's heart. And hit it. He felt as if it were exploding in his chest. If he married her, he couldn't stay away from her. That was a fact. He wanted her too desperately. He knew himself too well.

"I will ask for her hand," he answered before he could talk himself out of it yet again. "With your permission, I'll come to your house in an hour. I'll expect a few minutes alone with her."

The duke rose and set his glass on the table. "That's all I wanted to hear. Consider it done."

Chapter 26

When sorrows come, they come not single spies
But in battalions.
         —Hamlet, *act 4, scene 5*

Katherine walked through the front door behind her aunt. The afternoon card party they'd attended was crowded, loud, and quite enjoyable, even though the rain, which had been torrential at times, had moved the festivities inside the Windhams' house. No one let the pouring skies dampen their spirits or their zeal to win every game. Even Lady Leola, who often only tolerated card parties, seemed to have an especially jovial time, playing several hands before declaring it was time for them to go.

"I'm heading up to change and rest before the round of evening parties begin, my dear," she said. "You don't mind, do you?"

"Of course not, Auntie," Katherine said, taking off her damp bonnet. "It was a rather long event. I'm sure you must be tired. We stayed longer than I thought we would, anyway."

"And perhaps you should go up and get out of your wet shoes before you do anything else. You know what they say, cold feet will put a cold in your chest."

Katherine laughed as she laid her cape and gloves on top of her bonnet. "Auntie, I have on my leather high-top boots because it was raining when we left. My feet are dry."

Aunt Leola raised her brows but said nothing.

"What will I do after I marry and I don't have you to tell me I need to rest, to change my clothing, to rest my leg?"

"I would like to think your husband will take as good care of you as your uncles and I have." A rare serious expression settled on her face. For an instant, Katherine thought she saw tears start to pool in her eyes. "That is what he will promise to do when he says his vows. You will tell me if he does not, I trust?"

"When I marry," she answered cautiously. "Of course, if there's a problem, I will tell you."

"I will miss you when you leave this house, but it is time for you to have a home of your own. I'm going up. I'll see you later in the afternoon." She patted Katherine's cheek and started up the stairs.

Katherine supposed she would never outgrow her aunt's and uncles' affection to pat her cheeks. She started to follow Auntie Lee when she saw the duke walk out of the drawing room and saunter down the corridor toward her. He looked up at his sister. Aunt Leola paused on the stairs and stared down at him. He nodded once to her and then she continued on her way.

That was an odd exchange between them, and an unusual feeling that something wasn't quite right stole over her.

"Hello, Uncle," she said, reaching up to give him a kiss.

"How was your afternoon, dear girl?" the duke asked.

"Very enjoyable, and yours?"

"Good. Lord Greyhawke is here to see you."

Something was wrong. Katherine's stomach knotted. "Oh, I . . . well . . . Are you sure?"

The duke stared at her for a moment, and then his bushy brows drew together in concern. "I didn't think it would be a surprise to you that he asked to spend a few minutes alone with you considering your relationship with him."

Her breath trembled in her lungs. The duke was wrong. It surprised her greatly. There was usually only one reason a young lady would be left alone with a gentleman. If he had intentions of proposing. That thought weakened her knees and her palm pressed harder onto the handle of her cane. That couldn't be the reason, could it?

Surely not. He had told her many times, and again just yesterday, he would not marry. Had he changed his mind? Hope thudded in her chest and clamored throughout her being.

"Anyway, I've granted him that consideration," her uncle continued. "Do you have any objections?"

Did she?

No, of course not!

Reeling from the shock, from tamping down the joy that wanted to flood her senses at the possibility of marriage to Adam, she managed to say, "No, none."

"Then I'll give you some privacy with him. He's in the drawing room. I'll be next door in my book room."

"Thank you, Uncle," she whispered.

Her stomach was jumping as she walked into the drawing room, feeling as tight as the strings on a violin. Adam stood in front of the fireplace, handsomely dressed in fawn-colored trousers, dark red waistcoat, and black coat. His features weren't as welcoming as she'd hoped considering the assumed nature of his visit. That gave her a moment's pause. There was still something about this that didn't feel right.

Adam walked to meet her in the center of the room. His expression softened as his eyes swept her face. She wondered if he could see or sense her eagerness.

"You look lovely this afternoon, Katherine. The peach color of your dress enhances your skin and makes your eyes sparkle like emeralds."

"Thank you, my lord," she answered, still anxious that this visit might not be what she suspected.

"I see you have your cane. How are you walking?"

It had been such a natural part of her for so long, it wasn't easy to give it up. Katherine took her cane and laid it on the settee behind her. "I seldom use it when I'm alone."

"That's good, Katherine. That's very good."

His praise calmed her a little, and she cleared her throat. "Uncle said you wanted to talk to me. Alone. I must admit I'm quite taken aback by this."

"I've come to ask for your hand in marriage, Katherine."

A silent gasp escaped her lips, but once again she

sensed in him that all was not as it should be. "But you said you'd never want to marry again."

"That was my plan when I came to London. I had no idea I would meet you and that our relationship would progress as it has and open you up to ridicule and scandal."

She blinked slowly, convinced even more that all was not as it should be. "So you want to marry me to save me from scandal?"

"Your uncle is right. I have damaged your reputation more than once. It was never my intention to cause you harm in any way, and because of that I am honor-bound to offer for you."

Katherine's back stiffened. He wasn't saying exactly what she wanted to hear and that bothered her. "It sounds as if you want to offer for me to save your honor."

His forehead wrinkled in concern. "Katherine, that's not what I said."

"If not, then perhaps you should start over if you intend to ask me to marry you."

"All right, it's true that I have compromised you, but make no mistake that I am asking you to marry me because I love you."

His words astounded her. "Do you mean that? You love me?"

"More than you will ever know." Adam picked up her hand and kissed the back of her palm. "How could you not at least suspect that I love you? I can't keep my hands off you when we are together. Yes, I want to marry you and make you mine."

Goose bumps peppered her skin, and suddenly she

wished for her cane to help support her. "I never thought to hear you say that."

His gaze swept her face again. "I have wanted you since the first night I saw you standing so close to the dance floor. I meant it when I said I want you more than I've ever wanted any other woman."

"But you said you would never marry again."

"I never thought I would. I have resisted my feelings for you and denied my love because of genuine fear for you."

"What fear?"

"For your life if I take you into my bed and give you a babe. I have thought about this and there are things we can do to prevent you from getting in the family way. They won't be as satisfying, and we will have to be very cautious, but I swear to you I will do everything in my power to keep you from bearing a child."

Katherine's heartbeat seemed to stumble and then rumble like thunder across her chest and roar in her ears. What was he saying? "Things we can do? I don't understand."

"You don't need to understand them right now," he said softly. "I can explain them all later. None of them are one hundred percent guaranteed, but with a combination of all the things that are available to us, we can be fairly certain you won't have a babe."

Not have a child? But she wanted children. Katherine slowly pulled her hand from his grasp and stepped away. "Are you saying you want me to marry you, but you don't want me to have your children?"

Her words sounded bleak in her ears. He looked at her as if he couldn't understand why she wasn't comprehending him.

"You can't. I will not chance losing you the way I lost Annie."

Katherine stared into his eyes and for the first time saw how serious he was. How affected he still was by his wife's death.

For an instant, she was uncertain what to say. She had always thought him to be a complex man, a man troubled by his past, but this fear went far deeper than she had suspected.

"I see no reason why you should be afraid of losing me in childbirth just because you lost her."

"There is every reason to fear that. I have Dixon for my heir, so there is no reason to risk losing you to have a child."

Keeping her voice calm and her emotions in check, she said, "If we married, I'd have no problem being a mother to Dixon. He's a sweet child, and I could easily grow to love him. But I will have your word that I will have my own children or I will not marry you."

"Why are you being stubborn about this when you know how much I love you and want you?" he asked.

Angrily, she clenched her teeth a moment before saying, "So it's me being stubborn rather than you being completely irrational?"

"Yes, it is."

"It is a man's duty to give his wife sons and daughters."

"Not if it will kill her."

There was an uncomfortable edge to his voice. He took a step closer to her. Her hands closed into fists. "You don't know that it will, and you are being selfish."

His eyes narrowed, and his lips formed a crease of

frustration. "I am being kind and protective, which is what husbands also do."

"My aunt and uncles have pampered me for years. I will not let you do it, too. I may have a limp, but I am strong and healthy and there is no reason I can't bear you a son."

"Katherine, this has nothing to do with your limp. It has to do with me."

"Having a babe is my choice to make. If I am willing to take the chance, why would you deny me? You will trust me to walk, to dance, but you won't trust me to have your child?"

"My wife died trying to have my child!" he said earnestly.

"And my sisters and brother died without ever having the chance to grow up, marry, and have a family of their own. I will have children for them. I will name my children after my sisters and brother so their memory can live on. That is what husbands do. They give their wives babes and if you can't do that I will not marry you."

"Don't you think I want to?" he whispered harshly. "I can't."

Her throat burned and ached from holding in her grief, but she managed to whisper, "Maybe you are a beast. It's not natural for a man to not want sons."

Adam gently took hold of her upper arms. "For three days, I watched Annie die because the babe wouldn't come. Three heart-wrenching days. Hour after hour I listened to her scream in pain, until the only sound she could make was a pitiful moan. She told me she hated me for giving her the babe and it was my fault the babe wouldn't be born. When it was clear the midwife and accoucheur, the potions and teas, could do nothing for her, she begged me to end her life. She begged me to give her more laudanum to end her life. I would never put you through that, Katherine. Never. And yes, I was a beast after she died. I overturned furniture and tore down draperies. And it had nothing to do with my over-whelming love for her. It was guilt. Guilt because I swore to protect her and didn't. Guilt because in the end, I was her husband, I planted the seed that gave her the babe, and I couldn't save her. I won't risk your life for a son and I won't go through that agony again." He let go of her and stepped away. "I swear to heaven I love you more than my own life, but I cannot give you a child."

His words burned into her soul. At last Katherine under-stood.

"I'm sorry you had to go through that with your first wife. I'm sure it will be forever etched in your mind, but just because she blamed you doesn't make it true. Most any woman in pain would do the same thing. It is human nature, Adam. She and her baby were dying. She had to blame someone."

"If only that were true. It wasn't just Annie. The mid-wife told me it was my fault she couldn't have the babe. That no woman would be able to bear me a child because I am such a big man. I will always have big babes."

Katherine took a step toward him. "How can she know that?"

"I'm six feet four, Katherine. My shoulders are wide, my feet are big. I'd rather deny myself your love than cause your death."

She didn't believe what the midwife had said, but she

saw the emotion in his eyes, heard it in his voice. He wouldn't be swayed. Intense sadness buried deep in her soul.

"There are no guarantees in life for anyone, Adam. Risk is part of life. So is death. I've known that since I was seven. Most things that are worth having come with a little risk."

"But I won't risk your life. I won't watch you die, too. I love you too much. Getting you in the family way would be the same as pushing you in front of a runaway carriage."

Katherine blinked back tears and sucked in a huge, deep breath of courage. "Love is very powerful, and my love for you is strong and true. And as much as it breaks my heart, Adam, I cannot give up my dream of having children to marry you."

He jerked as if she'd slapped him.

"You made a vow, but so did I." She felt as if her words were being ripped out of her. "I will have children for my brother and sisters. I didn't have the pleasure of watching them grow up. I didn't get to see them play, laugh, and get married. But I will watch my own children do all those things. I'm brokenhearted their father won't be you. But you ask too much of me. Thank you wanting me, for loving me, and for showing me how deeply a man can desire a woman. For wanting to spare me Annie's fate, too. But my answer to your proposal remains no."

"Katherine."

He said her name so softly, she almost relented.

Swallowing a gulping breath, she added, "Don't worry about me, my lord. If the scandal breaks and Lord

Rudyard doesn't want to marry me, I will find a suitable match. I am the niece of a duke and the only heir to my father's fortune. Don't think for a moment I cannot find a husband even if my name is shredded by gossip. Now excuse me."

Somehow Katherine managed to hold her head high and calmly walk out of the room, up the stairs, and to the sanctuary of her room before she realized she had walked all that way without her cane. And that was when the first tear rolled down her cheek.

Chapter 27

Everyone can master a grief but he that has it.
—Much Ado About Nothing, *act 3, scene 2*

It had been a hellish day, and he was in a foul humor.

The first splash of brandy had gone down easily, so he'd poured another. He'd planned to spend the entire cold, wet evening at home and do what he hadn't done in well over a year, indulge in his brandy.

From the first night he'd seen Katherine, he'd known that she was wrong for him. She wasn't the kind of lady he could enjoy for a time and then leave. He sat in his book room with his booted feet propped on his desk, thinking that just maybe he'd return to his scoundrel ways of drinking and gambling the night away. But back when he was so young and carefree, he'd had very little control of his life. He hadn't wanted any. Hadn't needed any. Being free to do whatever he wanted when he wanted was all that mattered to him.

Now, he was an earl with a wealth of responsibility that he could have never imagined would be his.

He had Dixon and his future to consider, too.

But what he wanted was Katherine.

After he'd left her, he'd gone to the mews and saddled his horse. He'd ridden in the park until dusk. He'd thought about leaving Society as he had when he'd lost Annie, but he was a different man now, and that thought had quickly fled his mind. At the time, the isolation of the cold, damp coast was where he needed to be, but no longer. But he couldn't stay in London and watch the woman he loved marry someone else.

Adam sipped his brandy again. Yes, he would have to leave London and not return. He didn't want to see Katherine with Rudyard dancing at a ball or walking with the man and their sons in the park. No, he couldn't watch the woman he loved building a family with another man. And he had no doubt Rudyard would marry her, scandal or not. The man was a dandy, but he wasn't a fool.

The thought of her in any other man's arms made him feel as if there were a gaping hole where his heart should be.

A movement caught his eye and he saw Dixon standing quietly in the doorway. One day the lad would learn to talk more and announce himself, but for now, Adam would humor him.

"It's past midnight. What are you doing up at this hour? Is anything wrong?"

Dixon shook his head.

"Does Mrs. Bernewelt know you're down here?"

He shook his head again. "She smells better."

A smile spread across Adam's face. Leave it to his cousin to make him smile when he felt like hell. "Mrs. Bernewelt's hands?"

Dixon nodded.

"Good," Adam said dryly. "I'm glad to hear it. I finally did something right, and at least someone is happy. Which reminds me, I need to talk with her and make sure she's willing to go with us when we leave London."

Dixon walked farther into the room and stood in front of Adam's desk. His big eyes were full of concern.

Adam swore softly under his breath. "I hope she is. I don't want to have to interview for another governess."

"I don't want to leave. I like it here."

"So do I, but we can't stay. There are some things I need to do that can't be done from here." Adam rubbed his forehead. Katherine would know just what to say to settle Dixon, but Adam had no idea. "Remember, your home is where mine is. You go where I go. Understand?"

A wrinkle formed between Dixon's youthful eyes. "Where are we going?"

"To check the Greyhawke lands and estates. Meet the tenants and talk to the managers. It'll be good for you to go. It will all be yours one day."

"I like it here," he said again.

Adam understood Dixon's fears. He'd lost his mother, been sent to an orphanage, then been taken out to the coast and dropped at the door of a stranger. It was no wonder he didn't want to leave again.

"Look," Adam said, trying to think of what Katherine would say to calm the lad's fears. "This is something that needs to be done, and I've put it off for far too long as it is. It will be an adventure for your soldiers to go on. You can say they're going off to fight in a war."

"Can Miss Wright go with us?"

Adam rose in his chair and brought his feet down to the floor. "What made you say that?"

"Her hands smell nice."

"Everything about her smells nice," Adam said as a longing filled him to his core.

"She's pretty, too."

Oh, yes.

"No, she can't go with us."

Dixon's face relaxed into an expression of sadness. "Have you asked her?"

He had, and she wouldn't agree to his terms. He couldn't blame her. It was a hell of a thing to have to say to the woman you loved. Adam would give everything he owned to be able to take those words back.

"I can't. Now, you'd better find your way to your room before Mrs. Bernewelt finds you gone."

"I'll ask her for you."

Adam grunted a laugh. "It won't do any good, Dixon. She's going to marry someone else."

"That man in the park?"

"Yes." *Damn lucky man, too,* he thought. "Now go on back up to bed."

Listening to Dixon's small feet climb the stairs, Adam closed his eyes tightly. If he'd thought the outcome would be any different, he'd ask her to marry him a second time. But it wouldn't. He'd known from their first meeting that she had demons to deal with, too. She hadn't shared all of them with him, and he hadn't shared all of his until this afternoon.

The chair creaked as Adam rose and walked over to the side table, when from the front of the house he heard a knock. So did Pharaoh. He barked once and jumped up to investigate. Adam grimaced. Who would be coming to his door at this hour? Clark had already retired, so Adam put down his glass and strode to the entrance before Pharaoh woke up everyone in the house.

"Harrison," he said as the Pyrenees jumped on his friend. "Come in. I'll pour you a drink."

Harrison stepped inside but didn't close the door behind himself. "I'm not staying."

Adam tensed. He knew from his friend's tone and look of apprehension that something was wrong. "What is it?"

"It's Bray's wife. It's her time and she's having difficulty."

In the darkness behind Harrison, Adam saw Annie lying in bed, drenched in sweat, shrieking in pain, gasping for every breath. She swore she hated him for planting the babe inside her. She begged him to save her life and then begged him to save the baby's life.

"Adam," Harrison said.

Shaking off the memories, he whispered, "Damnation."

"He didn't want you to know. For obvious reasons. I've gone against his wishes to come tell you. I felt you should know. You don't have to go, but I knew it had to be your decision whether or not you went to stand beside him."

Old memories welled and threatened him again, but Adam fought them away. "Hell, yes, I'm going," he said. "It'll take time to get my carriage ready. May I ride with you?"

"Of course, let's go."

Thankfully, Harrison remained quiet and didn't try

to talk with Adam on the short ride to Bray's house. Adam was having a hard enough time keeping his own thoughts at bay without having to hear Harrison's as well. It wasn't something he'd allowed himself to dwell on, but at the back of his mind, he'd always known there was a chance something would go wrong with one of their wives during birth.

"Adam, you shouldn't have come," Bray said as he and Harrison walked into Bray's book room. "I didn't want you to. There's no reason to put yourself through—"

"Bray," Adam said, touching his arm to stop him. "I want to be here. How are things now?"

"As you know too well, the husband is the last one to be told anything."

Adam knew. The midwife had kept him out of Annie's room, too. After she'd labored more than a day and a half, Adam had defied the woman's orders and gone in to see his wife. The image of her distended, sweat-drenched body lying on the bed in that hot, dark room would always be with him, but now he had to block it from his mind.

"The midwife keeps telling me nothing is wrong. That it takes longer for some women to deliver than others. But I know the labor is going on too long."

Adam remembered hearing those same words.

"She's my wife, having my babe, and I'm locked out of her room," Bray continued. "I sent for the same accoucheur you brought in for Annie."

"Good," Adam said, but felt no relief hearing it. The man hadn't been able to help Annie.

"He's with her now. Hopefully he'll be down and tell me something soon."

"I'm sure he will," Adam said. "Where are her sisters?"

"The two youngest wore themselves out with worry and fell asleep. The older two are with Louisa." Bray rubbed his hands together. "I was sent word they were a comfort to her."

"That's good," Harrison said.

"Yes, but if someone doesn't come down soon with a report, I'm going to ignore the rules of propriety and go see for myself how she is doing, even if I have to knock the blasted door down."

"You remember how they are. For some reason they think the fathers will taint the birthing room," Harrison said.

"It's probably best we're not allowed in," Adam offered.

From above them, they heard Louisa cry out. Bray started for the door. "Enough of this foolishness. I'm going to see my wife."

Adam and Harrison looked at each other but said nothing. For more than half an hour, they took turns silently pacing in front of the fireplace, then over to the window and to the bottom of the stairs, and then back into the book room. Time was passing slowly for all of them.

Finally Harrison said, "I'm going to step outside for a few minutes. Come get me if there's news."

Adam nodded and walked over to the window and stared out into the darkness. He didn't know how long he had been standing there when he heard a voice behind him.

He turned. It was the male midwife who had tried to help Annie. "What did you say?"

"The duke has a son, and the babe and the duchess are in good health."

Relief flooded Adam. He hadn't realized until that moment that his legs were weak and his breaths were long and shallow. "You're sure."

"I feel confident they are. The duchess was sitting up in bed holding the babe when I left."

"That's good news."

"I remember you," the accoucheur said. "But I believe you're Lord Greyhawke now."

Adam nodded. "I guess there was no problem with the babe being too big to be born."

The man's brow wrinkled as he looked at Adam. "All births are different and some can be risky, but it really doesn't matter about the size of the babe," he said soberly.

Adam looked at the gray-haired man. "What do you mean? The size of the babe doesn't matter?"

"Large babes are born every day, my lord. What makes the difference is how the mother's body responds to the delivery process and how it pushes the babe out that counts. I'm sorry I wasn't able to do more for your wife. Not even forceps will help when the body doesn't cooperate and open up so you can get them in."

"Because the baby was so big," Adam said again.

The man's eyes narrowed as if he weren't following Adam's meaning. "You thought your wife couldn't deliver the baby because it was too big?"

"That's what I was told," Adam said cautiously.

"I'm sure your wife felt that way, but that wasn't the reason she couldn't deliver. Her body failed her by not responding to the labor and opening. It had nothing to do with the size of the baby. It could have been the size of my hand and it wouldn't have made any difference in the outcome for her. I have seen many small women, much smaller than your wife, have large, healthy babies. The body is supposed to open and make way for the babe to push through. Hers never did."

Adam felt as if his whole body were tingling. "So if I were to have another baby, there may not be a problem."

"There's no reason to think there would be. What happened to your wife had nothing to do with you or the babe. I'd say the odds were good that there wouldn't be a problem at all. It all depends on the mother. Some babes come fast, others take their time. But the mother's body has to do its part, too."

Adam walked over to a chair and sat down.

Chapter 28

I do believe thee: I saw his heart in his face.
—The Winter's Tale, *act 1, scene 2*

Oh, he was torturing her. Every time she looked his way, Adam was watching her. It didn't matter if he was talking to a group of gentlemen, to her friend Madeline, or to one of the dowagers sitting around the dance floor, always his gaze found Katherine's. And every time it did, he made her ache with longing. She'd tried not to look at him. Tried not to even glance in his direction. Oh, how she'd tried! But her eyes would not be controlled by her mind. Only by her heart.

What was he doing at the ball, anyway? He had stayed away all Season thus far. Perhaps he had come just to fill her with the pain of loss. She thought he'd already left London and that she'd never see him again. In truth, she hadn't wanted to see him. Her decision had been made, and seeing him only made her wish things between them could have been different. His reasons for not wanting children were valid, but so were her reasons for needing to have children of her own.

He couldn't change, but neither could she.

Katherine understood this and would have to bear the heartache, no matter how deeply it hurt her.

When she'd told the duke she'd decided not to marry Lord Greyhawke, he'd huffed out a low, exasperated sigh, turned his back on her, and walked silently away. That had stung. Aunt Leola had been more considerate and asked if she'd wanted to talk about what had happened. When Katherine declined, Aunt Leola hadn't pressed. She never would. She was much too polite to pry.

Katherine had worried that it would be unfair to marry Lord Rudyard knowing she loved Adam so deeply. But after much thought, she had decided she would be giving the viscount many things most people valued in someone they loved and wanted to marry. She would give Lord Rudyard loyalty, honor, and all the children he wanted. She would also give him control of a handsome fortune.

So with her promise to her uncle weighing heavily on her mind and only a week left of the Season, Katherine had planned to tell Lord Rudyard tonight that she would marry him. But just as her courage peaked and she was ready to say the words, Lord Greyhawke had walked into the ballroom, looking so dashing, so confident, that she felt as if her heart had melted into a puddle at her feet. It was as if he knew exactly when she had planned her acceptance and had come to disrupt her.

"You don't seem yourself tonight, Miss Wright. Are you tired?"

"No, my lord. I am well."

"Perhaps I should get you a cup of punch or another glass of champagne?"

"No, no more bubbles for me, but thank you, my lord. You do not have to stay every moment by my side. You should be dancing and enjoying yourself."

"I am quite contented being by your side, Miss Wright."

"But you are making me feel bad. I insist you find someone to enjoy the next dance with."

"Since you insist," he said with a smile, "I will. I don't think I've seen Miss Penny Marchfield on the dance floor this evening. Perhaps she'd like to give it a go."

"That would be so kind of you. I know she loves to dance and doesn't get asked as much as other young ladies do."

"If it will please you, I shall go ask her right now."

"Absolutely."

Katherine watched him stroll toward Penny. And she thought again what a nice man he was. If only she could develop those thrilling feelings of wanton desire for him that she felt with Adam, they would probably have a good life together.

Penny's face lit up like the glittering candles in the chandeliers that hung from the ceiling when Lord Rudyard asked her to dance. She looked over at Katherine and gave her a huge smile as the viscount led her to the dance floor.

Katherine laughed and waved to her. It felt wonderful to make Penny feel so special.

"Good evening, Miss Wright."

A shiver of anticipation skipped up Katherine's back at the sound of Adam's voice. She turned, curtsied, and looked up into his gorgeous eyes. "Lord Greyhawke."

"You're beautiful tonight," he said. "I believe you are wearing the gown you wore the night we met."

Katherine looked down at the gauzy pink gown. A warmth flooded her. He remembered what she had on that night.

"Yes, I was," she answered softly. "I'm surprised you remembered."

"I remember everything about you. Everything we said, every look and every touch."

Her throat went dry as his words washed silkily down her. "That is not something you should say to me here. Someone might hear you."

"It's true."

"Why are you here? I thought you might have already left."

"My business isn't finished," he said.

So he'd come to say good-bye. Her eyes moistened, but she quickly blinked the wetness away.

"Well," she said, suddenly feeling sad and angry at the same time, "Perhaps it will be soon. I know you are eager to leave. Now, if you'll excuse me, I see someone I'd like to speak to."

She turned to walk away, but he touched her arm and stopped her. "No, don't go. I'd like to talk to you."

It might be easy for him to have a long good-bye, but it certainly wasn't for her. "I really don't want to talk to you, my lord. I believe we said all there was to say to each other a few days ago."

"You are angry with me."

"Yes," she admitted. There was no reason not to when he was leaving.

"You're disappointed."

"That, too, not that you care or that it's any of your business."

"Broken-hearted."

She nodded, seeing no reason not to be honest but unable to say more. If he was going, she just wanted him to go.

"You love me."

"Stop torturing me, Adam," she whispered.

"I know you love me, Katherine."

She remained silent.

"I love you, too," he said softly.

"If you make me cry here in this room, I will hate you the rest of my life," she said earnestly.

He smiled. "I'm not going to make you cry, my love, and I'm not going to leave. I'm going to dance with you."

She opened her mouth to speak, but nothing came out. She was too stunned to do anything but blink.

"The next score that will be played is a waltz. I intend to dance it with you."

Frantically, she shook her head. "I won't. I can't."

"The first time I spoke to you, it was to ask you to dance. Do you remember?"

She nodded. "Of course. I'm not likely to ever forget that night."

"I know you have continued to practice."

Her eyes queried him. "How do you know that?"

"I know you."

"Even if I have, it doesn't mean I'm ready to dance at a ball with two hundred people watching me. I can't."

"You were already very good when we danced in your garden. I wouldn't ask if I didn't think you could do it. I have faith in you, and you can trust me."

"But I don't trust you," she said, near tears again. "Because you don't trust me."

"What makes you think I don't trust you?"

"You don't trust me to give you a son."

The quadrille ended and the dancers started leaving the floor.

"Dance with me and then we'll talk about that. I'm not going to allow your uncles, aunt, or Lord Rudyard to keep you an invalid. You don't need that cane, and you are going to prove it to everyone right now. Now, give it to me."

Other dancers started making their way to the dance floor and getting in the starting position for the waltz.

"You don't understand. I'm frightened."

"I've been frightened before, too, but someone that I love very much told me that life is full of risks and that anything worth having is bound to come with a little risk."

"Don't make a fool of me, Adam."

"I promise I'm not going to. The cane."

She looked down at her hand. The grip on her cane was tight but he was right. She did trust him. She lifted the cane and handed it to him.

"Ah, good evening, Lord Greyhawke," the viscount said as he walked up to them.

"Lord Rudyard," Adam said, and held the cane out to him. "Would you mind taking care of this for Miss Wright?"

"Ah, ah, of course not, but she needs this to walk."

Adam held out his hand to Katherine. "Not anymore."

Katherine placed her hand in Adam's and he escorted her toward the dance floor. He walked slowly and his grip was firm. Her practice had paid off. She knew her limp wasn't pronounced, and her knee and hip moved with more freedom than ever before.

When Katherine and Adam reached the dance floor, the other dancers parted, making way for them. Katherine heard whispers, gasps, and knew every eye in the room was on them. Her body trembled.

"Don't worry if you stumble or if I step on your toe. We will keep going. We won't stop. Understand?"

She nodded again, but said, "Everyone is looking at us."

"I want you to relax and enjoy your first dance."

He placed one hand to her back and pulled her into his embrace. That gave her all the confidence she needed.

"Let's show them how to waltz."

The music started, and on the right downbeat Adam stepped forward and Katherine stepped back. Their toes never touched as they moved across the floor. Katherine's chest swelled and her heart felt as if it might beat out of her chest. She was dancing at a ball with the most handsome gentleman in all of London. She was hardly breathing as she concentrated on her steps. She realized it was actually easier to follow Adam and to dance with the music playing.

Katherine knew she wasn't as graceful as the other ladies, but she didn't care. She felt as if she were. Just as in her dreams, she was dancing, flowing across the floor with Lord Greyhawke. The crowds blurred as she sailed from side to side in time with the music.

When the dance ended, the crowd erupted in applause. Only then did Katherine realized they were the only two on the floor. Her aunt and uncles were standing in the front row, clapping louder than anyone. She heard shouts and cries of "Bravo!" "Well done!" and "Splendid!"

She smiled at Adam, feeling as if she would burst with love and gratitude.

"Give them a curtsy, Katherine," Adam said. "They want a curtsy from you."

Adam continued to hold her hand. She held her dress out with the other and curtsied as the applause continued. All of a sudden, Adam dropped to one knee in front of her. The clapping stopped. The cheers from the crowd fell silent. There wasn't a cough, a sigh, or a whisper.

"Miss Katherine Wright, will you marry me and be my wife?"

Gasps sounded all around the room again, but none was louder than hers. Katherine questioned him with her expression. Her heart felt so full, she could hardly speak. "You know I can't," she whispered thickly.

"Let me rephrase what I asked. Will you marry me and give me sons?"

She was stunned into silence again.

"I accept your terms," he said. "The thought of you having a babe scares the hell out of me, but I will find a way to cope with that. We will have all the children you want." He smiled. "Besides, the thought of another man touching you scares me more."

Her heart leaped to her throat. "I don't believe you."

"I wouldn't be on my knees in front of two hundred people right now if it wasn't true, my love."

"I don't understand. You aren't making any sense, because last time I saw you, you were so adamant."

"I think you knew I wouldn't let anyone else have you. That I'd be back for you."

"No, I didn't know. How could I? I don't understand. What made you change your mind?"

"You mean other than my love for you and mad, raging jealousy at the thought of anyone else touching you? It's a long story and best told in front of a fire on a cold night when you're wrapped in my arms. Marry me, Katherine. Say you will be mine. We will have as many children as you want."

"Say yes," someone from the crowd called.

"After that proposal, she had better say yes," another person yelled.

"How romantic," still another commented.

"I love you, Katherine. Say yes."

Katherine looked down into his eyes. "Yes. A hundred times yes."

He rose and stepped closer to Katherine. "Some have called me a beast, and they will surely think so after I do this. But your acceptance needs to be sealed with a kiss." He pulled her into his arms and kissed her soundly on the lips.

But far from cries of beast, scoundrel, and rake, there were shouts of laughter and cries of hooray.

Chapter 29

I was won . . .
With the first glance . . .
—Troilus and Cressida, *act 3, scene 2*

Pale moonlight shone through the parted draperies. A bedside lamp bathed the room in a golden glow, and a low-burning fire warmed it. Katherine sat at her dressing table brushing her hair, waiting for Adam, feeling jubilant but a little anxious, too.

The wedding had been a quiet affair at the duke's home at half-past two. His dinner guests started arriving by half-past four. Though Katherine and Adam had tried to discourage it, her uncle had insisted upon a five-course dinner with dancing afterward to celebrate her long-awaited marriage.

Aunt Leola had told Katherine she had personally inspected the china and as there was no chip in any of it, there would be no reason for them to exchange plates. The Duke of Quillsbury was intent on marrying her off in a grand style. They'd had to stay at the celebration far longer than either of them had anticipated or wanted.

At last the bedchamber door opened and Adam walked in. An expectant rush shivered through her.

He shut the door behind him and turned the key. Katherine rose from her dressing stool and faced him. For a moment she felt wary, but then their eyes met across the room and held for what seemed like forever. Her love for him seemed to swell in her chest and overflow around her, calming her.

"Is Dixon asleep?" she asked.

"By the time his head hit the pillow," Adam answered, taking off his coat and throwing it onto the stool she'd just vacated.

Katherine smiled. "It was a busy day for him, too. It meant a lot to him that you wanted him included in the wedding festivities."

Keeping his gaze locked on hers, he walked toward her, removing his collar and neckcloth. "I don't think your aunt or your uncles were too happy about that. I think their brows were raised more than once at having a child at the dinner table, but as you so sweetly reminded them, Dixon is part of our family."

"They are old and set in tradition and manners."

Adam threw his neckcloth on top of his coat as he stopped in front of her. "Do you realize how inviting you are dressed in that white sleeveless gown standing in my bedchamber?" He paused and chuckled under his breath. "Of course you don't."

"I do know that pleasing you makes me happy."

"I am deliriously happy, but I'm thinking we have been married seven hours now and I've yet to give you a proper kiss, Lady Greyhawke."

"You mean like a first kiss?"

"That's your favorite kind, isn't it?" He slipped his warm, strong hand around to the back of her neck, pulled her gently to him, and brushed his lips across hers in a soft, brief kiss.

Her brow wrinkled, but she laughed. He knew she wanted long, deep kisses, not the mere touching of lips to lips. "There should never be more than one first kiss."

"I agree." Adam, pulled her close and gave her a long, passionate kiss that thrilled her all the way down to her toes, and contentment settled over her.

He raised his head and looked lovingly at her. "I love your hair flowing around your shoulders like this."

"And I enjoy seeing you dressed casually like this, without your coat and neckcloth." She ran her hands up his firm, muscular forearms and across his shoulders.

Adam seemed to study over what she'd said. "I like your hair down. You like me without my coat. Yet neither is a proper way to be seen in Society. What should we do about that?"

She pondered for a moment and started unbuttoning his waistcoat. "Perhaps we should spend a lot of time in our bedchamber."

"My thoughts exactly." He unfastened the last two buttons for her, shrugged out of his waistcoat, and sent it the way of his other clothing. "You danced beautifully tonight."

"It was better than a week ago when you proposed to me."

"Tonight is a night I will always cherish. You surprised everyone but me. I knew you could do it."

One day she would try to explain to him just how much it had meant to her, too. Not only the dancing that she had long dreamed about, but that he had come to her and bent his knee in front of everyone, asked her to be his wife. He'd kissed her soundly on the lips. Someday, she would find the words to let him know how much she treasured that expression of his love and devotion.

Adam looked around the room. "Where is your cane?"

"I have no need of it in here. I left it at the top of the stairs."

A smile broke across his face. Adam pulled Katherine back into his arms and kissed her hungrily again before stepping back.

"If I continue doing that, my love I will never make it to get undressed." He tugged on his shirt, pulling it from the waistband of his trousers.

Katherine helped him pull it over his head and toss it aside. She gazed at his strong, beautiful body. With an open palm, she reached up and caressed his shoulders and across his chest. She ran her hands tantalizingly slowly down his rippled ribs to the top of his trousers and back up again. His skin was smooth, firm, and warm. She could feel the rapid beat of his heart as her hand skimmed over it.

"You are a big, magnificent man, Adam. I have no fear of you or of one day having your child."

He looked deeply into her eyes. "I will have plenty of fear for both of us, Katherine, make no mistake about that. But it will not control me." He reached down and caught her up in his arms, then carried her to the bed and laid her on it.

With fascination, she watched as he stepped out of his shoes, unbuttoned his trousers, and slipped them

down his legs before crawling in beside her. Katherine
turned willingly toward him. He reached for the hem of
her gown and slowly lifted it up and over her head and
then flung it away.

She lay on the bed completely unclothed for him. She
watched his gaze sweep down her face to her breasts,
her stomach, and lower, before scanning back up to her
face. Appreciation shone in his eyes.

"You are beautiful, my love."

Katherine took in his fine, masculine body with the
same loving tenderness. "And so are you," she answered.

When his bare skin touched her breasts, a thrill of
excitement and expectancy spiraled through her. The
heat from his body immediately warmed her against the
coolness of the air. His hardness rubbed against the soft,
womanly part of her, and she welcomed it.

Their lips met in a tender kiss. Her lips parted, and
with her tongue she entered his mouth and tasted him.
Adam moaned his approval. Their tongues explored and
played together. He lightly ran his hand first over one
breast and then the other, his fingers teasing her with
feather-light caresses. He cupped one breast and
squeezed it gently, softly, torturously slowly, causing her
abdomen to contract in sweet pain.

"I like the fullness of your soft breasts," he whispered as he covered one nipple with his mouth. She
gasped with pleasure and arched her back. Shivers of
delight spiraled in all directions throughout her body
and amazed her with sensation.

He lifted, stroked, and molded her breast with his
hands. He sought and found her nipples with his mouth,
with his fingers, causing her to gasp with delight as a

soaring hunger gripped her. She spread her hands over his wide shoulders, strong back, and down to the flat firmness of his stomach, loving the feel, the firm texture, of his bare skin.

Their bodies entwined, they kissed and touched sweetly, lingeringly, for a long time, and each time enjoying the taste and touch of the other as passion and desire mingled and mounted inside them. They kissed fiercely. Their hands stroked endlessly from spine to waist, over hips and down thighs, sending chills of expectancy pulsing through them.

He kissed her sweetly, longingly, letting his lips leave hers and kiss their way down her chin, along the column of her throat to the valley between her breasts. His tongue traced a hot, moist trail from behind her ear down to her nipple, where he caught it up in his mouth and sucked gently again.

With loving hands, Adam caressed each breast before moving his hand down to her waist, over her stomach, down to her inner thigh, and over the most womanly part of her. She sucked in a deep but choppy breath at the new, glorious experience. He let his hand linger while they both enjoyed his touch.

She didn't know how long they kissed and touched, becoming familiar with each other, soothing each other, enticing each other with their caresses and murmured words of endearment. There were no inhibitions or hesitations between them.

Katherine moaned and sighed as waves of pleasure tightened her lower abdomen and between her legs. Something deep and wanton stirred restlessly inside her. Her hands left the broad sprawl of his shoulders to the small of his back and lower, to the firmness of his buttocks, and she kneaded his flesh.

She smiled when he moaned his approval.

Adam rolled her onto her back and moved on top of her, letting his body stretch the length of hers. His lower body settled between her legs, and he fitted his hardness against her. A delicious, languorous warmth spread through her, and she lifted her hips toward his. With a gentle push and a bit of pain, he entered her and she became his.

He started an easy rocking motion that was pure pleasure. She joined his movement, her arms circling his back and pressing him closer, harder, and deeper into her.

Their hips moved slowly at first, and as their passions mounted and mingled, so did their movements. Suddenly Katherine's body exploded into a sensation of pleasure that was beyond all comprehension.

"Adam," she whispered.

"Katherine," he answered as their bodies released and melded together as husband and wife.

Moments later Adam whispered, "I love you," as he snuggled his nose into the warmth of her neck.

For a long time Katherine lay breathless, fully contented, enjoying the weight of her husband's body on hers.

Finally, Adam rolled off her and onto his side. He faced her and snuggled her close to his chest.

Katherine gazed into his eyes and whispered with all the love she was feeling, "Thank you for saving Lord Rudyard from having to spend his life with me."

Adam rose up on his elbow and grinned. "You would have really married him?"

In all seriousness she said, "I would have. I promised my uncle. I felt you were lost to me."

He raked the backs of his fingers down her cheeks. "I was. I was told no woman would ever be able to have my child, and I believed it without question."

"And now you don't?"

"I've spoken with several midwives and accoucheurs, and they have all assured me there is no reason to believe you will have trouble bearing my child. The problem was with Annie and her body's inability to push the babe."

"I'm sorry for her and for your loss, too."

Adam nodded once. "And now I'm hopeful, but I will be cautious when your time is due. I may have to call in every midwife and accoucheur within one hundred miles of London to tend you."

Katherine laughed. "I promise you it will not take that many for me to birth your son, my lord."

"I believe that, too. I love you, Katherine."

"And I love you, Adam."

Epilogue

The sea hath bounds, but deep desire hath none.
—Venus and Adonis, *331–32*

Something disturbed Adam's slumber. His eyes popped open. Through the slit in the draperies, he saw a faint tint of pink in the dark sky. Dawn was on the rise. He listened but heard nothing. Perhaps it was Katherine mumbling in her sleep. He smiled to himself and snuggled closer to her warm back and caught the fragrant scent of her hair. Carefully, he pushed aside her auburn tresses and brushed his lips to her nape. Her bare shoulder twitched at his feather-light caress and he smiled.

Perhaps he would wake her and let her know he wanted her.

Then he heard the noise again. It was a soft knock on the door. A knock he recognized. Deciding not to disturb Katherine, he gently threw the covers aside and eased off the bed. He stepped into the trousers he always kept on the nightstand and buttoned them as he padded over to the door, unlocked it, and opened it just a little.

Dixon stood there, holding a candle. He looked up at Adam and said, "They're crying again."

Adam rolled his shoulders and sniffed as he stepped out of the room and gently pulled the door around. "The twins?"

Dixon nodded. "They woke me up. Again."

Adam frowned and rubbed the back of his neck, trying to think about what he should do or say. "Really?" he asked, stalling.

"The third time this week."

Adam knew. It was becoming an every-other-night occurrence for Dixon to find his way to Adam's bedchamber in the dark of night and knock on his door to complain. He didn't know why Dixon just couldn't sleep through crying. Their whimpers didn't seem all that loud to Adam.

"Well, they are babies," he answered, wondering what else he could say. "You know it's natural. Babies cry a lot. That's all they know how to do. That and eat."

"How many more are you going to have?"

The door opened and Adam felt his wife come up behind him and put her gentle hand on his shoulder. "I don't know. That's up to Katherine." He turned, looked at her, and smiled. "But as many as she wants."

"Thank you, my lord," she whispered into his ear.

Dixon rolled his eyes.

Katherine smiled at Adam and his heart melted. She was beautiful in her pristine white night rail, with her thick auburn tresses flowing across her shoulders.

She moved from behind him and looked down at Dixon. "Did the girls wake you again?"

Dixon nodded, paused, and then said, "Do you want me to go check on them for you this time?"

She glanced at Adam in surprise. "Would you like to do that for me?" Katherine asked him.

"I might as well. I'm already awake. I'm big enough now that I'm seven. The nanny can't rock both of them at the same time. I can help her if you want me to."

"Thank you, Dixon. That's very nice of you, and it will be a wonderful way for you to help. Tell Mrs. Foster I'll be along in a few minutes to help out, too."

Dixon smiled and turned away. Adam called to him and he looked back. "You be careful carrying that candle back to the nursery."

After Dixon disappeared into the other wing of the house, Adam turned and watched Katherine walk to the foot of the bed. She still had a bit of a limp, but it was hardly noticeable anymore. He closed the door and turned the key.

She picked up her robe and started to put it on, but Adam reached and gently took it out of her hands. He dropped her robe to the bed and slipped his arms around her slender waist and pulled her to him. The girls were almost three months old, and already Katherine's shape was returning to normal.

He'd worried every day when she was in the family way. All during her confinement, he'd stayed close by her side. And when her time came, it was quick. She'd not only given him one child, she'd given him two. And she'd had no trouble with either birth. She had been amazing.

He looked down into her eyes. "Why am I always

searching for something to say to Dixon, but you seem to know exactly what to say to make him happy every time you speak to him?"

"I suppose it comes naturally to me and not to you," she said with a teasing smile.

"In that case, let me say something that does come naturally to me. I love you, Katherine, and I'm thankful every day that I came to my senses and didn't let you marry Lord Rudyard."

"I love you, too." Katherine circled his neck with her arms. "And I'm quite happy about that myself."

"There's something else that comes very naturally to me," Adam said, backing her against the bed.

"That would be many things, my lord, so which one are you referring to right now?"

"This one," he said, and then swung her up into his arms and laid her down on the bed.

Her gentle laughter filled the room and made him desire her even more. "No, no, you rogue. You know we don't have time for this. The babies are crying and Mrs. Foster needs my help."

He lay down beside her and cuddled her in his arms. "And you will help her, but only after I have your help first."

She gave him a mock look of horror. "You beast. You would leave a baby wailing while you take the time to satisfy yourself?"

"Yes." He grinned. "But only because I know the babes are in no danger of not being properly cared for." He pulled her close and snuggled the warmth of her neck. "Now, I hope you have no objections if I kiss you like this, my lovely wife."

Adam kissed her hungrily, and she responded eagerly.

"But Mrs. Foster is expecting me," she argued in between his kisses and while her arms twined around his neck.

He kissed her cheek, below her eyes, and her luscious lips again. "I know, and you will join her. Just not for a few more minutes." He kissed his way down her neck. "Besides, you need to give Dixon time to feel like he is helping her, and . . ." He stopped and looked down into her sparkling green eyes.

"And what?" she asked with a suspicious expression.

He pulled on the ribbon that held the bodice of her night rail together. "And give me a little time to show you how much I love you."

She kissed his lips. "I think after almost two years of marriage, I know how much you love me. But I'm always willing to pretend I don't, so you can show me one more time."

He smiled. "You could never know. But, yes. Let me try to show you one more time."

Katherine sighed softy and wrapped her arms around his back and Adam thrilled to her touch.

Dear Reader,

I hope you enjoyed Adam and Katherine's story and the conclusion of the Heirs' Club of Scoundrels Trilogy. I have savored my time with all the characters in these stories. As with all the books I write, I'm always sad to see a story or a series come to an end.

The customs of childbirth that were followed during the Regency were very different from what we follow today. The birthing rooms were dark and hot. In most cases, only females were allowed inside, and husbands were kept away. Generally men knew little or nothing about childbirth. Terminology such as "in the family way," "with child," and "confinement" used in my story seems odd and stilted when used in dialogue, but in most cases I tried to keep the wording as accurate to the time period as possible. I do admit to using some literary license in the terminology and customs of the Regency for the sake of the story.

Most women were still using midwives during the Regency, but male midwives, or accoucheurs, were making headway into delivering babies for the aristocracy. It wasn't uncommon for there to be problems during or shortly after childbirth, where the lives of the mother and the baby were lost. Unfortunately, many women and babies died from the poor sanitary conditions or from over-medicating the mother.

If you haven't read the first two books in the **Heirs' Club of Scoundrels,** The Duke in My Bed *and* The Earl Claims a Bride, *both are still available at your favorite bookstore or e-retailer.*

I love to hear from readers. Please e-mail me at ameliagrey@comcast.net, follow me on Facebook at Facebook.com/AmeliaGreyBook, or visit my Web site at ameliagrey.com.

Happy reading!

Amelia Grey